Ovidia Yu is one of Singapore's best-known and most acclaimed writers. She has had over thirty plays produced and is the author of a number of comic mysteries published in Singapore, India, Japan, America and the United Kingdom.

She received a Fulbright Scholarship to the University of Iowa's International Writers Program, has been a writing fellow at the National University of Singapore and was recently inducted into the Singapore Women's Hall of Fame.

T0383919

Also by Ovidia Yu

The Angsana Tree Mystery

Ovidia Yu

CONSTABLE

CONSTABLE

First published in Great Britain in 2024 by Constable

1 3 5 7 9 10 8 6 4 2

Copyright © Ovidia Yu, 2024

The moral right of the author has been asserted.

A CIP catalogue record for this book
is available from the British Library.

ISBN: 978-1-40871-700-4

Typeset in Contenu by SX Composing DTP, Rayleigh, Essex
Printed and bound in Great Britain by Clays Ltd, Elcograf S.p.A.

Papers used by Constable are from well-managed forests
and other responsible sources.

Constable
An imprint of
Little, Brown Book Group
Carmelite House
50 Victoria Embankment
London EC4Y 0DZ

An Hachette UK Company
www.hachette.co.uk

www.littlebrown.co.uk

Dedicated with thanks to Professor Benjamin Ong and his team in the Division of Neurology, and Professor Koh Dow Rhoon and his team in the Division of Rheumatology, NUH, for keeping me functioning and writing.

Dragon Boat Dumplings

———◆———

'*A*iyoh, where is that driver?' my grandmother grumbled. 'Maybe he got lost. Don't know why they want to go and change road names. Now everybody is getting lost! Ask me my address, I also don't know! *Hiyah!*'

She was grumbling because, as of today, Saturday, 1 June 1946, British officials had decreed the road in front of our house would be renamed Mountbatten Road. It was cheaper and faster than building a monument to Lord Louis Mountbatten, though I suspected a repainted road sign wouldn't have the cachet of a new park or monument. Clearly the British were serious about keeping costs down.

The grand unveiling of the new road sign would take place at nine a.m., and Mountbatten Road, formerly Grove Road, would be blocked off from eight, which was why I was leaving so early.

'It's not yet seven o'clock, Ah Ma,' I said, 'and Hakim's been here a hundred times.'

Chen Mansion stood where it had always been, despite the address change. And even though I was twenty-six years old, I was back there with my grandmother, Uncle Chen and Little Ling, his daughter. While the rest of the world was moving forward, I kept being pulled back there. I wasn't sorry to be getting away for a bit today.

I stifled a yawn and pulled the light shawl more closely around me against the early-morning chill. I was wearing a light green and red print frock: green and red are lucky colours for Dragon Boat Festival and I was on a dragon boat mission, a week early.

'Maybe you shouldn't go,' Ah Ma said. 'Go so far alone and for what? When Hakim comes, just give him the food and her precious container and tell him to deliver it to the Pangs' place. No need to waste your time.'

I really didn't want to go. But if I wanted to succeed in making a point with my grandmother I had to see it through. 'I said I would go so I'm going,' I said. 'You know Pang Tai will be offended if you send back her *tingkat* with a driver. You should really come with me.'

Ah Ma snorted. 'In my old *tai chi* clothes? That would really offend the woman.'

Why was I heading out in the early morning in Dragon Boat Festival colours to visit the Pangs with a bunch of Ah Ma's *bak zhang* – sticky rice dumplings wrapped in bamboo leaves and tied with string into triangular parcels – made especially for the festival, as well as two bottles of Ah Ma's achar – turnip, cucumber, carrots and pineapple pickled in vinegar,

2

sugar and salt with lots of sesame seeds and crushed roasted peanuts? Because this was the formal return of Pang Tai's food container. The beautiful three-layered traditional blue-, pink- and green-painted enamel *tingkat* had been brought to us at Chinese New Year. Normally, all gift containers would have been filled with lucky food and given back when my family paid the obligatory return visits, but this year my family hadn't paid *any* return visits.

Most people were understanding. Chen family issues over Chinese New Year must have provided good gossip. But last Friday Pang Tai had asked for her container.

'So rude!' my grandmother said. 'Telling me to just wash and return empty! As though I have no food to give her!'

'Maybe she needs it?' I said. 'Maybe she doesn't know Uncle Chen's wife died.'

'Ha! Of course she knows. You think she wants her *tingkat* back? What she's after is your uncle.'

'Ah Ma!'

'That woman is dangerous. She treats her workers like slaves, and she has too many daughters.'

That was what set me off. As a woman who'd raised a polio-crippled bad-luck granddaughter (me) against the advice of family and fortune-tellers, you'd think Chen Tai wouldn't hold a woman's daughters against her.

'How can you say that?' I said. 'Women shouldn't put other women down.'

'You don't know what you're talking about.' Ah Ma's standard defence.

3

'Pang Tai has three daughters and Danny,' I said. This time I did know what I was talking about. Mei Mei, a sweet, silent woman, was ten years younger than Uncle Chen. Pang Tai had mentioned it several times on her last visit. The younger 'children', Girlie, Sissy and Danny, were about twelve, ten and eight years older than I was.

'I will bring her *tingkat* to Bukit Batok with *bak zhang* especially made for the Dragon Boat Festival. There's no point in offending people. You don't know when you might need to buy granite from them.'

I was only repeating to Ah Ma what she had said many times to me while I was growing up: be nice to people even if you don't like them. One day you might need to work with them. Given that the Pangs ran Singapore's largest granite quarries, surely it made sense to stay on good terms with Pang Tai.

'If you insist on going, I will call Hakim to drive you.' In other words, she knew I was right even if she would die before she said so. 'Better go early so you won't need to stay for lunch.'

I knew Hakim Harez from when he had driven Ah Ma about to collect rents before the war. He'd doubled as her security guard and babysitter, playing *tutup botol*, or bottle caps, with me while we were waiting.

Now Hakim was driving one of the pirate taxis that had sprung up to supplement limited public transport. They were a lifesaver for those living beyond the tram lines and bus routes and charged per person per ride. They were also

4

illegal, and it was understood that, if asked, you were merely 'taking a lift from a friend'.

'All the way to Bukit Batok to return a *tingkat*,' Ah Ma grumbled. 'So *ulu*. I don't know why anybody wants to live there.'

Ulu meant primitive or undeveloped. It was how people in the east of Singapore liked to see the area west of Bukit Timah Hill, the highest point on our island. When your entire island measures just over thirty miles from east to west, you make the most of tiny differences. Much of western Singapore was still plantations and primary forest – and quarries, of course.

What did Ah Ma have against Pang Tai? They were both widows who'd succeeded in keeping their families together. Shouldn't that have forged a bond between them? No. I'd seen Ah Ma's dislike in the way she politely pressed delicacies on her guest while praising her son's brains and her daughters' beauty. Danny wasn't clever and his sisters weren't pretty, and if the two women had liked each other, they'd have been gossiping and cackling while cracking pumpkin seeds in their teeth.

Uncle Chen wasn't any better. Pang Tai had asked if he could spend some time at her place. 'Now my husband is gone, I need something to bring masculine energy to the house.'

'Think about getting a pig,' Uncle Chen said. Pang Tai looked aghast, perhaps trying to decide if she'd been insulted. Maybe she just didn't like pigs. 'A good boar is better than any guard dog. It will keep burglars and monkeys away. And if you lend it to neighbours with sows, you can eat suckling pig all year.'

To be fair, Pang Tai wasn't the only one. Just months after his wife's death, Uncle Chen was showered with gifts and invitations and had refused to pay visits to any households with unmarried women. He and his wife had visited the Pangs on Ah Ma's behalf, often taking me with them, because Ah Ma claimed the long drive over the bad roads to Bukit Batok made her feel sick. 'And not just the roads. The air there is so dirty. Just drive through there and you're coughing for a week. Why do you think it's called Bukit Batok?'

While '*batok*' meant 'coughing' in Malay, it meant 'coconut' in Javanese, which was the more likely origin of the name.

Of course, what Uncle Chen or Shen Shen had said was, 'Our mother wanted to come to see you but she's too busy/ can't leave the house/has relatives visiting. He wasn't very good at lying but Shen Shen had been an expert. I would miss that side of her. But the excuses, like the visits, were just formalities to show our families were on good terms.

'No need to stay too long, *ah*,' Ah Ma said.

'You don't have to wait to see me off, Ah Ma.'

'Who wants to see you off? I want to do my morning *tai chi*. Just waiting for you to go.'

Ah Ma had practised *tai chi* for as long as I could remember. I'd always thought it was an excuse to be outside on her own, though sometimes she made the servant girls practise too. She'd tried to persuade me to join her, but I found the slow movements boring and pointless. These days she used the walking stick Dr Shankar had designed for her *tai chi* rod exercises. It was useful in other ways too. There was a ring below the handle that held Ah Ma's keys and the cloth pouch with her reading glasses. And the metal spike in its foot was good for poking at ripe fruit in trees and for stability on slippery or stony ground. Indoors the spike was protected by a cap ending in a wide rubber stopper, which Dr Shankar had also provided.

'It's a martial art that develops the *qi*. Good for self-defence,'

I preferred a more active kind of self-defence, but I was glad she could still do the movements. Her spiked walking stick was also useful for dismantling cigarette ends (which were just paper and dried leaves) and threatening miscreants who threw rubbish over the wall.

Hakim arrived punctually just before seven a.m. in a nice, fairly well-kept though not new car.

'*Salaam*, Mr Hakim, how are you today?'

Hakim Harez got out, grinning widely and bowing with a hand over his heart. 'Very good, thank you, Chen Tai. Miss Chen, how are you? Just a minute, ah, let me get ready the seat for you.'

He started spreading newspapers in the back. I sniffed. I smelt blood and fresh meat.

'Sorry, *ah*. I brought wife to market to sell chicken.'

Judging by the leafy fragments on the newspapers and the piece of cardboard he handed me to put on top of the newspapers, Puan Hakim had also harvested *daun kelor*, moringa leaves, and *bayam merah*, local spinach, for the market. I brushed off a scattering of soil from the vegetables as Ah Ma and Hakim chatted. A little dry earth was better than blood.

'Sorry to ask you to drive so far to so *ulu* place, Mr Hakim,' Ah Ma said. 'I give you eight dollars. Enough?'

She was being generous. The fifteen-mile journey would have cost about six dollars by trishaw, but that would have taken much longer and been far less comfortable.

'I cannot take money from you, Chen Tai.' I guessed Ah Ma had helped Mr Hakim to pay for his car. She was always helping people, and they all tried to pay her back, not always in cash. 'But why you want to send your granddaughter to Bukit Batok? Young girls should go to town, go Robinson's. Nice dresses there, imported from England.'

'Of course I must pay you. This is your business. My granddaughter has to pay family visit for me,' Ah Ma's mouth turned down at the corners to signify grief, 'now I am too old to go myself.'

'Of course you are not old, Chen Tai,' Hakim Harez said quickly. He returned two notes to my grandmother. 'Six dollars enough. If she needs to come back I'll take her for free.'

'Maybe you can drop me in town afterwards,' I said quickly. 'Can you give me about half an hour at the Pang quarry, then pick me up and drop me in town?'

I could tell Pang Tai that I had several visits to make and couldn't stay long. She would probably be as glad of that as I would. I could easily take the tram home from town.

'Where are you going?' Ah Ma asked.

I was tempted to say Robinson's, but Ah Ma knew me too well. With a crooked hip after childhood polio, I'd never enjoyed shopping for clothes I knew wouldn't suit me. And I knew she suspected I would try to see Le Froy.

I'd had an understanding with former Chief Inspector Thomas Le Froy: until we married at some unspecified point in the future, I would work as his assistant on the Public Health Services Bureau funds.

But Le Froy's duties had been abruptly suspended two weeks ago, pending an official investigation into the PHSB. 'Pending investigation' is what the British say when they've decided you're guilty and need time to decide what you're guilty of. The only reason I wasn't worried was that Le Froy didn't seem concerned.

I hadn't seen him since the office was closed. In fact, one of the points the investigation had already brought up was my lack of qualifications: I didn't have a secretarial certificate from an approved British institution.

I could almost hear Ah Ma thinking, *Ang mohs* don't like girls older than sixteen, but she saved us a good fight by not saying it out loud. I didn't need her feeling sorry for me: I could do that for myself. What had happened to me?

Before the war I'd been a promising top student whose teachers believed I could go on to university instead of getting married. Now it seemed I was too old to do either. Ironically, my work prospects were worse now than they'd been under the Japanese. During the Occupation, my Japanese language skills had been in demand. Now I couldn't get work as a teacher or as the reporter I had once been without qualifications.

'I want to go to town to see Parshanti,' I said.

Hakim looked at Ah Ma.

'Say hello to her mother for me. And tell her father I'm using his stick.'

'I drop you anywhere you want, Miss!' Hakim said. He helped me to settle the *tingkat* and food on the floor beside me and closed the door.

'Whatever you do, don't invite them for Dragon Boat Festival. That woman may come anyway but don't invite them,' Ah Ma called, as Mr Hakim put the car in gear and drove away.

Pirate Taxi Ride

'Your grandma is a good woman,' Hakim said. 'She always makes for me and my wife no-pork *bak zhang* for Dragon Boat Festival. I know all about Festival – last time in China one poet jumped into the river because the government is bad. So all the men row dragon boats to save him and all the women throw *bak zhang* into the river so the fish will eat it instead of the poet.'

'Yah,' I said, only half listening. Hakim had been telling me this story since I was a child. I had to remind Ah Ma to send some *bak zhang* to Hakim and his wife. The sticky rice dumplings I was carrying contained braised pork belly, mushrooms, dried shrimp and chestnuts, so couldn't be given to Muslims, like Hakim and his wife.

After almost two weeks of heavy rain, angsana trees all over Singapore had burst into bloom yesterday. It had been a glorious sight, people posing with flowering branches and taking photographs. It was a pity photographs aren't in colour, like paintings, to capture all that glorious yellow. Today there were yellow carpets on many roads, still beautiful, but in a few days the withered flowers would be a nuisance, clogging the drains.

It was nice being in a car. I thought again about learning to drive. I wanted to, but I'd been in the car with Parshanti driving and had seen the effort it took to manage the clutch pedal and the brake, especially for her many sudden stops. I was afraid my withered leg might not be up to it. But I wanted the independence it gave her. Also, I could help Uncle Chen.

Uncle Chen hadn't reopened his little shophouse in town after the war. Now Ah Ma had him driving merchandise around the colonial homes, especially the black and white houses in the north near Sembawang Shipyard and in the east near Seletar Airbase. The returning British wives were eager to buy the curtain material, pillows, pillow cases and sheets that Ah Ma imported from China, and Uncle Chen did good business selling the items door to door. That meant he was always home for dinner and sometimes Little Ling rode along with him, which they both enjoyed.

'Nowadays, if people jump into the river because the government is bad, no more people left to row boats or make *bak zhang*.'

'What?' I looked up and saw Hakim studying me in the rear-view mirror.

'How much did Chen Tai lose to those opium licences?'

The Japanese had banned opium on the island, but the returning British had auctioned opium-processing licences. Opium products, being heavily taxed, would generate funds to rebuild post-war Britain. The problem was, just two weeks after those licences had been paid for, the British had declared opium processing illegal. Now the government would not refund the money they'd collected for those licences, and anyone caught making or selling opium products would be subject to criminal prosecution.

It was whispered that the authorities had intended to ban opium all along. Auctioning licences was just their way of figuring out who was in the business . . . while pocketing some cash on the side.

'She didn't,' I said. 'My grandmother wasn't in the opium business.'

'Your *ang moh* boyfriend tipped her off because they are going to clamp down?'

'No! She was never in the opium business.'

'Huh.'

I don't think Hakim believed me, but my grandmother had seen the damage opium did, especially to the Chinese, and said no profits were worth that. Le Froy had been trying to get opium production banned since before the war.

'What's your *ang moh* boyfriend doing nowadays?'

We were moving fairly fast. I put my face out of the window and closed my eyes to enjoy the breeze, pretending I hadn't heard him. Hakim was a great one for gossip: he probably knew more about what Thomas Le Froy was doing than I did.

Le Froy and I had admitted to ourselves and to each other that we were in love when we'd thought we were going to die. But we didn't die, which made things awkward. I'd always sworn I'd never marry an *ang moh*, and I'd learned later that he'd sworn never to marry after his fiancée had died during his first posting out of England. I didn't deny or regret the joy I felt thinking of him. We just had to decide how to live with it.

At least Le Froy's position managing the PHSB fund gave him employment in Singapore after he was invalided out of the police force – at least until Jack Wilson was brought in by the British Military Authority to conduct his official inquiry into the fund's accounting.

I couldn't help thinking Governor Evans had set it up. He'd been biased against Le Froy ever since, as chief inspector with the police, he had applied the same laws to *ang moh*s and locals. Apparently that was discrimination against any British who had made the sacrifice to come out east.

I knew from Le Froy that the British were on edge. Now that the Japanese were gone, India and Indonesia wanted to shake off British rule, and Britain didn't want 'anti-colonial unrest' to spread to Singapore. But with all that going on, why were they worrying about a fully funded health-improvement project?

Unfortunately I could guess the answer to that. Over the last forty or fifty years, being male and British had been enough to guarantee a well-paid post almost anywhere in the Empire, other than Britain. Now that was changing. Those who hadn't yet made their fortunes were scrambling to remedy that. 'Guaranteed' investment schemes and dodgy 'big payout' companies were proliferating. Someone, resentful of Le Froy's refusal to invest public-health funds, must have accused him of making off with the money.

I knew nothing would come of the investigation. However much he scorned official protocol, Le Froy had been punctilious when it came to dispensing funds. I'd typed up all the transaction reports myself, with double carbons, one set for the governor's office, the other to the British Military Authority.

Even if Ah Ma didn't think Le Froy guilty of stealing money, guilt by association was enough for her. 'Since you're not working there any more, better you don't go near that place,' she had said. 'What happens if they go there, find something wrong and your fingerprints are everywhere?'

'Of course my fingerprints are there,' I said. 'That is where I work!'

When the motor-car slowed behind a moving bullock cart, I pulled my face in to avoid the smell.

'You know what they say about Le Froy?' Hakim Harez said, as though continuing a conversation. 'People say he's the one behind the opium ban.'

'Opium is bad for people,' I said. Why was that so hard to understand? Even the Japanese knew that.

It was understandable that those who'd paid for the last batch of licences were upset. Who could have seen this coming? Opium trafficking had been one of Britain's greatest generators of revenue for years.

'Nah. *Ang moh*s don't care what is bad for locals. The only reason they banned legal opium cooking is because the Chen family is taking over the opium monopoly.'

'What?'

'That is the marriage condition, right? Le Froy gives Chen Tai the opium market and Chen Tai gives him her granddaughter.'

I saw Hakim watching me in the rear-view mirror. If I got worked up, he would go, 'Joking, *lah!*' then tell everyone I wouldn't have been upset or annoyed if there hadn't been some truth in the rumours.

'Ha-ha,' I said lightly. 'Very funny.' Then I turned back to the window and the passing scenery. I wasn't annoyed with Hakim, who was only reporting to me what others were saying behind my back. Gossip was as much a part of his pirate taxi business as the driving. My grandmother always said, 'Let other people waste energy talking about you. Don't waste energy worrying about them.'

I wondered what she would say about this, though. Ah Ma hadn't been happy to learn Governor Evans had put Le Froy in charge of the health-services fund. 'Giving away money is not so easy. Those you give to say it isn't enough. Those you don't give to say you're crooked. And they all say you put it in your own pocket.'

Well, the official investigation would clear that up, wouldn't it? All that Le Froy had granted funds for were water pipes and sanitary sewage disposal, and that only after requesting tenders from several companies and picking a local contractor. Very likely this had upset the newly returned British officials, who were charged with getting enough money out of us to rebuild Britain.

They were also on the lookout for signs of 'unrest and insurrection', as had arisen in India and Indonesia. Their instructions were to keep the population divided along religious (India) and racial (Indonesia) lines. As long as the separate sectors were at each other's throats, they would need their British overlords.

This didn't work so well in Singapore. Most people had ended up there because they or their ancestors had fled from war, poverty or other people in their lands of origin. Survival and security – earning enough for food and shelter – were top priorities. And now the Japanese chokehold was gone, people weren't happy to submit to the returning British. But what alternative did we have?

Great Britain declared we were her main base in the east and would never be surrendered, but they'd said the same before the war and look how that had turned out. Britain had dissolved the Straits Settlements in April, meaning we were no longer part of Malaya, but a separate Crown Colony under a hastily patched-together civilian administration.

The biggest difference now was that before the war it had been difficult to find Englishmen willing to take up positions out east. Exorbitant salaries had been offered, along with houses and staff who were paid a pittance. Now locals wanted higher pay and we were flooded with stray *ang mohs* leaving India and Indonesia. They were turning up everywhere.

In fact, one was staring at me now through the car window. He was a short, rotund, sandy-haired man, wearing what looked like uncomfortably formal clothes – dark full-length trousers and a long-sleeved shirt. We were still on Hill Street, nowhere near Bukit Batok. Hakim had stopped the car just after the Hill Street police station and quarters. Once this area had felt like a second home to me, but it had been used as a prison and torture chamber during the Japanese time and I preferred to avoid it now. I wasn't superstitious, but I believe places carry echoes of the horrors they've witnessed – like scientists discovering bats can 'see' in the dark using sounds we can't hear.

The *ang moh* walked to the front of the car, apparently to check the licence plate. Was he some kind of motor-car inspector? New rules and posts were generated all the time.

'Don't say anything,' Hakim Harez said to me.

'What?'

'Nobody wants to drive to Bukit Batok so I said I'm going there, I bring him, *lah*. No need to say anything to Chen Tai.'

The entrepreneurial Singapore spirit had raised its mercenary head again.

At least the stranger was a welcome distraction from the coming visit. It wasn't Pang Tai's simpering or Danny's heavy-handed teasing I minded so much as the Pang girls. Still living at home in their thirties and forties, was that how my future would be?

The *Ang Moh* in the Front Seat

———◆———

'Wilson? Going Bukit Timah fire station?' Hakim Harez called through the front passenger window.

The man looked suspicious. '*Mr* Wilson,' he said. 'You're the driver Peters hired?' He looked as if he was waiting for Hakim to produce identification.

'Bukit Timah fire station,' Hakim repeated, and pushed open the passenger door.

Instead of getting in, the man opened the back door and looked at me. 'Get out,' he said. He made shooing gestures as though he was chasing chickens away from spilled rice. 'And take that stinking cardboard with you. What an awful smell! You no understand-oo English-oo?'

Hakim patted the seat beside him. Of course I understood that he wanted me to move up front with him so the *pukka sahib* could have the back seat to himself. But I didn't want to. When I was a child, being allowed to sit in front with Hakim had been a special treat. He shared with me his

19

kacang sipat – salty, spicy broad beans fried till they split – but not his cigarettes while we waited for Ah Ma to collect her rents. But even children understand 'First come, first served' and I didn't like this man taking for granted that the back seat was automatically his.

I looked at Hakim. He was wiping his steering wheel with great attention. He wasn't a confrontational man but he was a master of not getting involved. Whichever one of us ended up in the back seat would have been fine with him – as long as he was paid.

'Women, huh! Hey, Driver.' Wilson thumped the front seat till Hakim looked at him, 'Get her out of there.'

Hakim stared at him blankly, then he peered at me. Ah Ma had booked him to take me to Bukit Batok, so he shouldn't have picked up an additional passenger. Then again, my grandmother always approved of extra business.

I didn't blame Hakim, given that the additional male passenger should have known to sit in front with him, leaving the back seat for Chen Tai's granddaughter. But how had someone who didn't know that Hakim drove for Chen Tai arranged for Hakim to pick him up?

As always when there was more going on than I understood, I sat tight and said nothing. The sweet, floral scent of angsana blossoms came through the open door.

'Well?' Wilson said. He tapped my shoulder and swept out his arm in an arc to show me the direction in which I should exit. I'd once watched an *ang moh* trying to teach a dog to fetch a stick with almost the same gestures. The dog, a Singapore Special, had ignored him. Having sniffed the stick before it was thrown and known it wasn't edible, it sat and licked its backside instead.

I didn't lick mine, but neither did I move out of the car.

'Your girlfriend?' Wilson said to Hakim. 'Do something, will you? '

Do something? Wilson seemed unfamiliar with Singapore – at least with how Singapore pirate taxis worked. But his uneven skin colour, the spider veins on his nose and neck and red, scaly spots on his hands showed he'd been out east long enough to suffer from the equatorial sun.

Not long enough, however, to impress his fellow officials, as his lack of an official car and driver showed. At least he didn't seem inclined to drag me physically out of the car.

But why was he heading to Bukit Batok or Upper Bukit Timah? There wasn't much in the quarry district to interest an *ang moh*. I wondered whether someone was playing a trick on him. *Ang moh*s were fond of playing tricks, especially when they got drunk.

'When he say "Wilson", I thought you Indian,' Hakim said. 'You not Indian.' He shook his head and reached to pull the door shut, as though the racial deception had been deliberate and was enough to forfeit the booking.

'What did you say?' I wanted to laugh at how shocked Mr Wilson looked. 'You dare call me a dirty Indian? I'll have your licence. I'll have your job!'

Hakim wouldn't have done that before the Occupation, but after you've seen Caucasians bowing to Asian *kempetai* you understand that white men are just men. For all their crazy cruelty, the Japanese had given us that. *Ang moh*s like

21

Le Froy, Dr Leask, Harry Palin and Mrs Shankar had been in Singapore long enough to see themselves as local, not better than locals.

'No licence, no job for you to take.' Hakim put the car into first gear.

'Stop! Your orders are to take me to the Bukit Timah fire station!'

I guessed Wilson was military or ex-military.

A gust of wind scattered a last few angsana blossoms over him. Wilson brushed the petals off his head and scraped a flower out of his collar, crushing it. Lovely as they are on the tree, their fragrance is strongest when crushed.

'Orange blossom.' Wilson sniffed his fingertips. 'Smells like orange blossom. Fake, of course. Like everything else in this damned place.'

Hakim released the handbrake and revved the engine. 'Who's going to Bukit Timah fire station?' he called out of his window, away from Wilson.

Wilson threw his briefcase into the front seat, climbed in after it and pulled the door shut behind him.

'So why are you heading to Upper Bukit Timah?' Wilson turned around to ask me, as the car moved off with a grinding of gears. I remained blank. 'No speak-oo English-oo, eh?'

He seem not to mind that apparently I didn't understand him. 'There should be some way to make something of these trees out here. Find a way to make them last longer, put them to some use. There's so much damned waste, that's what I can't stand. No one cares. Lazy locals, incompetent officials.'

I don't think Wilson was listening to himself. He was one of those people more uncomfortable with silence than stupidity. I'd often wished angsana flowers lasted longer too, but never thought of making it a government issue.

'Another race, another species . . . Of course I acknowledge intellect in other creatures. I once saw a pig in a circus they swore could count. If you tried to short-change her on apples she would grunt and snort and kick up an awful racket. But it turned out her handler was giving her signals all along. She was clever enough to grunt or not grunt, that was all. Her handler was using her to swindle fools in the audience.'

As we left the city, heading north-west down Bukit Timah Road, the landscape grew more rural. To our right I could see the primary forest that covered the granite heart of our island. Rubber, pineapple and mangosteen plantations and the *attap* huts the workers lived in edged the road. Many had been badly damaged by bombing during the invasion, but Nature recovers fast and sweet-potato vines, with bright blue to violet highlights from butterfly pea flowers, grew thick over the wrecked cars and ruined homes.

At the seventh milestone of Upper Bukit Timah Road, where Chun Tin Road and Jalan Jurong Kechil branched off, the Japanese had tried to create 'Beauty World' – an amusement park where Japanese propagandists for the 'Greater East Asia Prosperity Sphere' had held rallies and screened Japanese movies. Not surprisingly it had failed. All I saw as we drove past was a hotchpotch of zinc and *attap*-roofed shacks.

Even with Wilson talking to himself in the front seat, it felt more peaceful out here than it did in the city centre, where the land was increasingly crushed beneath housing and offices packed close together. And though it was not as developed as the residential east, the greenery and fresh air reminded me of the Singapore of my childhood. I remembered walking along goat trails, like the ones we were driving past now, muddy tracks that remained waterlogged for weeks during the annual monsoon. But this annual inconvenience had left rich silt that resulted in an abundance of vegetables and fruits.

The roads grew steadily worse after we left the modern macadam construction behind. The unsurfaced gravel was bumpy and made Hakim worry for his tyres and suspension as we passed streetlamps and telegraph poles that were still lying by the roadside. The power and water supply systems destroyed during the war were still being replaced.

Finally Hakim pulled to the side of the road and halted. 'Here?'

We'd stopped not far beyond the eighth milestone of Bukit Timah. I knew where we were because we'd just passed the Amoy canning factory with its giant Green Spot bottle standing outside – it had been something to watch out for when I'd gone with Uncle Chen and Shen Shen on Chinese New Year visits to the Pangs.

'Bukit Timah fire station.' Hakim pointed.

'Are you sure?' Wilson said.

We were looking at two buildings. One was like offices, with a large garage or storehouse beside and a little behind

24

it, wooden structures that were more like fire hazards than a fire station. A notice with the Crown Colony coat of arms read 'Bukit Timah Fire Station, 260–276 Upper Bukit Timah Road. (Residences Under Construction)'.

It didn't look as though the construction was ongoing. Behind the main buildings foundations had been laid, but the work had stopped long enough for the recent rains to have flooded the site. The residences, which were probably housing for the firemen and their families – how else would they get people willing to work out here? – wouldn't be ready for a while.

Wilson got out, throwing a few coins onto the seat, then slamming the door. Hakim was collecting and counting them, so I watched as a tall, Indian-looking man opened the door to Wilson, who waved his arms and gestured towards the car. He was clearly complaining about how he'd been treated. I guessed it was the man at the fire station who'd hired Hakim.

I didn't recognise him, but he stared at me in a way that made me think he knew me.

Satisfied, Hakim tooted his horn and waved out of the window as he drove off. Wilson ignored him, but the man from the fire station waved back. I'd been right about that, then. Hakim knew people everywhere.

'Old friend,' Hakim said, though I hadn't asked.

I could relax. Now Wilson was gone, it was good to be moving fast in a motor-car outside the city.

Suddenly we swerved, then stopped so suddenly I was jerked into the back of the front seat and the *bak zhang* tumbled onto the floor. 'Hakim? What happened?'

OVIDIA YU

Two thin women in *samfoos* were in the middle of the road, holding each other and weeping. Hakim must have been driving at 30 m.p.h. at least but he'd manage to swerve to a stop without hitting them.

'What are you doing in the middle of the road?' Hakim's voice showed how shaken he was. 'Want to die? Go and die somewhere else. If you damage my car I will kill you! This is expensive car, okay! Miss Chen, where are you going?'

I thought I recognised them – the two Pang sisters – and had climbed out of the car to hurry to them. Though we'd been bumping into ruts and over stones I stepped out into mud and possibly worse, but I ignored it and focused on the moaning women. They held both of each other's hands in a way that would have been comical if they hadn't been so terrified.

'Sissy? Girlie? What's wrong? What happened? Are you all right?' I spoke only basic Cantonese, but they caught their names and looked at me, blinking. 'It's Su Lin, Chen Su Lin, Chen Tai's granddaughter.'

'Su Lin! Come and help us!' They each took one of my hands, pulling me into their circle.

'Are you all right?' I couldn't see any injuries on them. 'What happened?'

'I should drive you to the house, Miss Chen.' Hakim had followed me out of the car.

Sissy and Girlie looked at him suspiciously and edged me away from him.

'It's Mei Mei! You must come and help her!'

'What's happened to her?'

'Please come and help Mei Mei! Quick!'

'What happened? Where is she?'

'Come!'

'Where is she?'

'At the Death Pool!'

The Body at the Death Pool

———◆———

The Death Pool was an old quarry that had been closed after several deaths due to rock-wall collapses. It had already been long abandoned when Danny Pang brought visiting children to the clearing where the old foreman's shack stood. That was where, in the old days, the quarried rocks and gravel had been weighed and loaded onto lorries, but now it was just a rock plateau with three large trees at the edge of the huge pool of dark water.

Danny scared us with stories of men who'd died in the quarry. Then he'd hold us off balance over the edge, saying the ghosts were hungry and wanted our *ang pows* – the Chinese New Year red packets containing money that children were given for good luck. Most children meekly surrendered them: Danny had bullied for profit as well as for fun.

Once, when Mei Mei came to find out what was happening, because I refused to surrender my *ang pows*, Danny pushed her in. Luckily she managed to cling to the rocks at the edge and climb out. I remembered thinking how unfair it was that Pang Tai scolded Mei Mei rather than Danny, and Uncle Chen told me to keep quiet when I tried to protest.

Anyway, as I followed Sissy and Girlie up the winding lorry track that branched off from the road, I guessed where we were heading.

'Is Danny up there? Is this one of his jokes?' I asked.

'No. Only Mei Mei is there,' Sissy said. 'Danny is at the number-four quarry.'

'Mei Mei said don't tell him,' Girlie added.

'Why?'

'We're not supposed to go up there, but then sometimes . . .'

'Sometimes we have to go,' Girlie added.

I'd not thought Danny Pang would be so protective. But maybe he'd changed. If you had three sisters living in semi-wilderness surrounded by quarry labourers you had to be careful.

Even before we reached the plateau I heard moaning. The girls pointed, 'Mei Mei's up there.'

The lorry track took the long way around, but the steep goat path on the right led directly up. Holding each other's hands again, Sissy and Girlie clearly meant to stay where they were. All right. If Mei Mei was hurt, the shortcut could make all the difference. I hitched up my dress, wishing I'd worn something more practical, and started up the path.

The gravel on the slope was moss-covered and slippery. I slipped and landed on my knees more than once and wished I'd followed the road. Though I insisted childhood polio hadn't handicapped me, it had left me unsuited to climbing slippery slopes with sharp gravel shards, thick roots and muddy slush. I was sweating and scratched when I finally stood on the plateau overlooking the Death Pool.

Somewhere a kingfisher was demanding, 'Cake? Cake! Cake? Cake!' A sweet fragrance came from the carpet of yellow surrounding the three old angsana trees. I'd forgotten how huge they were, at least ninety feet tall and five in diameter. They had a peaceful presence – until you saw two people beneath them . . . and the blood.

There was blood all over Mei Mei's *samfoo*. She was keening softly, leaning over a man's body covered with a scattering of yellow flowers. As I walked towards them, the smell of death was mixed with the fragrance of angsana. It wasn't just for flowers that death comes suddenly.

'Mei Mei!'

She jumped and looked terrified.

'It's Su Lin. Chen Tai's granddaughter. Do you remember me?'

'Su Lin?'

'What happened? Are you hurt?'

Mei Mei shook her head. 'I thought it was Stinky at first. I thought it was Stinky and he was dead.'

I squatted and looked at the body as I kept an eye on Mei Mei. As I told the police later, it was the body of a thin man who might have been Chinese or Malay. I wanted to make sure he was really dead and not in a faint, so I touched his neck. I jerked away in shock when I almost dislodged his head. What seemed a very fine line of red turned into a gaping raw wound. The front of his throat was cut almost to the bone. The man was definitely dead.

Mei Mei laughed. 'I thought his head would drop off! I thought it was Stinky! I thought he was dead but he's not!'

I wondered if she was in denial or had dementia. I lifted Mei Mei's hands off the body, checking her for injuries. She didn't seem hurt.

Of course she was in shock. Anyone would be. The bizarre wound reminded me of the old superstition that warned of demons hatching inside your body if you ate food stolen from prayer altars. Once the demons hatched, they exploded out of you, making you bleed from your mouth, ears and eyes . . . but nothing had exploded out of this man. Something had cut his throat from the outside.

Mei Mei had quietened and was watching me. There were bruises on her face and arms and I wondered if the dead man had caused them.

'Do you know who this is?' I asked.

Mei Mei nodded. 'Ah Kok,' she said. 'I thought it was Stinky,' she repeated. 'I was sure it was Stinky!' She started to laugh again. 'It's not funny. It's not funny at all. It's horrible. I don't know why I'm laughing.'

'Was he your boyfriend?' I asked. 'Did you come up here to meet him?'

'No! No, not my boyfriend. Don't say things like that!' She seemed angered by my question, but the next moment she was laughing again. 'Why does everybody think he's my boyfriend? Why would I want a boyfriend? I'm going to live here and work for my mother for ever.'

I almost asked why she had come to meet the man up here if he wasn't her boyfriend. Instead I realised the thing to do now was call the police and get Mei Mei away from there. It was a dangerous area, with the steep drop down to the rocks surrounding the Death Pool. I didn't want the police to come and find two bodies.

'Can you go back to the house and call the police?' I said.

'No, I can't.' Mei Mei shrank back from the body now, though she'd been holding it before. She looked as though she was going to throw up.

I dug into my cloth pouch and pulled out a paper packet of dried salt lime strips. 'Take one,' I ordered. 'It will settle your stomach.' Mei Mei refused, but I forced one into her palm, wincing at the blood and dirt there. She closed her fingers over it numbly. I had to move her hand to her mouth to get her to eat it. The blood on her fingers looked gruesome but she didn't notice.

Dried salt limes are good for soothing you whether you're coughing or thirsty or have just seen an almost decapitated body and need something to stop you throwing up. I stuffed a couple into my own mouth, grateful for the sour, salty shock. It helped to steady me.

I moved her away from the body, careful not to step on or dislodge anything that might be evidence. Mei Mei's face and arms were bruised, the red of fresh injury. I wondered what had happened. Had she defended herself against the man and killed him? Had someone else caught them up here and attacked them? Was the killer still about?

I looked around the little clearing. Could someone be hiding behind the three huge angsanas? Or in the old shack? Up here we were out of sight of the active quarry and the house. What had brought the dead man up here? And how had Mei Mei known to come up here to find him? I couldn't see anyone.

From what I remembered, there was another steep path at right angles to the one I'd climbed up. It ran down the slope to the back of the Pang house. Presumably that was the way Mei Mei had come up. These paths and the long winding lorry track were the only ways to get up here, but anyone might be waiting along any of the paths.

I had to find help, but which path to take?

The blood pooled around the body was already darkening. I saw there were deep cuts in the victim's fingers too. The tip of one had been nearly severed and I saw strange sparks of light there when the clouds moved and the sun caught it. It was almost as though the goddess Dian Mu had slashed his throat and fingers with her swift, deadly lightning bolts. But we were in modern Singapore, not ancient China.

Mei Mei was moaning again. She was genuinely upset, but I also had the feeling she was acting more upset than she felt to hide her . . . relief? I turned to her, then jumped when I saw movement at the top of the trail from the road. It was only Sissy and Girlie, still holding on to each other. I had no idea how long they'd been watching, but I was glad to see them.

'Come here. Do you have a phone in the house?'

'Yes. No.'

'Yes, but not working.'

'Can you send someone for the police?' I said.

'Police?'

'There are no police here.'

I remembered Hakim Harez. 'You know the driver who brought me here? Remember the car I came in? Find the driver and tell him to let the police know there's a dead body here. And he should tell Le Froy.'

Sissy and Girlie stared at their bloodied sister. They seemed more struck by the state of her than by the dead man on the ground.

'Ma will scold you for spoiling your clothes,' Girlie said.

'Ma will scold you,' Sissy agreed.

'Go!' I said. 'Now. Quick. Take Mei Mei with you. Tell the taxi driver to inform the police. And take Mei Mei back to the house. I will stay here with the – with the man until the police come.'

I'd thought someone ought to stay with the body till help came, but I wasn't so sure it was a good idea after they'd left.

A String of Flying Seeds

I'd already checked that no one was lurking around, but if Sissy and Girlie had come up without my hearing them, why not the killer? And why had staying with the body seemed a good idea? It felt wrong to leave it, even if the victim was dead, beyond minding, at the mercy of flies or birds or anything that might crawl out of the Death Pool.

And, yes, I regretted thinking of what might come out of the Death Pool. There were too many flies around. I flicked them away, a few inquisitive ants too, but did 'preserving evidence' mean chasing ants away or leaving them as 'natural'? Sherlock Holmes would probably have known how someone had been killed from the kind of ants on a body, but I wasn't a supernaturally intelligent fictional character and I preferred to stay away from ants. I noticed that, although the man lay at some distance from the rocky drop to the water's edge, his sandals and legs were wet and covered with algae scum. His shirt was wet, too, with more than blood, and his fingernails were crusted with pond dirt and fibres from some kind of sacking, as though he'd been trying to rip something apart.

I went to the edge of the Death Pool and looked down the steep drop to the dark water. I couldn't see anything he might have tried to push into or pull out of the water. I spotted a couple of angsana seeds and reached for them.

Angsana seeds are brown and circular, with a bulge at the centre and often a little tail. They look like little flying saucers or stingrays. We'd all played with them as children. These seeds looked like they'd been threaded on a string that had snagged on a rock. I couldn't tell if the dark stain on them was blood.

The angsana trees here had shed all of their blossoms, but it would be some time before the seeds formed. The ones I'd found must have come from a previous season. The angsana is valued in traditional medicine as well as for its durable and strong hardwood. The bark is used to treat diarrhoea and dysentery; the gum soothes lumps and bumps and mouth sores; and the leaves are steeped for potions. But these trees had been badly treated. Someone had made horizontal cuts about an inch deep around the trunks, which left resin oozing out, like blood from a slashed arm. It would be easy to collect, but would continue oozing, making it harder for the trees to recover. There were dark scarred lines of crusted sap from previous cuts and I could see dead branches that hadn't survived them.

I couldn't tell what had made those marks – no saw or axe with which I was familiar. A younger, frailer tree could be killed in that way. Cutting one groove at a slant and inserting a shunt was slower, but the sap would flow for up to five hours and the trees could adapt better – look at how rubber trees survive, despite years of daily tapping.

Was that why Mei Mei had come up here? Whoever was collecting the resin was an impatient, selfish person. I decided that someone who showed so little respect for the life blood of a tree was quite capable of murder.

But feeling sorry for the trees was a pathetic attempt to distract myself from the dead man beneath them. Nevertheless you shouldn't ignore small wrongs because other wrongs seem more important.

I could see no one in the foreman's shack but went to take a closer look. It wasn't much more than three sides of wood planking with an *attap* roof overlooking the quarry below. There were some sacks, a scattering of granite chips and the rock dust that lay everywhere. I noticed some *langau* or blowflies. Slightly larger than houseflies with a metallic sheen, they are usually the first to arrive when an animal is wounded or dies.

The plateau seemed the only level area around the Death Pool. Sheer rock face rose on its far side: that was where the active quarries were. Other than the steep goat trail up from the road, and the path branching off it that led down to the back of the Pang house, there was the curving lorry track.

I walked down to the bend in the lorry track to see how far it went. There, another steep trail branched off, seeming to lead down towards another small plateau. I sniffed. I could smell badly prepared charcoal that gave off more stench and ash than heat. It was hard to tell through the thorny overgrowth but it looked as if someone, perhaps one of the Pangs' workers, had set up a cooking area there.

'Don't move!' a man's voice said.

The murderer? I spun around, but it was only Danny Pang.

'I said, "Don't move"! There's a black snake behind you. Very poisonous. By the time you hear it hissing, it's too late. You're dead.'

And then I heard the hissing.

I scrambled away. If it was already too late it couldn't hurt, and as Froy says, it's harder to hit a moving target. I stumbled and fell but continued crawling away as fast as I could, until I realised Danny was laughing. Of course he was the one hissing.

It was the kind of trick Danny had played in the old days. Drat him – and me: I'd fallen for it.

I got to my feet and smoothed down my dress. My knees and palms were scraped and sore.

'Come on,' he said. 'Can't you take a joke?'

I reminded myself that people deal with shock in different ways and maybe being an idiot was Danny's method.

'Why did you run away? I told you, don't move. If there was really a snake, you would be dead and serve you right.'

'But there wasn't.'

'Hah!' Danny said, 'I'm trying to teach you a lesson but you're too stupid to learn. Girls are so dumb. You and my sisters, all so dumb. Why did you tell Sissy and Girlie to call the police?'

I pointed towards the body under the trees. Danny kept his eyes away from it, but I could tell he knew it was there. 'Mei Mei had quite a shock.'

'Well, who told Mei Mei to come up here? If you're so clever, answer me that!' Danny was looking for a reason to be angry. I couldn't believe he'd once reminded me of Uncle Chen – who had to be prodded into doing anything.

'How's your ma?' I asked. The youngest child, Danny had always been close to his mother. 'Is she at home?'

'Why is that your business? What are you going to tell my ma?'

'I hope she's okay, that's all. Mei Mei was quite upset. Women get upset when things like that happen. And Ah Ma gave me some *bak zhang* for all of you. I must have left them in the car.'

I hoped the food was all right and was reminded of how shock makes people react strangely. Look at me, worrying about *achar* and *bak zhang* at a time like this.

'My ma is in the house. Where else would she be?' Danny didn't look angry any more, but again he asked, 'What are you going to tell her about . . . ?' He waved at the body without looking at it.

'I think most likely it was a tiger or wild boar.' A sharp claw or tusk might have slashed the poor man's throat. 'Mei Mei probably frightened it off before it could drag him away.'

'Huh.' Danny glanced at the body and looked away. 'So why are you here? Waiting for *hantu, ah*?'

Even though he laughed, Danny was clearly uncomfortable talking about *hantu* or ghosts. Most people were, whether they admitted it or not. Likely there would soon be whispers that spirits had come out of the Death Pool and killed the man. A little shrine would appear under the angsana trees, so that if the dead man's spirit tried to return to his body, it would realise it was dead.

'Do you know why Mei Mei came up here?' I asked.

'Exactly!' Danny said, 'Why did she?' He was working himself up again.

'Look . . .' I put a hand on his arm to stop him. Danny shook me off impatiently but I had to say my piece before he saw his sister. 'I know you're angry with Mei Mei but it's no use shouting at her. Do you know if she came up here to meet somebody?'

I wasn't just being a busybody. These were questions the authorities would ask, and they might be gentler with Mei Mei if I could give them some idea of the situation. 'Why would Mei Mei meet anybody?'

'Why would Mei Mei meet somebody here?'

'Do you know if Mei Mei had a boyfriend? Wait – don't get angry. I'm not accusing her of anything but I think she went to *paktor* with somebody and they had a fight. '

Paktor in Singlish covers everything from a casual date to a passionate relationship. Danny gaped at me, shaking his head slowly. I couldn't tell if he was more shocked that his sister might have been seeing someone or that she might have killed him.

'Danny, listen to me. Someone hit Mei Mei. There are bruises on her face and arms. If the man who is now dead attacked her and she defended herself, they can't blame her for killing him.'

Danny stared, processing this. At least he didn't flare up again. I suspected his anger was a defence when he felt threatened, meaning he didn't see me as a danger. Men weren't so difficult to handle if you were used to dealing with children and animals.

'Mei Mei said he's called Ah Kok or Stinky,' I said. 'Did you know him?'

'Of course,' Danny said. 'I know him better than my stupid sister!'

Ah Kok

———◆———

'His name was Khoo Kheng Kok. He was my friend, not Mei Mei's. People called him Ah Kok. He used to work for me,' Danny said.

'I'm sorry,' I said.

'Ah Kok's father was my pa's foreman. They disappeared at the same time. The Japanese took them away. So when I took over from my pa, Ah Kok got his father's job. Now . . .' He shrugged.

'I'm sorry,' I said, but returned to a more important point: 'Have your sisters rung the police yet?'

'The telephone line's not working,' Danny said. 'Somebody has to go to the fire station for that.'

So there was a purpose to that ramshackle fire station, after all. Well, unless I wanted to walk to the fire station myself (I didn't), I might as well put this time to good use.

'Of course you don't want to get Mei Mei into trouble, but if you know anything about her and Ah Kok you should tell the police, okay?'

Danny glanced at Ah Kok's body, then turned to stare at the dark water of the quarry pond.

I normally found it peaceful to be around water. But this wasn't the living, moving water of sea or stream. Rather, it was stagnant, with flies and other insects. It reminded me that the Dragon Boat Festival was also a time to counter bad vapours – we were coming into the warm season when people got sick easily and epidemics spread. Though mostly they didn't die with their throats slashed.

'We used to go swimming down there,' Danny said. 'Can you believe it? Me and Ah Kok and Stinky.' Danny's eyes were still on the dark water. 'When we were small. They told us, "Dangerous! Stay away!" but you know what boys are like, right?'

Stinky – that was the other name Mei Mei had mentioned.

'You and Ah Kok and – Stinky? You were good friends when you were young?'

'Yah. The three of us were friends. And we all made it through the Japanese killing Chinese men and boys. We were the "Lucky Three" – that was what people called us. But then I had to take over the quarry and they were working for me and, I don't know, after that, we were not so close.'

'Can be hard when your friend becomes your boss,' I said.

'I didn't show them any favouritism. I had to tell them, "You cannot bully the workers just because you're the boss's friend."'

'Not your fault,' I said. 'Do you know if Ah Kok had problems with anybody else?'

'Stinky,' Danny said quietly. Now he looked at me, as though challenging me to deny it.

I remembered Mei Mei saying she'd thought the body was Stinky's . . .

'Where's Stinky now?'

Danny shrugged, taciturn again. 'Don't know. Haven't seen him.' Clearly he suspected something there, too, but was unwilling to say it.

'I know you don't want to get your friend into trouble, but something happened between Stinky and Ah Kok, right?'

'I heard Ah Kok shouting at Stinky for getting my father and his father taken away by the Japanese.'

'You mean he was an informer? But that was in Japanese time. Why did he bring it up now? When did you hear?'

'This morning.'

Ah. That could have led to a fight and—

'Do you believe him?'

Danny shook his head. 'I don't know what to think. I told them to get out of my office and fight somewhere else. I don't know why they came here.'

'Do you know where Stinky is now?'

'He's supposed to be supervising quarry fourteen and he didn't turn up. But . . .'

'But what?'

'Stinky had been staying with my family for years. My pal, my bro, you know? But recently he started pestering Mei Mei.'

'Mei Mei?' Maybe I shouldn't have dismissed her as an old maid.

'I had no choice but to kick him out of the house. I never fired him, though. He could have gone on working. He was my old *kaki*, my bro. But Mei Mei is my sister, you know what I mean?'

I'd never had a brother to watch out for me in that way but I could imagine. Like Uncle Chen but less bossy. It would have been nice. 'Would it have been so bad? I mean, if he and Mei Mei got together?'

'Ma called him "that Indonesian",' Danny said. He shook his head. 'His pa was Chinese but his ma was Indonesian. She was a bar-girl.'

Singaporeans might overlook race and religion, but protective mothers are in a category of their own.

'What's Stinky's real name?' I asked.

'Teo Shin Yi. He came to stay with us after his ma died. His pa was my pa's old friend, but he was dead.'

I didn't remember Stinky, but if he'd grown up with the Pangs, likely he'd been one of the children I'd encountered during past Chinese New Year festivities.

'And Ah Kok's name was Khoo Kheng Kok?'

Danny nodded, 'He wanted to be Mei Mei's boyfriend, but Stinky also liked Mei Mei, so . . .'

I was learning a lot about Mei Mei.

'Your ma didn't like Ah Kok either? He was Chinese, right?'

'We had nothing against Ah Kok but he was only earning sixty dollars per month. If Mei Mei wants to marry, why not marry somebody who can help the family instead of becoming an added burden?'

I knew Danny meant well but he had no idea of how to talk to a sister about her suitors. I couldn't say much about Mei Mei's choice of men as the only one I'd met was dead. And who was I to talk anyway? My options weren't much better.

'You're their boss, couldn't you help with the salary?' I asked.

'I told Mei Mei to wait until I can increase Ah Kok's pay to a hundred and sixty dollars a month. But what can I do? Everybody needs granite for their roads, their buildings, but nobody has money to pay me until their construction is complete. How am I supposed to pay my suppliers and my men? And now sections eighteen and nineteen are flooding. There's still a lot of good rock, which shouldn't go to waste, but the stupid fools refuse to work there. They say the walls are not stable – if they weren't stable they wouldn't be walls. They would be floors, right?'

Despite all the problems, he seemed happiest talking about the quarry.

'Do you think Ah Kok and Mei Mei came here?' I could imagine how romantic this place might be (minus the dead body), with a carpet of blossoms and the scent of the angsana. 'She said not, but she might have been lying,' I said.

'She might,' Danny agreed.

Mei Mei was his sister, but from what I'd seen of my friend Parshanti and her brother growing up, sisters lied to brothers more than they lied to anyone else.

Danny looked strained and exhausted and I felt sorry for him. Whatever Mei Mei's relationship with Ah Kok, Danny had been his friend since they were boys. It was tragic that they'd survived the war and the deaths of their fathers only for things to end up like this.

When he started down the goat path to the road I went with him. We'd see anyone approaching from the road, though not from the house – and it wasn't likely his sisters would come from there.

'There were workers up here earlier.' I remembered the damp charcoal I'd smelt. 'Somebody was cooking.'

'Nah. The workers don't cook for themselves,' Danny said.

'There's a clearing – a little way down the lorry road?' I'd caught a glimpse of what had looked like embers under a cauldron support.

'Nah,' Danny said again. 'Hey! Your driver put your food on the roadside before driving off.'

'Oh, no!'

I'd forgotten all about Hakim picking me up – forgotten about him altogether. It must have been well over an hour since he'd dropped me off and I hadn't even seen Pang Tai yet. Or were all social niceties thrown out the window when there had been a death in the vicinity?

'He was going to drive me back,' I said, suddenly exhausted.

'I can take you,' Danny said. 'The quarry is closed for the rest of the day. Always like that when there's a death on the site. The workers are used to it. They're all in the dormitories – see?' He pointed further down the main road and I peered through the thorny shrubbery.

'Why is there barbed wire around the workers' quarters?'

'From the Japanese time. That was when it went up.'

Of course. Under the Japanese, everything had changed. But now things were starting to change back.

'Can you give this food to your ma? From Ah Ma. She made *bak zhang* for you all, for the Dragon Boat Festival. Sorry we're returning your ma's *tingkat* so late.'

'Give them to her yourself,' Danny said. 'I'll drive you over to the house.'

'You have a motor-car?' If it was a motorcycle I didn't think I could manage the *tingkat* and my grandmother's extra food.

'Better than a motor-car.'

What Danny had was a small pickup truck, with a rickety shelter rigged over a high-sided loading bed and a row of benches on each side. It was clearly used to transport workers as well as goods, though any adult occupants would have knees overlapping. Right now it was empty, except for a heavy tarpaulin, some sacking and ropes.

We put Ah Ma's *bak zhang* and pickles into the back and I managed to climb up into the two-seater cabin while Danny watched me and laughed. Gentlemanly behaviour went only so far.

'I should have put you in the back. It took you longer to get in than it will to drive you there.'

'I could have walked to the house,' I said, 'or I could have sat in the back.'

For some reason this made Danny snort with laughter. 'I promise you, you wouldn't like it there.'

Before he started the engine, I heard a vehicle approaching from the direction of the main road. Danny got out of the pickup at once. I did the same, more slowly. Was it the police?

The beaten-up jeep that appeared didn't look like a police vehicle. It stopped at the foot of the trail and I heard a familiar high-pitched voice complaining about the road conditions. Wilson got out of the vehicle, which I saw was driven by the tall, dark fire-station officer.

'Do you know who that *ang moh* is?' I asked Danny. 'What is he doing here?'

'Must be from the government.'

He seemed to recognise the fire-station officer, though. I could tell because he looked away when the officer grinned at him.

'Who's that?' I asked.

'How would I know?' Danny said.

'Peters!' Wilson said. 'There's no quarry pond here. You've got the wrong place again. What are you looking at?'

Wilson glanced round, but didn't register us two locals at the foot of the track.

Peters winked at me, then turned to Wilson. 'Up there, sir. We can drive around by the road, takes fifteen to twenty minutes. Or we can walk up the track.' He gestured at the goat path behind us. 'It'll take five to ten minutes.'

'I'm not getting back into that thing.' Wilson took in the path and finally registered us. 'You two, get away from here,' he said. 'This is government business.'

'. . . from the Pang house,' I heard Peters say, as they started up the goat path. And then, 'A Chen, I think . . .'

Wilson turned back to us, lost his balance and fell, swearing. I felt a mean pleasure that even with two good legs he wasn't doing much better on the uphill path than I had.

'Can we bring the food up to your house?' I said to Danny, who seemed torn between keeping an eye on me and watching Wilson and Peters. 'I want to give it to your ma.'

'Yah.' The mention of his mother activated him. 'Hurry up. Why are you so slow?'

The Pang House

———◆———

'Pang Tai, my grandmother says she's sorry she took so long to return your *tingkat*. And she made some *bak zhang* for you and your family.'

'Chen Su Lin! You are still here, *ah*?' Pang Tai looked surprised to see me, but recovered fast. '*Wah*, Chen Tai is so good, so generous! Everything is so upside down here today that I have nothing to give you in return. Sorry, *ah*, excuse me one minute. Sissy! Girlie! Come and take all this to the kitchen.'

Pang Tai, talking non-stop, disappeared into the back of the house. Danny hurried after her. I wondered what she'd heard about the dead body from her daughters – maybe she was hoping it was one of Danny's jokes.

I followed Sissy and Girlie to the kitchen, 'Where's Mei Mei?' I asked.

'Mei Mei?' Sissy said.

'Why Mei Mei?' Girlie said.

'I just want to see if she's okay,' I said. 'Finding a dead body must be so scary, right?' I gave a shiver of exaggerated fear.

'Mei Mei is crying,' Sissy said. 'In our room.'

'Mei Mei's upset,' Girlie said. 'She won't come out.'

'Can I go to see her?' I headed down the corridor to the bedrooms, wondering if the girls were still sharing the room nearest the back door to the kitchen I remembered from the old days.

Indeed Mei Mei still shared the same room with her sisters. It was so crowded with things that it was hard to tell, but they might have been sleeping on the same mattresses. She was curled up on one, still wearing the blood-spattered clothes. And I'd been right about the bruising on her arms and face.

'What happened? Who hit you? Was it Ah Kok?'

Mei Mei just shook her head. When I asked if Stinky had hit her, she turned away, but I felt sure I was right. Was she so terrified of him she couldn't even say his name?

'Why did you go up to the Death Pool?'

Mei Mei shrugged. 'Needed *kino*.'

Kino, or dragon's blood, was the milky red angsana sap. I guessed Mei Mei needed it for her cuts and bruises. Did that mean she was the one who'd tapped the trees so brutally?

'I found these up there.' I showed Mei Mei the strand of flying angsana seeds I'd found.

She snatched it from me. 'Where did you get this? Who gave it to you?' She examined the seeds. I saw terror in her eyes as she spotted the traces of blood. 'Tell me!'

'They were up by the Death Pool,' I said. 'Caught on the rocks near the water.'

'No, no, no . . .' Mei Mei opened a rattan box drawer and tucked the string of seeds into a cloth with a dried stalk and blooms. Then she closed her eyes and started moaning again, like she'd been doing over the body, as though all hope was lost. I didn't think she was putting on an act – but she'd had the presence of mind to put away the angsana seeds . . .

'You didn't make food for the workers today,' Sissy said. She and Girlie came in and sat side by side on another mattress.

'You need to make food for the workers,' Girlie said.

'There's not enough rice left.' Mei Mei tried to cover her face, but winced. Her right wrist seemed to be giving her pain.

'You should see a doctor about your hand,' I said.

'It's okay.' Mei Mei lifted her arm, then spoiled the effect by whimpering.

'You should see a doctor,' I said again.

'No.' Mei Mei shook her head.

'Or why don't you come back to Chen Mansion with me?' I said. 'Our neighbour is a very good nurse. If the bone is broken, she can splint it for you. She takes care of a lot of women who don't want to see man doctors. And she won't charge you. She's Malay but she can speak some Cantonese and I can translate for you.'

'I don't think my mother would like it,' Mei Mei said. 'She doesn't like me to go out.'

'You numbskull!' Pang Tai had reappeared and found us. 'Why were you sneaking around and finding dead bodies?

If you stay here and do your work we wouldn't *kenah* anything like that!'

So the man wouldn't have been dead if Mei Mei hadn't found his body? I reminded myself Pang Tai was probably also in shock and not to judge her.

Mei Mei looked guilty to me too, and I had the feeling she was hiding something. But some people automatically act guilty when they're being questioned.

'I know it looks like she killed him, but we don't know what happened yet. Don't be angry with her,' I said. 'She was there by the body, covered with blood. Maybe he attacked her and it was self-defence. Get her to tell you what happened before the police come.'

'Yes,' Pang Tai said. 'You are very wise.'

She rearranged her face and smiled at me. 'How is your uncle? So sad to hear what happened to that wife of his . . .' She was wearing gold earrings and two gold chains and her eyebrows freshly drawn on. To impress me? That was unlikely. I wasn't worth impressing. More likely it was to show respect for my grandmother, whom I represented.

Compared to Pang Tai, Ah Ma seemed old and shabby, as if she wasn't bothering any more and didn't care what people might think of her. I felt embarrassed for her.

'*Wah*, Su Lin. New dress, right? So pretty. But it's dirty. Wasted!'

Pang Tai had the flat, round face of a farmer's wife but her cheeks were whitened, her hair blackened, and as she chatted she casually flicked her fingers so I could see the rings she was wearing. I wasn't sure, but I think she'd slipped those on too, when she went to put on her entertaining-a-guest outfit.

'Your poor uncle shouldn't have any trouble getting someone to look after him and his little daughter – how is she?'

She looked more avid for gossip than sympathetic. 'Ah Ma is looking for a new servant girl to look after her.' So far none had measured up.

'Servant girls are no use!' Pang Tai said. 'He should get her a new mother!' I saw her glance at her three daughters.

'My uncle is very well,' I said. 'He's spending a lot of time with his daughter.' Actually, Uncle Chen was blossoming. Being a widower seemed to suit him.

'He has only one daughter, right?' Pang Tai shook her head sadly. 'No sons.'

I knew it wasn't fair to hold that against her, but I did. At least my grandmother valued her granddaughters.

Danny opened the door. 'Have the workers been fed yet?' He might have been talking about pigs.

'Mei Mei usually makes food for them,' Sissy said.

'We just bring it down. We do the washing,' Girlie said.

I remembered the cooking fire I'd seen off the lorry track leading to the Death Pool. 'Can't you give the workers food and let them cook for themselves?

'No,' said Girlie. 'The workers are not allowed to cook.'

'No,' said Sissy. 'The workers are never allowed to cook.'

Mei Mei lay there with her eyes shut.

My life's goal had always been to get away from cooking and other domestic chores, but I was good at them, thanks to my grandmother. Ah Ma believed that clean bedding and clean floors were an extension of personal hygiene, and preparing a meal for twenty or more was a matter of basic organisation. 'I can help,' I said.

Even if no one in the house felt like eating, food had to be provided for the workers. I'd learned from my grandmother that that was a responsibility you took on once you had someone working for you.

And maybe Mei Mei would be more disposed to talk if she didn't have meal preparations hanging over her.

Ah Ma's kitchen was a model of practicality. Of course it was the Chinese amah *jies* and the local servant girls and house-boys who kept it clean, but everyone knew it had to be maintained according to Chen Tai's standards. Most of our pots and pans and spatulas were old and worn, but everything in view was regularly used to feed the household, and there were larger vats to feed the hordes on special festival days.

The charcoal chips container, the pig bin and the chicken bucket were emptied, washed and set upside down to drain, the bins of rice and barley, the tins of rock sugar, dried chillies, dried mushrooms, lotus buds and ginkgo nuts regularly topped up.

I'd taken such organisation for granted until I'd seen kitchens in other family homes. Like the Shankars': there was order, but it was obvious only to Mrs Shankar. And like the Pangs': I couldn't make sense of how their kitchen was arranged . . . or perhaps it wasn't arranged at all. If Mei Mei and her sisters were doing the cooking for their household as well as for the workers in the dormitories, why were certain goods locked into cupboards? And why were there only two or three cups of powdery rice left? That was hardly enough to feed all the men I'd seen behind the barbed-wire fencing. I found a cache of century eggs stored in dragon pots behind the kitchen.

Pei dan, or century eggs, are duck, chicken or quail eggs preserved in a mixture of clay, ash, salt, quicklime and rice hulls for weeks or months. The yolks become a dark greenish grey and have a creamy consistency. The whites turn into a translucent dark brown jelly.

Thanks to the war years, I was familiar with stretching food resources. One big pot of rice porridge would fill their stomachs at least. And there were bean sprouts, bean curd and fermented stinky tofu 'cheese' made of fresh bean curd preserved with salt, rice wine and chilli.

'You're giving them so much food, *ah*?' Danny said.

'*Wah.*' Pang Tai had come in behind him. She started to say something about the food, but I'd noticed what Danny was now wearing.

'You're wearing the same jacket as Ah Kok?'

'It's the foreman's,' Danny said. 'Keys, torch, alarm whistle, everything.'

'What if it was you they wanted to kill?' I said. 'You look like you're about the same height. From behind, in the same jacket, maybe they killed the wrong man.'

'Ha!' Danny said. 'Trying to scare me, are you? I'm not scared!'

'What?' Pang Tai said. 'Why would anybody attack Danny?'

'Why would anybody do anything to Ah Kok if he was just working for Danny? You don't understand,' I said. 'I'm just saying that if somebody didn't know Danny, and Ah Kok was good friends with Danny—'

'Everybody is good friends with Danny. Danny has many friends. What are you trying to say about him? Stinky and Ah Kok were his good friends. For many years they were all good friends. Stinky was like a brother to him.'

'And somebody killed Ah Kok!' Why couldn't they see what was so obvious?

'I don't know anything about that,' Danny cut in. 'Why do you say things like that? Why do you talk to my mother like that after she's been so good to you?'

Danny might have been the strongest and loudest but no one would have called him the brightest. I turned to Pang Tai. If I could make her understand, she could explain it to Danny better than I could.

'Whoever killed Ah Kok might have thought he was attacking Danny. You must tell him to be careful.'

Pang Tai stared at me. Then she turned to Danny, who was also staring at me, his mouth open.

'I'm sorry,' I said, 'but I have to say it. You might be in danger. In fact, whoever did this to your friend might have been after you.'

'Danny?' Pang Tai looked at her son. I saw that she'd understood me perfectly but wanted to make sure that he did too. It was automatic little gestures like this that probably made her an easier woman to live with than someone like

Mrs Shankar, who always said what she thought and wouldn't hesitate to call you stupid if you were being stupid.

'Danny? Danny, look at me and pay attention. What is Su Lin saying?'

'That whoever killed Ah Kok might try to kill me.'

Pang Tai nodded, acknowledging this. Then, as it sank in, she shook her head slowly. 'No . . .' she said.

'Don't look like that, Ma. You know that nothing is going to happen to me. I can take care of myself.'

But they still hadn't got the whole thing. 'You must be careful, Danny. I know that Stinky is your friend, but if something happened that made him attack Ah Kok – Danny, you mustn't trust Stinky just because he's your friend. If you know where he's hiding you must tell the police, okay?'

'Please,' Pang Tai said to me, 'please, you must help my son.' She held out her small, perfectly manicured hands to me. When I took them in mine, they were very cold. She put her head on my shoulder and wept. 'Stinky's father was close to Danny's. My late husband insisted we take the boy in, even though his mother was a bar-girl. I couldn't kick out the boy because Danny's father insisted that he stay. I never thought it would put my own son at risk. Su Lin! You must help us. I am depending on you. Danny, come with me! Danny, come, I want to talk to you.'

After their mother and brother had left, Sissy and Girlie helped to pack the food, fitting it on the trolley around the rice-porridge pot they would push across to the dormitories.

'At least Mei Mei has stopped shouting,' Sissy said.

'No more shouting,' Girlie agreed.

'Who was Mei Mei shouting at?' I asked.

Sissy and Girly looked startled, as though they hadn't realised they weren't alone. I hefted the wok onto the edge of the basin and turned my back to them. 'I get scared when people shout,' I said absently, as I scrubbed.

'So do I,' Sissy said.

'I think she was shouting at Stinky,' Girlie said. 'I was scared too.'

'Mei Mei shouted, "I hate you! I wish you were dead!"' Sissy said, not to be outdone.

'Danny said not to tell the police,' Girlie said.

'I'm not the police,' I said, into the silence that followed.

'Yah.'

'Yah, so it's okay.'

'The *ang moh* police at the Death Pool want to see you.' Danny appeared in the doorway.

Sissy and Girlie screamed and put their arms around each other.

'Shut up, you idiots,' Danny said. 'The police want to see Su Lin!'

Suspects on the Scene

———◆———

A young policeman was waiting outside the front door. 'This way, miss,' he said, and walked me back up to the Death Pool.

I'd not seen him before. Most of the experienced police officers who'd survived the Occupation had been posted up-country to Perak and Kedah for 'retraining' or to help re-establish borders. They would also root out vigilantes and rogue Japanese soldiers from the jungle.

I'd never thought I'd miss Prakesh Pillay and Ferdie de Souza so much.

'I said, secure the scene!' Wilson was saying, to another policeman, as we arrived. 'I ordered the quarry shut down until further notice. Don't just stand there. Tell them to stop work and round them up.'

My police escort went to stand beside his colleague. The two acknowledged Wilson's orders but didn't do anything. They looked like a bicycle patrol who had been flagged down and were waiting for someone in authority to appear. A piece of tarpaulin had been thrown over the figure under the trees, but nothing else had changed.

'The quarry has already stopped work.' Danny had followed us. He spoke to the policeman in Malay. 'The workers are back in the dormitories.'

'That one again,' Wilson said, without looking at him. 'Tell him to go away and get his boss here. I just hope to God the man speaks English. There's been a murder. Doesn't anyone here understand that?'

The bicycle policemen looked uncomfortable. I guessed they knew Danny owned and managed the quarry. But Wilson, who'd taken charge, wasn't listening to them.

'I speak English,' I said. 'This is Mr Pang, big boss of Pang Quarry. I can translate for you.'

Maybe it wasn't my smartest move, since it drew Wilson's attention to me. But I'd been working in a hot kitchen for the last half-hour and I wanted to get all this sorted out so I could leave with a clear conscience.

'That's her,' Wilson said. 'I told you to arrest her.'

What?

'Sir, you said bring her,' the policeman who'd accompanied me said. 'You never said bring where.'

'You're all fools!' Wilson said, then turned on me. 'You speak English. You lied to me in the car. Who are you, really? Who sent you to spy on me? And why did you kill that man?'

'What?'

'Arrest her,' I said. 'Why are you standing there like idiots? I don't care if you don't have handcuffs – just tie her up with something so she can't run off again.'

'On what charges are you arresting her?' Le Froy said.

I spun around. Le Froy was no longer in uniform, but his presence still gave off an aura of authority that made the two policemen and even Danny stand up straighter. This wasn't just because he was an *ang moh* – Wilson certainly didn't have it.

'Su Lin,' Le Froy said, 'what are you doing here?'

I saw he had come up from the lorry track, walking around the police vehicle that had been parked across the road to block access to the crime scene. Of course, anyone could just walk around the motor-car as Le Froy had just done and there was no way to block off all the ill-defined goat paths. Just seeing him made me feel a hundred times better. I was smiling from sheer relief. It was like in the old films where the music switches from a minor to a major key when the hero arrives and you know everything's going to be all right. Though this wasn't a movie and I had no idea how it was going to turn out.

Le Froy gave my shoulder a quick squeeze. I saw the flare of interest in Danny Pang's eyes and the disgust in Wilson's and thought simultaneously that Le Froy shouldn't have touched me and that he'd let go too soon.

No, I wasn't being rational. Yes, I was glad he was there.

'It is murder,' I said.

Le Froy's eyes were warm and happy to see me. 'You've seen the body? Not a quarry accident?'

'No. This quarry has been closed down for years. Since before the war. And it wasn't—'

'I have undeniable proof,' Wilson interrupted. 'That girl was in my car coming out here. She somehow found out about my meeting and forced – or paid – my driver to transport her. That driver must be found and interrogated right away.'

'You want her arrested for coming out here in your car?'

'It wasn't his car!' I said.

'I want her arrested for the murder of Danny Pang, owner of the Pang quarry. I came out here by appointment to meet Mr Pang this morning, but she got to him first and killed him.'

'Hah?' Danny might not speak good English, but he could follow it well enough to understand he'd been killed. This was the first time I'd seen him look so shaken.

'Danny Pang,' Le Froy said, 'murdered.'

Before Wilson could come up with undeniable proof that Danny was dead, Fahey and several other policemen came down the lorry track.

Michael Fahey was now Detective Chief Fahey and had become acting head of Singapore's Detective and Intelligence Unit after the departure of Rob Johnson. He and Johnson, an old college friend and the governor's stepson, went a long way back. My distrust of Governor Evans and his family covered Fahey, too, and I didn't understand why Le Froy couldn't see they were all the same.

Fahey might retain some naive, youthful idealism, but in the end they all served the hand that fed them.

Fahey's officers were carrying evidence bags and I realised they must already have gone over this area before they'd walked along the trails. I wondered if I ought to mention the angsana seeds I'd found – but they were with Mei Mei and I didn't want to compromise her.

'Finally!' Wilson seemed peeved yet relieved to see Fahey. 'I don't know why you're wasting official time. It's obviously a case of two family triads competing to control the opium black market. Anyway, everything's under control. I didn't mean you to come out – I just needed someone to take this culprit in for questioning. This overlaps with my investigation so I suggest you leave the documentation to me.'

'Sergeant Gomez?' Fahey said to the policeman who'd escorted me from the house. 'You spoke to some of the workers?'

'Yes, sir. I interviewed several of the men, sir. They all said the same thing. That the spirit of their old boss and foreman came out of the water and killed the victim,' Sergeant Gomez said. He referred pointedly to his notes to show he was not making it up.

'But Danny Pang isn't dead,' Le Froy said.

'I saw the body myself,' Wilson scoffed. 'The man is definitely dead. And she,' he pointed at me, 'is responsible. I practically caught her in the act earlier. Look at her – covered in blood! You were looking for the weapon? You'll probably find it on her.'

'I'm not dead,' Danny said loudly. He was starting to look upset again. Chinese people believe it's bad luck to say someone is dead when they're not because words have the power to make things happen.

'And who are you?' Wilson demanded.

'I am Danny Pang,' Danny said.

'You are a liar,' Wilson said. 'You're with her. Part of her gang.' He turned on me. 'I didn't know who you were. Then my man at the fire station saw you and told me you're from the Chen family. Gangsters. Rivals of the Pang family. And what do you know? Just after you turn up here, Pang turns up dead.'

'Shouldn't you have a stenographer present before interrogating her?' Le Froy asked mildly.

'It's no use trying to hide behind all your police talk—'

'I'm not with the police.' Le Froy turned to face Wilson, exaggerating his limp – one of his feet had had to be amputated. 'Neither are you, as far as I'm aware.'

'You're just trying to make trouble for me because I'm getting too close to the truth. I'll have to report this to the highest authorities.'

'Please go ahead.'

'What are you doing out here, Wilson?' Fahey asked.

'I told you. I had a meeting. If you'd got me a car and a half-competent driver as I requested—'

'Who with?'

'That's confidential.'

The look on Danny Pang's face told me he knew something about this meeting. 'Danny?' I prompted. 'Did this man come here to meet you?'

'I think maybe he came to meet Stinky. I know that sometimes people think Stinky is me.'

I looked around the clearing. Now the body was covered up, it was a pleasant place. There was probably more life here now than when quarrying was still taking place. There were birds, lizards, snakes and definitely bugs. I could understand Mei Mei coming here to meet a boyfriend, but – 'Why here?' I asked. 'Why were you meeting someone all the way out here?'

Looking around, I realised that George Peters, who'd come up with Wilson earlier, was no longer anywhere to be seen.

'It's confidential,' Wilson said. 'I don't have to tell any of you anything.'

We heard the mortuary van groaning and grinding its way up the lorry track long before it arrived. It was really their supply truck, but carried corpses, with cardboard taped over the back windows. One of the police officers moved their vehicle to the side of the road and everyone was silent as the workers, helped by the corporals, loaded the dead man into the back of the van.

'I have the car here,' Le Froy said. 'Let's find some lunch and get you cleaned up. It'll give the mortuary people time to come up with something.'

He was right. There was no point in speculating until we knew what had happened to Ah Kok.

'Wait!'

Danny Pang caught up and grabbed my arm. 'Where are you taking her?'

'Back to town,' Le Froy said, in Cantonese. 'I'm not arresting her. But she doesn't live here so she doesn't have to stay.'

'Tell him I need to talk to you,' Danny said, as though he hadn't just heard Le Froy speaking Cantonese. 'In private.' He pulled me aside.

I saw Le Froy shaking his head. He didn't object. He must have thought Danny wanted to make sure I wasn't being kidnapped by this *ang moh* with a car.

And I wasn't sorry to let Le Froy see I wasn't entirely without protectors even in the *ulu* west.

But my welfare wasn't Danny's main concern.

'Do you know what the police are going to do?'

'Danny, how would I know?'

'They are going to find out who killed Ah Kok, right? And they should look for Stinky also. Stinky has contacts in Indonesia. His mother's people are from there.'

'Danny, do you think Stinky killed Ah Kok and ran away?'

He shook his head. I could tell he was looking for a way to get something off his chest without blatantly betraying his childhood friends, and talking was difficult for him.

'Just tell me what you know. You want to find out what happened to Ah Kok, right?'

Danny nodded. 'Stinky and Ah Kok were fighting over Mei Mei.'

'What?' I couldn't help it. 'Mei Mei?'

My shock made him grin. 'Whichever of them married Mei Mei would be marrying into the Pang family.'

Ah, that made sense.

'And lately documents and money have gone missing from the office. I don't want to tell the police because – you know.'

'Because you suspect Stinky took them and you don't want to get your friend into trouble.'

Danny nodded.

'Look, if he did things like that to you, he's not a friend. Remember that.'

'Yah.'

Danny Pang didn't look happy as I walked off with Le Froy, who'd parked further along the lorry road. I waved to Danny, but he turned away. I wasn't surprised. Uncle Chen wouldn't have been happy seeing me go off in a car with a white man either – not even with Le Froy, whom he knew and trusted. It was just a Chinese man thing.

And Danny Pang didn't know Le Froy could be trusted. I would explain it to him another day.

It surprised me. I was so used to not caring what people thought of me. Was it Le Froy? No. I didn't want Danny to think badly of me.

At least I hadn't invited the Pangs over for a meal during the Dragon Boat Festival – but maybe compared to finding a dead body on their property, that wouldn't have been so bad.

'What are you doing here?' I asked Le Froy. 'Did Fahey call you in?'

If Fahey had reinstated Le Froy in the Detective Unit I might see him in a slightly better light. Though I couldn't see Governor Evans allowing that to happen.

'Not at all,' Le Froy said. 'Given Fahey invited himself to breakfast with me, I thought it only fair the entertainment should be on him.'

Le Froy's Breakfast

———◆———

I saw the little bundle on the front seat of his car and recognised it for what it was – his uneaten *kaya* toast wrapped in a banana-leaf packet.

I'd seen it happen countless times – a sudden call, the adieus and pushing back of wooden stools as men prepared to leave their unfinished breakfast, and the speed with which the stall-keeper shouted, 'Boss! Wait!' and rushed after them while wrapping the remains of their food. It was a small thing, no more than he would do for any regular with an unpredictable schedule, but the little bundle on the seat was evidence that, whatever the bigwigs said, locals accepted Le Froy as one of them. Or, at least, as a regular who could be counted on to pay for his food. Which, in Singapore, was pretty much the same thing.

'You had breakfast at the *kopitiam*?'

'Tried to. Fahey came and joined me.'

I found that hard to imagine. Fahey was still uncomfortable with street food. He wasn't one of my favourite people, not least because he'd taken over Le Froy's former position as head of the Detective Unit.

When I'd first met Chief Inspector Thomas Le Froy, I'd been surprised to learn he preferred local restaurants and hawker stalls to the Anglo eateries. I'd been impressed that at the Keong Saik Road *kopitiam* near his lodgings the stall-keeper knew him well enough to shout, 'Breakfast, boss?' without asking him what he wanted. That was reserved for regulars who came for their daily serving of thick-cut *kaya* toast, soft-cooked eggs and *kopi,*

But I was the one who'd introduced him to the 'right' way to eat his eggs – he'd been tapping a hole in the top of the egg and scooping out the contents with a teaspoon, as though he were seated at an English breakfast table in front of a porcelain egg cup. Not until I'd introduced him to the crack, swirl and slurp had Le Froy acquired a real appreciation for soft-boiled eggs with the white fully set but not solid, and the yolk liquid gold but fully warmed through, accompanied by white pepper and a dash of soy sauce.

He'd told me that during his wartime imprisonment he'd found himself yearning for a soft-boiled egg. He had kept himself going by replaying how I'd explained adding salt and pepper to the egg mix – how it was always better to taste the mix sooner rather than later. And he'd yearned, hoped and prayed that I was alive and we would survive the Occupation to eat soft-boiled eggs together again.

I knew he was really telling me how much he'd thought about me.

'Fahey? What did he want?'

'The usual. Telling me not to provoke the higher-ups. Warning me that the locals, as well as the the higher-ups, blame me for the ban on opium processing,'

'That was Governor Evans's decision, not yours.'

'They're losing a lot of money and it's easier to blame me than the governor.'

'Did he manage to eat a *kopitiam* breakfast?'

'I tried to introduce him to bulletproof *kopi*,' Le Froy said.

'No good?'

'Not yet. But I haven't given up on him.'

Even though the British might have introduced condensed milk to our local coffee, it was the slab of oily butter stirred into Hainanese coffee that made it 'bulletproof *kopi*'. It was a little too strong for me, but Le Froy could take it.

Le Froy had come out of the war looking years older and minus one foot. But the greatest change the war had wrought was his new conviction that outsiders – British administrators – had no business running things in Singapore. This worried me. I couldn't imagine the British ever allowing us locals to run our own country and I feared it would turn the other British against him so that he was sent back to England.

Yet Le Froy had refused the offer of a pension at home and had returned to the Crown Colony to oversee the Public Health Services Bureau, a position Governor Evans had created for him – not at his request. Le Froy pointed out that a health fund for locals should be administered by locals and submitted a list of names he considered qualified to form a committee. He learned later that Governor Evans had thrown away the list and told London, 'Le Froy says either give him the position or he'll hand the money to a bunch of monkeys.'

London had given him the post.

Had that prompted the official investigation into the PHSB I'd been hearing rumours about? Apparently the order had originated in London, but what if Governor Evans had given Le Froy the post so that Wilson would have an opportunity to unearth something damning about him?

'I almost persuaded him to try *kaya* toast, but the man didn't like the idea of coconut jam.'

I snorted. *Kaya* tastes much better than the over-sweetened, artificially coloured imported jams the Westerners ate. 'He must have had a reason to want to talk to you in the *kopitiam* instead of in his office or at the club,' I said.

I knew Le Froy wasn't comfortable with the regard – almost hero worship – in which Fahey held him. I also knew Fahey wouldn't barge in on Le Froy's breakfast unless he wanted to talk to him out of the earshot of other *ang mohs*.

'Nothing. Just to warn me about what the governor's good lady is up to back in London. I told him I don't need to know what the gossip papers are printing.'

'What is she up to?' I asked.

'Apparently the *Sunday Pictorial* has her saying I'm a traitor. That I'm deliberately cutting down revenue for Britain to spite her husband and destroy his career.'

'Didn't the Foreign Office agree opium was a vice that needed to be eradicated?'

'Everyone agrees opium is bad, but they know someone will profit from it, so why not us?'

That made sense. After all, Stamford Raffles had established Singapore as a British port mainly to safeguard British opium trade routes between India and China. And before the war, opium and opium contracts contributed up to 60 per cent of government revenue in British-controlled colonies like Bencoolen, Penang and Singapore.

'People still blame you for closing the opium factories and packing plants, and the ban on the consumption and possession of opium,' I said. I'd heard the gossip too. 'They say Governor Evans would never have come up with it on his own. Since one in every four Chinese adults is addicted to opium they'll get it somehow, and someone else will take the profits.'

'I wouldn't say one in four,' Le Froy said. 'They don't realise how many Chinese died since we were last in charge here.' He looked up the path we'd just descended and I suspected he was wondering if this most recent death had been opium-connected, too.

'Dr Shankar's being pressured to sell medicinal opium, with huge taxes added on. They told him that if he refuses it'll drive people to the illegal markets and that will make the Chinese syndicates more powerful.' Parshanti's pa had said not to tell anyone about that, but I didn't think Le Froy counted.

From Le Froy's lack of surprise, I guessed Dr Shankar hadn't thought he counted either.

'People will talk no matter what we do,' Le Froy said. 'And if we don't do anything they'll talk even more, so we should just get on with what we think is right. Fahey's not a bad sort. There's pressure on him for setting up an office for me in the Dungeon and he can't help worrying.'

'For himself?'

Le Froy shook his head. 'That he's not doing his duty unless he warns me. I offered to sign an affidavit saying I've been duly warned.'

I had to laugh. I'd tried to warn Le Froy not to get on the wrong side of his own people plenty of times too.

'How's the phantom pain?' I asked. Dr Shankar had explained the pain Le Froy had felt in his amputated foot should be abating as his nervous system got used to the loss. He had been trying traditional Chinese massage and acupuncture rather than taking Western medications. He said it was because he wanted to be aware of the signals his body was sending him, but I suspected he was worried about addiction to painkilling medicine.

'At least Fahey isn't a racist oaf like some of the men posted out here,' Le Froy said, avoiding the subject as usual. This, more than anything else, had taught me a lesson. I had never believed Le Froy – or anyone else – could overlook my polio-withered leg. But now I saw that his missing one foot made very little difference to how I saw him. It was only one tiny part of the whole package. Of course it affected how he did things, but the greatest difference it made was to how he saw himself.

I finally believed what he and so many other people had tried to tell me over the years – that they didn't see me as a cripple. Ironically I don't think Le Froy believed it of himself. I hoped that would come with time – I wasn't going to have a foot cut off just to convince him.

'Fahey may not be racist,' I said, 'but he believes in the absolute right of the British Empire to rule all for the good of all.'

'I once felt the same way,' Le Froy said. 'Now I'm just the cynical outsider.'

'No,' I said. 'Now you're the local insider. It's not for you to help Fahey do his job. Let him make his own mistakes. He'll discover there are flaws in the system he's here to uphold.' Although those who refused to see their own flaws often ended up more comfortable than those who could see only those flaws. I didn't know which group did more damage.

'Aren't you worried about the investigation they've landed on you and your department? What's Wilson supposed to investigate? The department isn't six months old. What accounts, what records is he supposed to be checking? This is just someone in London trying to make trouble.'

'If someone makes a complaint, the Home Office is obliged to investigate,' Le Froy said. 'Especially when money is involved, as in this case. The people have to believe we are honest. The appearance of honesty is just as important as the actuality. You know that as well as I do.'

'I just don't trust Wilson. You know he was involved in an incident in Indonesia and was shipped out here? He's probably got high-up connections who bailed him out of trouble.'

Le Froy reached for the packet of *kaya* bread. 'Soggy,' he said. He unwrapped it and flung it away, with its banana-leaf wrapper. Immediately birds swooped on it.

'There were more than twenty deaths, including civilians,' I persisted, repeating what I'd heard from Parshanti and Nasima, a neighbour with connections in Indonesia. 'It was hushed up. Officially it was a landslide caused by floods.'

'It is the rainy season in Indonesia,' Le Froy said.

'Yes, I know.'

'Anyway, a young sergeant in uniform khakis turned up looking for him,' Le Froy changed the subject. 'There was a report of a body found in a Bukit Batok quarry. We thought dynamiting had triggered a rock slide or set off a dormant Japanese bomb. Fahey started calling for volunteers in the *kopitiam* because if other men were trapped there might still be a chance to get them out if we worked fast. He said he'd worry about jurisdiction after everyone still breathing was hauled out of there.'

I hadn't realised Fahey had changed so much. There'd been a time when he wouldn't have snatched a baby from a burning building unless it had papers proving it was the legitimate offspring of British citizens.

'I asked the sergeant which quarry it was and the nearest numbered track, but he didn't know. He did say it wasn't an accident but had happened near the Pang quarry. There was one dead local man and one injured local woman. I knew the Pang quarry so I gave Fahey directions, then decided to come along and see for myself.'

He paused. 'That was when Fahey told me he'd heard that that ass Wilson was heading out to a quarry in the area today. Wilson had wanted him to provide transport but, unfortunately for him, Fahey had no vehicles or drivers available. Wilson told him he intended to collect proof that the Pang family was fighting the Chen family for control of the black-market opium trade. Fahey was worried that if someone was killed this could turn into an all-out triad war.'

'An all-out triad war?' I said. 'Fahey missed out on a great career in sensationalist journalism.'

'Better a fool who asks questions than one who doesn't,' Le Froy said. 'To be fair, he was quoting Wilson.'

'Speak of the Devil . . .' Wilson was picking his way down the path in our direction. 'Let's go – now!'

In Le Froy's Car

'Excuse me,' I said.

When Le Froy opened the passenger-side door for me, Wilson pushed past me and sat down. 'Ah, that hits the right spot,' he said. 'Can't wait to get out of this place.'

I don't think he was trying to be rude. He genuinely didn't see me, like you don't see a lizard on a wall or a bird on a lamp-post. I almost laughed at Le Froy's expression, though.

Wilson reached to pull the door shut, but I moved in and blocked it with my body, thanks to the laws of physics. Someone doesn't have to acknowledge your existence for you to block their path.

'Excuse me,' Wilson said.

'Excuse me,' I said.

Just hours ago I'd refused to let him move me to the front seat so he could have the back for himself. Now there was no way I was going to let him take it.

Wilson looked at Le Froy and held up his hands. 'I'm throwing myself on your mercy. Fahey's making his men go over the area with a fine-tooth comb and my driver's gone off and abandoned me. I'm not waiting out here till they finish. You're about to transport that one to Police Headquarters, right? I'll be fine dropping off there too.'

Le Froy looked at me. I couldn't tell what he was thinking. I kept my face calm and blank – thanks to years of watching Ah Ma's mahjong games, that wasn't hard.

'It's okay,' Wilson said. 'I was in the taxi with her earlier and, yes, she stinks, but it's not so bad if you keep the windows down.'

Now Le Froy looked so angry that I touched his hand lightly just to indicate that I was all right.

I saw Wilson notice this because his face changed. I saw surprise, disgust, then fury, and guessed he was one of those racial purists like the Japanese, only he probably despised the Japanese as much as they despised him. Of course, both groups despised us.

'It would be better if you waited for the police transport,' Le Froy said.

'Hey, don't abandon a colleague to fraternise with the locals.' Wilson, his transport to town at stake, managed to sound almost polite.

'I will fraternise with whomever I wish.' Le Froy's light, reasonable, conversational tone was dangerous. I'd heard him use it (in at least three languages) to people who, choosing to be unreasonable, had ended up arrested – or dead.

81

Wilson got out of the car. Maybe he was cleverer than I'd realised. I must remember to be more careful around him.

As he walked away I heard him call, 'He's going off with that cripple. I think he wants to question her.'

That stung – I'd thought I was walking pretty evenly. And didn't Wilson realise the man he was speaking to could equally be described as 'that cripple'?

It was only as we drove off that I realised Wilson, in his own way, had been doing what he could to protect Le Froy's reputation. It didn't make me like him – but maybe I hated him a little less.

'Thank you,' I said. 'I think you saved my life, getting me out of there.'

'What were you doing there? Chen Tai's not trying to match you with that thug, is she? I thought she'd agreed to stop?'

Le Froy knew what I'd gone through with people trying to marry me off. After all, a connection with the Chen family was probably worth at least as much as a connection with the Pang quarry.

'It's not Ah Ma's fault. The Pangs were offended because we didn't return their Chinese New Year visit, so I said I'd go. And Danny Pang's mother doesn't want him to marry me any more than he does. But I feel sorry for his mother – her husband disappeared during the Occupation and she's feeling lost and helpless. Pang Tai wanted Uncle Chen to help her run the quarry since he'd closed his shophouse, but Ah Ma said she needed him. Ah Ma doesn't like Pang Tai. She thinks that because she herself managed to take over her late husband's business, everybody should be able to.'

'Not all women are as strong and clever as your grandmother,' Le Froy said.

'She can't see that. She thinks they're weak and lazy. And I think Ah Ma's still afraid Pang Tai's after Uncle Chen – for herself or one of her daughters.'

'Then why didn't she send your uncle to pay this visit? Let him make clear that the memory of his wife is enough for him to stay single for the rest of his life.'

That made me laugh. It was probably true, though not in a romantic sense.

'I think Uncle Chen's scared of Pang Tai.'

Now Le Froy laughed and I risked asking, 'That man Wilson is the Jack Wilson who took your job, isn't he?'

'He didn't take my job. He's investigating my accounts.'

I was sorry I'd brought it up. It seemed just the mention of it made Le Froy look rumpled and tired. And I'd always believed there was nothing more tiring than worrying about something out of your control.

'What happened back there?' he asked.

Now that was better. Ghoulish as it might sound, Le Froy and I had got to know each other over a series of dead bodies. And although, when we were apart, I'd worried and fretted (pointlessly, I know) as to where our strange relationship was going, now we were together, just being with him was enough. Besides, it's probably always easier to work out the details of someone else's death than your own life.

I told Le Froy how I'd found Mei Mei over the dead man's body. 'She was in shock and she was moaning, but it wasn't grief. If anything, it was relief.'

83

'Hysteria?' Le Froy suggested.

'No – quieter. It was flooding out of her, like the whoosh of cold sweat after the Japanese *kempetai* bayonets the person standing next to you and moves on. You're not crazy, you know you're still stuck in the shit, but you're alive – and that was what she kept saying, that she thought it was Stinky who was dead, only it wasn't.'

'Stinky's the one who's missing?'

'Yes. They grew up together, Danny, Ah Kok and Stinky. The boss's son, the foreman's son and the half-Indonesian son of the boss's dead friend.'

Le Froy nodded. It was good to be with him again. I forgot about Wilson and stretched my legs out. At the very least I'd delivered Ah Ma's *bak zhang* and returned Pang Tai's *tingkat*. My duty was done.

'You don't think Mei Mei killed him? Why?' Le Froy said.

'She might have. I don't know her very well. But if she did, I don't think she's a good enough actor to pretend she didn't. She's always been the good girl. The unmarried sister, the spinster aunt.' That was the fate that loomed ahead of me if I didn't do something about it. 'Someone told me you made the governor ban the legal sale of opium so that you could hand the monopoly to my grandmother.'

'I heard that too,' Le Froy said. 'In lieu of a dowry, since apparently I can't afford one. How is your grandmother?'

'She's all right. Health-wise at least. Flooded with government forms. She doesn't like paperwork.'

'They're probably aiming to prove your family is trying to corner the market in illegal opium now that the government certificates are banned.'

'What?' Ah Ma had stopped dealing in opium even before the Japanese ban. 'Why?'

'My fault, I'm afraid.'

'You told them my grandmother was dealing illegal opium?'

'Of course not! But people looking for ulterior motives will find them. Why else would the British ban official opium sales if not to benefit on the black market?'

Le Froy didn't have to explain why my family had come under suspicion. Many of Ah Ma's businesses and rentals had probably dipped into the opium trade.

He slowed down to manoeuvre around a cart. Its pair of bullocks had stopped to chew roadside sugarcane. Their Indian driver was chewing too, and raised his whip in salute as we went by. Le Froy, as was his manner, returned the gesture and called a greeting as we passed.

I couldn't say Le Froy lived like a local because he moved more easily between different groups of people than any local could, explaining *ang moh* ways to the locals and local ways to the *ang moh*s. I remembered when he'd thought I was going to die and how he'd acted to save me. I remembered, too, that the worst thing about dying was that I'd not told him how I felt about him. In that mad moment, just before certain death, it had all felt completely right. The problem was, we hadn't died. And it can be a lot harder to live with lifelong love than die in a glorious moment for it.

'When they don't find anything they'll move on,' Le Froy said. 'We just have to let them look. And they just have to show that everything's investigated and correct.'

For a moment I forgot what he was talking about. 'That's what Ah Ma said.'

'Great minds,' Le Froy said. 'I've got a desk in the Dungeon. Fahey's arranged a desk and typewriter for you, if you want it.'

My old table and typewriter, I supposed. The one I'd used when I'd worked as the Detective Unit's local liaison. They were still using the filing system I'd set up when I was working in the Archive Room, which we'd known as the Dungeon.

His mention of Fahey made me look out of the window.

I shouldn't have had anything against the man. He had always been polite and respectful to me. But it was as if there was a Fahey-shaped *hantu raya* inside me that I kept feeding with resentful thoughts and information I picked up. The *hantu raya*, or 'great ghost', is a traditional spirit that takes on forms created by your obsessions.

Except the *hantu raya*, in exchange for this *saka*, or feeding, is supposed to serve its master. Instead I was at the mercy of these pointless resentments. I couldn't say any of this to Le Froy, who owed Fahey for the office space he'd given him after the interloper (who I now knew as Jack Wilson) had commandeered his office.

'Fahey doesn't like Wilson either,' Le Froy said casually. 'That's something you two have in common. Fahey's not so bad.'

'I never said I didn't like him.'

But I didn't trust him. He'd been appointed to his post by Governor Evans, who didn't have a stellar record in selecting staff.

Was that my only reason for not trusting Fahey? Well, it irked me that Le Froy seemed to be mentoring him. Even though Fahey's only qualifications for his job were that he was male, white and university-educated.

I might have been university-educated if not for that stupid war.

It seemed a good time to change the subject.

'Jack Wilson thought he was going to the quarry to meet Danny, but Danny didn't know anything about it. And he thought Danny had been killed. Maybe he had something to do with Ah Kok's death – because he thought he was Danny.'

'Wilson arrived at the quarry in the same car as you. Meaning you're his alibi,' Le Froy said.

'No, he didn't. We dropped him at the Bukit Timah fire station and the man there had a jeep. They could have driven up really fast . . .' But no. The body I'd seen had been dead for some time. 'I just think he's involved somehow. Why was he going out there? Why did he lie about having a meeting with Danny?'

'Or maybe Danny lied about not having a meeting,' Le Froy said. 'Would he?' This was how he'd worked with and trained his sergeants in the old days: he'd taught them to make conscious deductions. If your reasoning worked but your answer was wrong, it meant your original facts were wrong or you had left something out.

'Danny's self-conscious about not speaking English. He wouldn't have agreed to meet Wilson, who only speaks English.'

'Was Ah Kok's English good?' Le Froy asked. 'Or Stinky's?'

'Stinky's English is,' I said, remembering what Mei Mei had said. 'Stinky can speak, read and write English, Dutch, Chinese and Malay.'

Le Froy looked more interested, 'So it might have been Stinky who arranged to meet Wilson?'

I'd thought the worst scenario was that Stinky and Ah Kok had fought over Mei Mei and Stinky had killed Ah Kok and run off. But this was probably worse.

Cousin Larry Leask

———◆———

The hospital mortuary van was still being unloaded when we drove around to the car park behind the mortuary wing. There was always a strange smell here, not because of the mortuary but because this was also where the hospital's rubbish collection area was.

I saw a strange *ang moh* man standing a small distance away watching the unloading of the corpse with a cigarette and some interest. He transferred his interest to Le Froy's car when we stopped just inside the unloading zone.

'Le Froy!'

He didn't respond. But that didn't indicate the man was a stranger to him. He was focused on the men setting up the van's back ramp and went to them, haranguing them to be careful with the body.

I remained by his car. I couldn't make out most of what he was saying but snatches, like 'urgent' and 'decomposition' and 'don't compromise the evidence', came my way. He'd clearly expected them to have taken the corpse inside and under Dr Leask's eyes long before now.

Le Froy followed the covered stretcher through the mortuary doors but I remained outside. I understand the importance of post-mortem results but, as with the results of digestion, I'd rather not observe the process of elimination.

'If he makes enough trouble here they may send him back to the Public Health, er, Infrastructure Department just to get him out of their hair,' the strange man said. 'Larry Leask. How do you do?'

I was pleasantly surprised. Any *ang moh* meeting me for the first time as I was getting out of Le Froy's car would probably have assumed I was either a servant girl or a prostitute. Either way they wouldn't have introduced themselves to me. Even better, I realised I knew exactly who he was. 'You're Dr Leask's chaplain cousin, and you've come to officiate at his and Parshanti's wedding!'

'Bingo!'

'I thought you weren't expected until a week before the day?'

'I like to exceed expectations!'

Though Dr Leask hadn't quite said so, I'd gathered his family had been shocked that, instead of rushing home to the family in Scotland once the war was over, he'd announced he was remaining in Singapore to marry someone they'd never met.

Dr Leask had stuck to his guns, despite mutterings about Chinese voodoo and Indian witchcraft, but I knew he and Parshanti had been unhappy that there wouldn't be anyone from the Leask side of the family at their wedding. When his cousin Lawrence had offered to come and conduct the ceremony it had seemed like a blessing from the Leask family.

I suspect this meant more to Mrs Shankar than it did to her daughter. Her own family had never forgiven her for marrying the Indian medical student who'd lodged with them, however much they'd liked him until then, and she didn't want her precious Parshanti going through the same thing.

It showed, I thought, how deep the hurt was and how much the Shankars loved each other.

'Am I that famous on this island, then?' He struck an American film-star pose and grinned widely. 'I'll need to get my teeth whitened!'

I had to laugh. His teeth looked white enough to me for a movie poster.

'I'm afraid not. Parshanti told me about you, that you were coming and you would be staying at the Farquhar Hotel—'

'Not my idea or my money, I'm afraid. Cousin Robert – that's Gordon's father – made all the arrangements.'

'That's where they're setting up tents for the war-crimes trials, right?'

Larry Leask nodded. 'That's partly how he got me in. I'm the army chaplain on call, tending the souls of the good men testifying.'

So he wasn't here just for Dr Leask and Parshanti. In effect, he was paying his own way. I wondered if Parshanti knew that. She'd been reluctant to talk about Cousin Larry and I'd wondered if she was worried about how much he would cost, staying at a hotel instead of bunking in with Dr Leask.

'I'm sorry I don't know how to address an army chaplain,' I said. 'Is it Father or Colonel or Reverend Leask?'

'We're British Army officers but we don't hold standard officer ranks,' Larry Leask said. 'We're designated "Chaplain to the Forces" or "CF" so my full designation would be "The Reverend Lawrence Leask CF". The nominal military rank would be major, but I'm usually addressed as 'Padre' at work. Away from work, I'd much rather you call me Larry.'

I didn't see why Parshanti disliked him. I was finding him charming.

Larry looked enough like Dr Leask to make clear that they were related, but you wouldn't mistake one for the other. They were both tall men with white-blond hair and blue eyes. But Lawrence's hair was thicker, his shoulders broader and, like many new arrivals, he looked better fed and better dressed than his cousin, whose sun-browned skin and lean jungle-toughened limbs made him look like a local islander who just happened to be *ang moh*.

'Where the hell is Leask?' Le Froy bellowed from the doorway.

Lawrence Leask gave an exaggerated shrug and shouted, 'Try the wards!'

Le Froy disappeared again.

'I hope that wasn't a friend or relative of yours in the wagon of death?' Larry turned abruptly back to me. 'Or of Le Froy's? I'm afraid, after so many deaths, it's easy to forget—'

'Oh, no,' I said quickly. 'I know what you mean. I thought that once the Japanese were gone we would all live happily ever after. Instead there are all these stupid little problems.'

As I spoke, another car drew into the compound and Jack Wilson got out. He didn't glance at us but headed into the building with the same air of officious entitlement that he'd tried to enter the taxi.

'And there's a stupid little problem for you.' Larry said exactly what I was thinking.

I couldn't help laughing. 'Do you know him?'

'We've met. Unfortunately. I hear Wilson got shunted over here on an important confidential mission. You know what that really means, right?'

I couldn't tell if he was asking if I knew what Wilson's confidential mission was, or what the word 'confidential' meant, I played it safe.

'It means he got sent here on an important confidential mission.' I echoed his tone, mimicking his sibilantly hissed 'confidential'.

(Incidentally this is a big part of why Singaporeans do so well in academic tests. Thanks to our long years as a colony, we learned that if you repeat to people exactly what they've said to you, exactly as they said it, they tend to think you're as clever as they are. Which is good, given most people who set academic tests believe they're the cleverest ones around.)

Larry laughed, and I was pleased with myself. He was nothing like I'd expected an army chaplain or cousin of Dr Leask to be.

'It means they don't have any idea what to do with him. He was involved with something in Indonesia, something big and bad enough that they had to get him out of there. Apparently he's got important connections so they transferred him here instead of shipping him home in disgrace . . . or in a coffin.'

'What happened in Indonesia?'

'Did you hear about the flash floods?'

'Of course.' I nodded. Rainfall across the region had been higher than usual, with massive flooding and landslides in Indonesia. Our neighbour, Nasima, was among those who'd been raising funds and sending supplies to help villagers driven from their homes. 'There's always flooding here during the monsoon season. The only reason it doesn't kill as many people here as it does in Indonesia or Malaya is because there are fewer people in Singapore.'

Larry nodded. 'From what I hear, this flood took place not long after the Battle of Surabaya.' He offered me his cigarette packet and lit one for himself when I shook my head.

We'd all heard about the Indonesian nationalists who wanted independence rather than resubmitting to Dutch rule. They were fighting British troops because Britain had decreed that Asian countries freed from the Japanese had to be returned to European rule. The biggest clash had been in Surabaya City last October, with people coming from all over Indonesia to take a stand against the British. It had paid off, because now independence for Indonesia was being seriously discussed.

'A landslide triggered by flash floods destroyed two villages. Volunteers from the Indonesian military moved in to rescue and extract as many people as they could before it was too late. The soldiers anchored themselves to form human chains, passing villagers from man to man out of the danger zones to safer ground. But then a squadron of British troops came to help with the rescue operation, saw the Indonesian Army uniforms and fired on them. A good many soldiers were killed, as well as the civilians they were trying to save. All in all, at least two hundred people died in the chaos.'

'That's terrible. But why? Are you sure?' Though our newspapers and radio reports had covered the flooding, they hadn't said anything about this incident. 'I didn't hear about it.'

'Everyone in the force is talking about it. But the papers aren't allowed to print anything. Bad for our reputation, shooting people we're supposed to be there to protect.'

'Was Wilson involved? Are you saying that's why he was sent here?'

'Who knows?' Larry shrugged. 'Doubt if he knows for sure. All I can say is he was shipped out within a week of the incident, so there must be some connection. He might even have been told he was being promoted, transferred here from Indonesia. It must have been frustrating to find no increase in pay or power.'

'Is he a soldier, then?' I'd thought Wilson was a civilian pencil-pusher brought in to make trouble for Le Froy.

'Wilson was a soldier, with connections in high places, which explains why he wasn't put in the brig or sent home,' Larry Leask said. 'But now he's set on scoring points rooting out illegal opium factories. Governor Evans is saying Wilson's like Le Froy was in his heyday. Le Froy closed down all the Chinese gangsters and triads and Wilson's getting rid of the opium traffickers.'

I wanted to say they were nothing alike – Le Froy had been a police chief inspector doing his job, not some administrator pulling rank where he wasn't wanted.

And Le Froy was still very much in his heyday . . . Something in the way Larry Leask was waiting for me to answer made me wonder if he'd said that just to provoke a reaction.

Luckily there was a commotion at the mortuary entrance as Dr Shankar and Le Froy came through the doors, Wilson scuttling behind them. I couldn't tell if he was hurrying them out or trying to detain them.

'Without doing a full autopsy I can't say for certain but clearly the poor man's throat was slit. I can't say what was used, but if you produce the knife we should be able to match it. And there are traces of glass, but a glass knife? No. More likely glass had shattered nearby, then ground into powder underfoot and contaminated the wound.'

'You have no business here!' Wilson said officiously. 'I've already taken action. You're going to find out very soon that you can't just walk into official government premises without authorisation.'

Dr Shankar nodded, 'Ah, yes. I owe you thanks for my presence here, I believe.'

'What?' Wilson looked offended at such a possibility. 'Oh, no. I assure you I would never do anything to help—'

'You reported Dr Leask for allowing me into the mortuary premises?'

'Oh. Yes, I did. And I assure you the authorities take an extremely serious view of security breaches, especially in such a case as this—'

'Dr Leask explained to those authorities that he was extremely understaffed and I have been offered and accepted a locum position.' Dr Shankar beamed down at the spluttering Wilson. 'At satisfactory pay. So, I must thank you, sir.'

'Well, we'll see about that. Deserting his post in the middle of the day. Nowhere to be found! That man Leask is a slacker, a charlatan and an incompetent quack!'

'Oh dear,' I said. 'Poor Dr Leask.'

'Dr Leask is an excellent doctor.' Dr Shankar was no longer smiling. 'His first responsibility as a doctor is to his patients. I believe he is attending to a woman who had an unfortunate encounter with hot oil and is in extreme pain.'

'Holding up a murder investigation to treat some useless old fool who had an accident in the kitchen?'

'It was some time before the unfortunate woman made it to the hospital. Now it seems that cleaning the maggots out of her wounds is a matter of some urgency.'

Wilson charged back inside, in the direction of the hospital wing this time.

Dr Shankar nodded formally to Larry Leask and me before following him.

I hoped that for Dr Leask's sake, as well as his poor patient's, Dr Shankar and the ward assistants could hold Wilson at bay.

'Nothing's going to happen for a while,' Le Froy said. 'Not with the island's one official pathologist refusing to look at any dead bodies till he's finished extracting his maggots. Come on, we'll find somewhere out of the sun. Get a drink or have lunch.'

He spoke to me, ignoring Larry Leask, who was standing there looking bland. Maybe disappearing into the background was a quality chaplains had to cultivate – to be present without interfering.

'I don't feel like eating. I want to wait till I know what happened.' I remembered my initial assumption that Mei Mei had killed the man. I wanted to be proved wrong so I could assure Danny and Pang Tai that Mei Mei wasn't a killer.

'You're not upset, are you? Want me to run you home?'

Though his eyes were on the hospital building, I suspected Larry Leask was listening. It made me uncomfortable.

'I don't want to go home yet. I want to go back to the Pang quarry. I cooked lunch for the workers because Mei Mei was too upset and I used up the last of their rice. They need to eat even though they're not working today. Did you know they've stopped work at the quarry? If they're late on deliveries it means they may not get paid and Danny's already worried that not enough money is coming in.'

'They'll work something out. It's a business they've been running for years without you rushing over with supplies.'

I knew that was true. But why did it sound so condescending?

'I'll run you home,' Le Froy said again.

'I don't want to go home yet.'

It wasn't that the people at Chen Mansion wouldn't be interested in what had happened at the Bukit Batok quarry. They would be all too interested and that was the problem. My grandmother, especially, would want all the details. And I wasn't ready to go into it with her.

And what was going to happen at the Pang quarry? With the police investigating the body there, it was likely that the workers would decide to leave, either because they wanted to avoid the authorities or because of the bad luck and evil spirits that a murder set loose. And who could blame them?

'I'll leave word with the police to make sure the workers have rations,' Le Froy said. 'Going through the right channels will keep them fed longer.'

'Or get them deported,' I said. In my experience, the British seemed to think that moving people, whether beggars, squatters or single mothers, out of the area where complaints had been made about them automatically solved the problem.

Laksa Lunch

———◆———

'I'm not hungry,' I said. 'I'll go over to the Shankars' shophouse to see if Parshanti's at home.'

'You can't turn up there just before lunchtime to tell her there's been a murder and you haven't eaten yet,' Le Froy pointed out. 'That would really trigger an emergency.'

I had to laugh. He knew Mrs Shankar almost as well as I did – probably better, given they'd grown up in the UK and come to Singapore as adults. It was hard to remember Mrs Shankar was Scottish. Even other Indians, who'd tried her curries and *kootu*, Dr Shankar's favourite dish of lentils and vegetables, assumed her fair skin came from some northern Indian ancestors. Mrs Shankar said she took it as a compliment to her cooking.

And, yes, it would definitely add to Mrs Shankar's stress if I turned up just before lunchtime without having eaten. 'You're right,' I said. 'I should eat something first.' Maybe I could also find out more about what had happened to the poor man. 'But I'm really not hungry. I don't think I can eat rice.'

'*Laksa*, then,' Le Froy said.

The thing about *laksa*, rice noodles with spicy seafood and coconut gravy, is that you can eat it whether or not you're hungry, whether it's a hot day or there's a thunderstorm, whether you're feeling happy or sad. As a child, you feel grown-up eating *laksa* because it's mildly spicy, and in later years, your eyesight and teeth almost gone, slurping the soft slippery noodles feels like a return to childhood.

Le Froy and I ended up on stools in front of a stall that sold good, cheap Singapore-style street *laksa*. Though I still felt guilty when I thought of the thin rice-porridge meal I'd put together for the workers, I could smell the lemongrass in the simmering coconut soup and was looking forward to my bowl.

Wisely, Le Froy waited till we had finished before saying, 'That girl Mei Mei who you found with the body, she's a friend of yours?'

'She's not my friend. I mean she is – a family friend. But I don't know her very well. She's much older. I remember when I saw her at Chinese New Year in the old days she was practically a grown-up. She was responsible for serving drinks and snacks and keeping the other children quiet while the adults talked.'

'But naturally you don't want to believe she killed this man.'

'I don't think she did,' I said. 'She was so upset. But I think she knows more about it than she's saying. I thought if I got a sack of rice and brought it out to them, I might get a chance to talk to her if she's calmed down.'

And there would be rice for the family and their workers.

'Fahey knows what he's doing,' Le Froy said. 'He'll talk to everyone there and get the whole story.'

'He'll talk to them,' I said, 'but they might not talk to him. A lot of people aren't comfortable talking to the police. Fahey may know his job, but . . .' I shook my head.

'But what?'

'He's not like you.' I remembered the impression I'd had of Le Froy long before I'd met him in person. He was head of the Crown Colony Police Force, but unlike the other big shots, he was willing to work with locals of any race or religion. He was also regarded with respect as well as terror by gangsters and business people . . . and he took off his shoes when he came into your home. It was the ultimate mark of respect and few *ang mohs* observed it.

'Lucky for him!' Le Froy said lightly. 'Why are you in such a hurry to talk to Mei Mei?'

There was no point in asking how he'd deduced that. Anyway, he was right.

'I was hoping to talk to her before she meets up with Stinky and they put together a story.'

'Ah. You suspect "Stinky".'

'I just think Mei Mei went up to the Death Pool to meet him. Why else would she go there alone in the middle of a busy morning? She was supposed to be making food for the workers but she went up there instead. And Danny couldn't find Stinky anywhere after that, so I'm sure he and Mei Mei are involved somehow. Danny said Ah Kok and Stinky were interested in Mei Mei. What if Ah Kok found her and Stinky meeting there secretly and lost his temper? I saw bruises on Mei Mei's face and she has an injured hand. If Ah Kok hurt her, Stinky might have tried to stop him and ended up killing him.'

Le Froy nodded, but I knew he had heard me and would pass it on.

I felt disloyal to Danny for giving the police, via Le Froy, all this information on his friend. But if Stinky was a killer hiding somewhere around the quarry, wasn't it best for everyone that the police had the information as soon as possible?

Anyway, there was another subject I wanted to bring up. 'I just met Chaplain Lawrence Leask, Dr Leask's cousin,' I said. 'Parshanti told me he's horrible and to keep clear of him, but I thought he seemed nice. What do you think?'

'No thoughts.'

'He said Wilson was transferred here from Indonesia because of some problems there. During the monsoon floods,' I said. I didn't believe in gossip, but this was information, not gossip.

'The Indonesian military was using their flood response to entrench their position with the people. The British had to keep that in check,' Le Froy said.

'By opening fire on flood victims and their rescuers?' Just saying it made me angry.

'Of course not. Parshanti doesn't like Leask's cousin? Why?'

'I don't know. She just said she hated him and didn't want to talk about it. But he seems nice enough. I was surprised.

I had the impression Leask's family weren't . . .' I made a little *moue* with my mouth like Parshanti had done when telling me about them.

'Well, you know the Leask family doesn't like the idea of their boy marrying a girl they've never met. It's understandable.'

'So you don't think Parshanti and Dr Leask should get married?'

Le Froy looked at me. He didn't have to point out that that wasn't what he'd said, I knew that, but I was angry he'd neither denounced nor denied Wilson's involvement with the shooting of flood victims.

'That's what you implied,' I said. 'You think it's understandable that Dr Leask's family doesn't think Parshanti is good enough for him.' The betrayal I felt wasn't just on Parshanti's behalf. 'All his family is going to hate her, aren't they? And that will be understandable?' Again, I wasn't asking just for Parshanti. Though Le Froy and I got on fine, except when he didn't condemn the British for firing on locals, I knew he was part of a family and society that would condemn him for marrying me.

'Understanding how people feel doesn't mean I agree with them. The Leask family doesn't like their son marrying a stranger. They've never met Parshanti Shankar, so of course they're concerned. Knowing her and knowing her family, I personally think Gordon Leask is a very lucky man.'

Maybe that helped a little.

'But it's not just his family, is it? Mrs Shankar's worried too. She doesn't want to upset Parshanti, but she told me that if they ever decide to return to Britain, Parshanti will be judged by everyone. She's always dreamed of going to England, and I'm afraid it will be a huge disappointment. And if that happens, it'll spoil everything between the two of them—'

'Eat your *laksa*,' Le Froy said. 'You always say it should be eaten hot. "Hot and spicy",' he quoted me.

I knew he was trying to distract me. We both knew what I was really worried about, which I couldn't put into words. 'It's all right. I understand it. That's just how things are and nothing anybody can say will change that.'

'They don't have to live in England,' Le Froy said. 'Or here. There's a whole world out there. Australia, Iceland, South Africa, the border between China and Tibet . . . They could travel across the Americas by rail, or sail across the ocean to Hawaii.'

I felt suddenly, unexpectedly, tearful.

'I apologise.' Le Froy looked as awkward as I felt. 'Some people find the uncertainty inherent in multiple possibilities overwhelming and upsetting.'

His language was convoluted, but I knew this reflected how he felt. Luckily, I didn't feel convoluted at all.

'I love you,' I said.

'Thank God,' he said. Then, unexpectedly, he closed his eyes. Now I studied him I saw he looked drained and exhausted. Was Wilson's investigation getting to him? Or something else? For all his reason and practicality, both very Singaporean traits, Le Froy had a suppressed emotional side that occasionally, like an ingrown toenail, surfaced and gave him trouble.

'Can you imagine two people travelling the world?' I asked.

'It depends where their duty lies,' Le Froy said. 'Duty, calling, responsibility . . . whatever . . . to reach full potential individually and as a couple.'

Again I knew he wasn't just talking about Parshanti and Dr Leask.

Did I want to travel and see the world? Of course I did. Didn't everyone? If this life is all one can be certain of, seeing, doing and experiencing all you can is almost a responsibility. However, I wasn't certain I wanted to live a nomadic life indefinitely.

But what were my alternatives? Living in Singapore and being treated as a lower-class citizen by the *ang mohs*? Or living elsewhere and being treated as a foreigner by everyone?

During the war, Japan had made Singapore the central command for their military operations in South East Asia. They'd come to value our deep, sheltered natural harbour, four airports and industrious workforce. Would it really make a difference whether we worked for the glory of Britain or Japan?

'Harry Lee enrolled at the London School of Economics earlier this year, but now he's talking about switching to Cambridge to study law.'

'What?' I was distracted by the sudden non sequitur.

'Have you thought any more about going to university?'

That took me back. When I'd first met Le Froy I had just got my School Certificate and was full of dreams of university, but that felt a lifetime ago.

'I wish I had gone. But I have other priorities now.' I grinned. 'Wilson's a university graduate. Can you imagine being in a college surrounded by Wilsons? You'd be arresting me for murder!'

It was a joke, but the mention of murder sobered us both. I scooped a last delicious cockle out of the dregs in my *laksa* bowl.

'Where are you going after this?' I asked.

'I'm staying in Singapore as long as they'll let me.'

That seemed a strange way to put it, but I was glad.

Although 'I meant now, after this. When do you think they'll get official cause of death? Can you find out if they've located the murder weapon?'

'There's no point in you going back to the quarry,' Le Froy said. 'I know they're friends of yours, but I think you should stay clear of this one.'

'Why? Wilson is trying to make trouble for them, and people will listen to him rather than to them—'

'Wilson's fighting his own demons.'

Was Le Froy being deliberately self-destructive? Even Larry Leask could see that Wilson was a troublemaker.

'I'm going to the Shankars' place,' I said.

107

The Shankars

---◆---

'Yes, we're closed! It's got my poor dear man so stressed, though he won't admit it. The police came round, saying they've received information that Shankar's Pharmacy is a front for opium-trafficking and Dr Shankar is selling excessive amounts of opioids and providing cover for opium transactions. They took away all our imported tobacco.'

Mrs Shankar was the only person in the shop when I pushed open the pharmacy door despite its 'Closed' sign.

'I saw Dr Shankar at the hospital just now,' I said. 'But the closure is just temporary, right?'

'I'm so glad they took him on to keep him occupied. Yes, the closure is temporary, we hope. But at the same time he's got this slimy government man coming in and saying if he's willing to dispense opium for "medical reasons" he can make the investigation go away. Ha! Entrapment, that's what it is! He even told me that if I wanted to help my husband out of his unfortunate situation, I would tell him, this government man, who his contact was. "Get thee behind me, Satan!" was what I said to him.'

'Was Jack Wilson the slimy government man? Don't trust him! He's been going after Le Froy too.'

'Indeed! None slimier! And don't worry, dearie, I wasn't born yesterday. If you ask me, it's really Le Froy he's after because he said—'

But before she could say more, there were women's voices outside.

'Mary, the sign says "Closed".'

'I can see that, Amy, but that's just the pharmacy sign. She's a seamstress, not the pharmacy.'

'Customers. Excuse me a minute, dearie.' Mrs Shankar smoothed her hair and her dress and hurried to the door as two *ang moh* women looked in. 'I'll be right with you, ladies!'

'Your sign is very misleading. Mary and I thought you were closed.'

'Amy and I might have gone away after seeing it and then you'd be out of business.'

Mrs Shankar's dressmaking business wasn't likely to close down any time soon. It seemed there were always strange *ang moh* women in the Shankars' shophouse, these days. I'd heard Dr Shankar suggest he close the pharmacy and work as his wife's dressmaking assistant.

'I'm very sorry, ladies,' Mrs Shankar said. Then, quietly, to me, 'Su Lin, you'll wait in the kitchen? You'll stay for lunch, of course. Parshanti should be back with Dr Leask soon.'

It was thanks to Governor Evans's recently departed – for England, not the afterlife – wife that Mrs Shankar's dressmaking skills were in such demand. Mrs Evans had worn (mostly unpaid for) Mrs Shankar's morning dresses, tea frocks and evening gowns to events at Government House, advertising Mrs Shankar's skills better than any mannequin.

Mrs Shankar had a good eye, could tell what would suit her clients and, very importantly, what would wear well in our equatorial climate. As a result, she had more dress orders than she could fulfil.

I half listened as today's clients checked on the progress of dresses they'd ordered to take back to England with them, although they probably wouldn't say where they'd had them made, so it didn't take long.

'So sorry, Su Lin.' Mrs Shankar came to kiss me when the two ladies had finally left. 'Busy, busy, busy, these days.'

'You look like you enjoy the work,' I said.

'Oh, I do!' She laughed. 'I always enjoyed making dresses for my dolls and for me. Not playing dress-up but making things pretty. And now they bring me lovely fabrics and trimmings and pay me to play with them – this is my dream come true. When I was a little girl all I wanted was to use beautiful things like these to make beautiful dresses.' She held up some fabric and trimmings for me to admire. 'Aren't these gorgeous? I've set aside some of this lace for your bridesmaid's dress. I'm trying out an idea that I just pinned out. It's not ready to try on yet but would you like to see it?'

'I think not just now, thank you,' I smiled to soften the disappointment. I didn't have enough energy to make enthusiastic sounds about a dress I knew I wouldn't look good in.

'You'll join us for lunch, of course?'

'I've eaten,' I said, 'but thank you. Do you know where Parshanti is?'

'I never know where that girl is.' Mrs Shankar sat down at her Singer sewing machine. 'Just let me get this done and I'll be with you. Nothing those fancy sillies couldn't tuck in for themselves with a needle and thread in less than five minutes, but if they're willing to pay me, I'm willing to do the work.'

Spoken like a true Singaporean!

'I can't help thinking of my old home back in Edinburgh, now my girl might end up there. Or at least she'll see it when they go to visit Dr Leask's relations in Aberdeen. I remember how the mica in the granite there made the whole city glitter and twinkle in the evenings and early mornings, even in the dark winter. Like there's something magic under all the looming, gloomy buildings.'

'Do you miss it very much?' I asked.

'Can't say I thought about it once I chose a different life for myself. I remember the terrible winter we had when I was just seven years old. The snowdrifts were up to my chest and I swore that one day I would move somewhere where the sun shone all year. When it gets too hot here, I remember that!

'It's just that my Shanti marrying a Scotsman makes me think of home. Who would have thought something like that could happen? But if I miss anything it's the freedom to roam without people looking at you like you're some crazy loon or lost *ang moh*. That and the coolness of the hills. The little hills here make me think of home, like when I was up on Government Hill. Just looking at the sky and the tops of the trees I could have been back in Scotland. But every part of Scotland is so different. Here it's pretty much the same whether we're down here or up in Malacca or Klang. Same trees, same creepers, same bugs. But it's alive,' Mrs Shankar smiled, 'not grey and cold, which is another way I remember my childhood home.'

Parshanti arrived home arm in arm with Dr Leask as we were setting the table. I couldn't help noticing how Dr Leask's face lit up when he looked at her. And I was glad to see Parshanti smile back at him. She was glad to see him too. If only they could go on feeling like that, surely everything else could be worked out.

Larry Leask followed close behind. He smiled at me but saved his biggest greeting for Mrs Shankar. 'How's my lovely lady?'

'Oh, you great silly boy, go on with you!' I could see Mrs Shankar was taken with Larry, who flirted with her gallantly.

'You're having lunch here? Again.' Parshanti was openly rude to him. 'Without letting anyone know?'

'Of course I knew Larry was joining us for lunch,' Mrs Shankar said. 'I sent a runner this morning, inviting him to join us and he accepted. There's that nice bit of mutton I made into a curry, but there's far too much for us.'

'Why didn't you say so? Anyway, you know Pa loves left-over curry. He always says it tastes better the longer you keep it.'

'It was while Mrs Frobisher and her sister were still here and then it slipped my mind.'

I didn't understand why Parshanti was so snippy with her mother. Mrs Shankar was clearly enjoying Larry Leask's company and stories of home. At the very least he could update her on all the old haunts she'd not seen since she'd come out east.

'I thought you were going to end up working through lunch again,' Mrs Shankar scolded Dr Leask. 'Did you get everything finished or do you have to rush back? I'm glad Shanti went to get you. Shanti, you didn't see your pa there, did you?'

'I saw him,' I said. 'He was working on the body from the Bukit Batok quarry. Did you see it?' Then I couldn't help asking, 'I know you were busy when they brought it in, and I hope the poor burned woman with maggots is all right, but did you have a chance to see what happened to the dead man?'

'Not yet. Terrible job, quarry blasting. But better than having no job at all. Just one man? That's a small blessing, at least.' Dr Leask was perched on the little bamboo stool just inside the doorway that separated the shop from the living quarters of the house, bending over to unlace his shoes.

'I hope the poor man's family will be taken care of after his accident,' Mrs Shankar said. 'You'll let us know if there's anything needs to be done for his family? I can speak to my customers about raising funds. They all have too much money and too much time on their hands.'

Dr Leask's house shoes were waiting for him as he arranged his shoes against the step and peeled off his socks.

Apart from him and Mrs Shankar, in her cushioned slippers, the rest of us went barefoot in the Shankar home, following the local custom.

'It wasn't an accident,' I said. 'Definitely not blasting. I don't know what it was, but the man's throat was sliced through to the spine. I tried to test for a pulse and his head almost came off!'

Larry had kicked off his own shoes as he came in. 'Could have been a guillotine,' he said. 'You know the guillotine was intended to be a humane instrument? A swift, painless decapitation, compared to botched sword and axe beheadings or hangings. And look at the halal meats. Westerners come here and say they can't eat halal because it's Muslim. It's ridiculous! Halal meat comes from healthy animals that are reared in clean environments. The animal must be slaughtered with one cut that severs the trachea, oesophagus, carotid and jugular ... more or less what would have happened here. The cow – or the man in this case – would lose consciousness within five to ten seconds of the cut. No one likes thinking about it, but wouldn't you rather know your dinner didn't suffer?' He caught Mrs Shankar looking exasperated. 'Sorry. I got that from your husband. He took me on a walk through the wet market and was explaining about the different slaughtering methods.'

As far back as I could remember, Dr Shankar had been fascinated by strange deaths and diseases, driven to try to solve or cure them.

'I heard about the body. I thought it was a quarry accident,' Dr Leask said. 'That's why I thought I'd come back and have lunch first. You said Dr Shankar looked at it?'

I nodded.

Dr Leask didn't look upset that a possible murder victim awaited him in the mortuary. More as if the older doctor had opened a present he'd overlooked.

'I'm sorry,' I said quietly to Mrs Shankar.

She pressed her hand on mine lightly. 'It's not your fault, dearie. If I have a passion for stitching up clothes, my man has one for cutting up people.'

Even though I told them I'd already eaten, Mrs Shankar had set a place for me and insisted I join them.

'The Bukit Batok quarry? I'll drive you if you show me where the body was found,' Parshanti said.

'You're not going anywhere near there,' Mrs Shankar said. 'You should stay away from the Bukit Batok area,' she added to me, as I went to help carry the rice and hot dishes out to the table. 'The quarry workers keep to themselves and don't like outsiders. They're all going to move on. They never stay in one place for long. People don't like hiring former quarry workers – there's nothing in town for them once the quarries are dug out. No one in town will take them on. They'll just have to move to where they can find other quarries. Until they're overtaken by machines.'

Parshanti winked at me before turning to her mother. 'Danny Pang, the quarry owner, is about five years older than we are,' she told her mother.

'Closer to ten years older,' I said.

'Anyway, his father died during the war and he's been running the family business ever since. His family own the land the quarries are on. They're locals, not quarry people. His family has known Su Lin's for decades.'

Mrs Shankar immediately looked more interested. I winced inside. Mrs Shankar was one of the best and sweetest women I knew, but she was also one of the biggest gossips and a matchmaking addict. She'd been forced to curb her tongue during the war and now . . .

'It's been a long time since I saw your granny, Su Lin. Maybe I should take her some of my carrot cake.'

'Ah Ma will be happy to see you any time, Aunty Shankar. But she doesn't have any plans to match me with Danny Pang.'

'Oh, dearie, I would never dream—'

'Of course you did, Mam!' Parshanti squeezed her mother's shoulder affectionately. 'You're always asking, "Has Su Lin said anything about her and that man?" and "Have you warned her they say he might have a wife and a family back in England?"'

Mrs Shankar focused, embarrassed, on her mutton curry. But I could tell she didn't mind being teased by her daughter. Now they'd got her safely back with them, her parents didn't mind anything she said.

'I was just returning the visits for the family,' I said. 'We didn't return any Chinese New Year visits this year, so Ah Ma sent *bak zhang* and sweet snacks for the Dragon Boat Festival.'

'How many sons in the family?' Mrs Shankar asked.

'Just Danny. He only has sisters. All older than him.'

'Oh!' Mrs Shankar was captivated. 'Sisters? How many? Can they sew?'

Dr Leask had eaten even less than I had, and was fidgeting now. 'Not an accident then? The man couldn't have cut himself and bled out?'

'Cut right into the bone,' Larry said unexpectedly. 'Dr Shankar said he hadn't made a full examination but the tissue, fascia, muscles were all sliced through. Could you pass me the *sambal kangkong*, please? He said it must have been fast. A cross between garrotting and beheading almost.'

'Excuse me,' Dr Leask said.

'See why some murders are best kept secret?' Larry Leask winked at me.

Post-mortems

———◆———

After the two doctors had returned to the hospital, Parshanti and I did the washing-up while her mother returned to her sewing machine.

In the old days, Parshanti had hated washing up and would only touch soapy water with gloves on because she was afraid of getting the 'dishwasher hands' that the ladies' magazines warned about. But now she worked quickly, competently and without complaining.

The Parshanti who'd come out of the jungle after the Japanese left had assisted Dr Leask in tending the sick and wounded under the worst conditions. I couldn't imagine the things she must have seen. She wasn't the same as the girl who had gone in. But I had changed too. We all had. At least Parshanti and I were still friends.

I looked at her as we worked in companionable silence. Parshanti was at least two inches taller than I was now – it was hard to believe we'd been the same height on our first day at school – and slender. Though no longer as skinny as she'd been when she came out of the jungle, she had not regained the plumpness in her cheeks. And though she was growing her hair again, it was far from the thick curly black mass that had once reached down to her hips when left unpinned. She pushed it back now as she leaned over and said, 'Sorry about that awful man. He just follows Leasky everywhere and it's impossible to shake him off. Sometimes I think he's deliberately trying to come between us.'

For a crazy moment I thought she was talking about Le Froy, but I saw she was glaring at Larry Leask who was talking to Mrs Shankar at her sewing machine. They seemed to be laughing about something.

'That's a super idea, Larry! Now you're here you should definitely watch the dragon boat races.' Mrs Shankar stopped treadling her machine and turned to us. 'Su Lin, you'll take Larry to watch the dragon boat races, won't you? Su Lin's practically family and she can tell you much more about the festival than I can. But I don't think they'll let you row. They've got clans and teams, and they train for months beforehand and take it very seriously.'

'Mam!' Parshanti sounded furious, 'You're not to try to match Su Lin with that – with anyone. She's not interested!' She dug an elbow into my ribs. 'Tell my mam you're not interested in any of her matchmaking.'

I knew I didn't have to say anything: the Shankars were old friends.

'Who said anything about matchmaking?' Mrs Shankar demanded. 'A visitor from a far-off land is here wanting to see the sights and I can't ask a friend to show him around? Anyway, Su Lin has a tongue in her head and can speak for herself. Why not let her decide?'

'Because she's too polite to tell you what she thinks and you know it!'

'Hey,' Larry Leask said, holding his hands up in mock surrender, 'I was just looking to experience some of the local sports, not to make trouble.'

'Then why are you here?' Parshanti snapped.

Even I winced. The man was a visitor to the island and a guest in their house. Mrs Shankar left her sewing machine to go to Parshanti, who'd abandoned me and the kitchen sink to stand in front of Larry Leask and glare at him. She pulled her daughter away and they went into a heated muttered conversation.

Over the years I'd heard enough of their spats not to worry. Indeed, the unnatural politeness in the Shankar household immediately after the surviving members of the family had been reunited had made me uncomfortable. They'd talked to each other as though they were strangers. Now they were back to fighting like family.

But, of course, Larry wasn't to know that.

'It's all right,' I told him. 'Please don't mind them. They're like this all the time. They don't mean it.'

He grinned. 'I don't mind at all. I have sisters. Makes me feel right at home!' He moved to my side, 'I'll help you with the rest of that. Let me dry while you put things away, because I don't know where everything goes yet.'

He sounded like a man well trained by his sisters, but I found myself wondering if he had deliberately provoked altercations between them.

I didn't understand Parshanti's hostility towards him. She made up her mind about people fast then seldom changed it, but I hoped she would change her mind about Larry Leask. After all, he was going to be her cousin by marriage. That had to outweigh whatever bad first impression he'd made on her. And I found him charming.

'We have to go now.' Parshanti pulled me out of my thoughts. 'Su Lin has to get home. Ma, I'm going to take the car and drive her.'

'I thought Su Lin was going back to the mortuary to hear what my cousin says about the body she found,' Larry said, catching Mrs Shankar's attention.

'What? Oh, yes, I do have to go,' I said, as though I'd not heard him. 'Yes, please, Shanti, that would really help.'

I could be a good friend even when I didn't know what was going on.

Outside, I tried to keep up with Parshanti as she hurried down the road away from the house.

'Speak English, can't you? Why are you so stupid?'

A soldier was berating an old hawker woman who was often there.

Last year, you could be beaten up if you were caught speaking English. Now we were back to believing anyone who didn't speak English was stupid.

'What's wrong?' Parshanti stopped.

'I can't make this old fool understand!' the soldier said. 'I don't want any more of her stinking snacks, I just want my money back!'

The old hawker woman grinned, 'Long time no see, missy! You want *kari pok*?' Her *kari pok*, or fried curry puffs, were delicious, though perhaps spicier than the soldier was used to, given how red his face was.

'You tried to poison me! I want my money back!' the soldier said.

'Next time,' I said in Malay. She nodded and switched back to her doleful and confused expression for the soldier.

'Come on.' I pulled at Parshanti. 'She's all right.'

'You can't just let him bully the *mak cik* like that!' *Mak cik* means 'aunt' in Malay, and in Singlish is a respectful way to refer to any older female.

'She's fine. I promise you!'

'Why did you find that body?' Parshanti said. 'Why do things like that keep happening to you?'

'I didn't. That was Mei Mei.'

'Danny Pang's oldest sister. Do you think she killed her lover? I can imagine wanting to do that sometimes!'

'I think she knows more about what happened than she's saying. And if Danny's involved – though I don't think he is – it's probably because she's pulling his strings. But I'm sure Wilson had something to do with it.'

'Jack Wilson! He's trying to get Pa to say Le Froy's crooked!'

'Has Dr Shankar told Le Froy that?'

'Pa told me Le Froy says not to get involved.'

'He's so frustrating sometimes,' I said. 'So blindly British. He accepts everything this unqualified outsider Jack Wilson does! Even Larry Leask who just got here can see he's a crook. Why can't Le Froy?'

At the mention of Larry, Parshanti pursed her lips and clammed up.

'What?' I said.

Typically, Parshanti changed the subject. 'You like Danny Boy?' she said. 'Why don't you think he's involved?'

'I don't dislike him. I just don't think he would bother to lie about it if he killed someone. He'd just say they asked for it. And he'd believe it too. That's why I don't think he had anything to do with it. He'd never be able to keep quiet about it.'

'So you *don't* like him.'

'Whether I like him or not has nothing to do with anything.'

'Of course it does. When you get information on a crime, you always have to consider who you're getting that information from.'

'What?' That might be true, but I hadn't expected to hear it coming from Parshanti Shankar. 'Have you been reading mystery stories?'

'No. Just listening to Leasky when he reads the war-crime-tribunal reports.'

We left it at that. Neither of us was following the war-crime trials that were going on. Of course justice had to be done, but I didn't want to relive the times we had only just escaped from. Both Dr Leask and Le Froy seemed addicted to reading, discussing and arguing about the reports.

'I think it's because they didn't get a chance to fight,' Parshanti said.

'They also serve who only stand and wait,' I intoned. Thanks to our shared Mission Centre School education, Parshanti recognised the quotation and laughed. I remembered Miss Ferguson telling us that 'Pandemonium', Milton's capital city of Hell, literally meant 'all demons' and how irrelevant seventeenth-century poetry had seemed to me then – until we found ourselves living in a city filled with demons. It was not just the Japanese: their presence had turned some of our own people into demons.

And I found myself wondering whether little Miss Ferguson had missed her childhood homeland all her life as Mrs Shankar had.

Without discussing it, we'd automatically headed back to the hospital and had ended up in front of the waste bins by the mortuary doors.

'Anyway,' Parshanti said, 'this dead man, could he have killed himself?'

An unfortunate number of people had survived the Occupation only to commit suicide on learning their families and loved ones had died.

'He didn't kill himself. I don't think it would have been physically possible,' I said. I remembered Mei Mei's strange manner. 'And there's no proof that Mei Mei killed him.'

'You think she did kill him!' Parshanti pounced. 'You said that as if you didn't want to accuse her without proof but you really think she did.'

'No. It's just she was behaving so weirdly. She was covered in blood because she'd been holding the body, and she was crying and laughing.' I grimaced at the memory. 'She kept saying she thought he was dead until she turned him over and he wasn't. But he definitely was. It was obvious.'

'That's just hysteria,' Parshanti said. 'The shock. I expect she meant to say she found him lying there and didn't know he was dead until she turned him over. She's trying to say she shouldn't have touched him.'

'She said she thought it was someone called Stinky, only it wasn't.'

'It sounds like Mei Mei's in love with Stinky. And if she thinks he probably killed this guy she's not going to tell anybody anything about it, is she?'

That pretty much summed up how Mei Mei had behaved.

'We should go and talk to her before she's over the first shock,' Parshanti said.

'After, you mean,' I said.

'I mean before. Before she's got time to come up with a story and before everyone tells her not to say anything.'

'And you're just going to say, "Did you have anything to do with murdering that man? Can I ask you some questions about what happened?"' I don't know why I was mocking her for suggesting we talked to Mei Mei. It was exactly what I wanted to do.

'But we should wait until we know what happened to him,' I said. 'That's why I want to know what Dr Leask decides in the post-mortem.'

'Good luck with that,' Parshanti said grimly. 'If Fahey's involved everything will be "confidential".'

'Won't Dr Leask tell you later?'

'He wouldn't tell me anything that everyone doesn't know. What's the point of being a girlfriend if you don't get to hear secrets?'

I'd felt the same about Le Froy.

Parshanti was right. Dr Leask didn't tell us anything we'd not already learned from Dr Shankar. But I suspected there wasn't anything more to tell.

'It must have been a very thin, very sharp blade. There are marks on the bone. Whatever they used, it cut deep. I'm surprised they didn't take the man's head off. And the cut goes all the way around the neck, like a garrotte. I've never seen anything like it. The victim might have been taken by surprise from behind, but even if not, I don't see how he could have done anything to stop it once it was around his neck. His fingers would have been sliced through.' Dr Leask paused, 'It makes me think of the aluminium wires used to cut cheese blocks in my youth. They were pretty powerful – those cheese rinds were thick. But I've never seen anything of the sort out here. People here aren't much into cheese-making.'

'So you'd say the killer was efficient?' Fahey asked, coming out of the mortuary.

'The doctor's on a break,' Parshanti said quickly.

Parshanti and I had been talking to Dr Leask just outside the door. Since he didn't smoke, Dr Leask granted himself stretch breaks and he'd been filling us in as he swung his arms forwards and backwards and twisted his torso in circles. I hoped our presence wouldn't get him into trouble.

Fahey was surprisingly mellow. He lit a cigarette. 'I'm on a break too,' he said. 'They didn't do a very efficient job of getting rid of the body, though. They left it right next to the quarry pool. If they'd bothered to tip it into the pool it might never have been found.'

'They might have been interrupted,' Dr Leask said, 'by the girl who found the body.'

'Why didn't they kill her too then,' I asked, 'and put both bodies into the Death Pool? But there was a lot of blood. That makes most people panic. They often don't realise how much blood comes out of a pig, for example, and how slippery everything gets.'

'Perhaps you interrupted them,' Fahey said.

That sounded like something Wilson would have said. Next he'd be accusing me of helping with the murder.

'Where's Wilson?' I asked Dr Leask. 'I thought he would be here, trying to find reasons to arrest me.'

'He was here,' Dr Leask said. 'A messenger came for him and he had to dash off. What's murder when there's a chance to shut down another illegal opium factory?'

'A sure thing in Bukit Batok,' Fahey said. 'But he didn't say why, exactly. I let him take one of the department cars.'

I had a sudden awful feeling that I knew where Wilson was headed and what he was up to. 'Shanti, can you drive me to Bukit Batok?'

'Why? Do you want to buy a sack of rice first?'

'No. Can we just go? Now? Please?'

Parshanti knew me well enough to trust the feeling I couldn't put into words. We dashed back to get the Shankars' car from the alley behind their shophouse.

Cooking Opium

———◆———

'I think that was why Wilson went up there originally. He must have been tipped off that someone was cooking opium there. I even know where—'

'What?' Parshanti demanded.

'Keep your eyes on the road! I thought it was the workers cooking food, but Danny said they don't cook for themselves. But then the body was there and the police were there—'

'So why didn't he just tell the police about the opium? It would have saved him making another trip.'

'I think the police got there before he had time to set it all up. He got Hakim to drop him at the fire station where he had a driver waiting for him. That was how he got to the quarry. He's already been here! If there's any opium down there he set it up himself – or that man he met at the fire station did.'

There was indeed something brewing in the cooking area I'd seen from the side of the lorry track leading to the Death Pool.

'How can you tell it was even Wilson?' Parshanti demanded. Thanks to the police vehicles and the mortuary van, the trail and the vegetation on both sides of it were criss-crossed with a mass of tyre marks. 'And where is he now? Oh, wait – down there?'

Peering over the rocks, I saw someone standing far below us, where the lorry track branched off from the supply road. Wilson was standing beside a small Police Department Ford. Now he'd set the scene, it was unlikely he would come back until he had reinforcements.

'Are you going to warn Danny and his sisters? What if they can't prove it's not theirs?'

'We don't have much time.'

But time to do what? Anyone who's walked past an opium den would recognise the smell at once. It had a strong, pungent odour, whether it was being cooked or smoked, and it could be detected from quite a distance. Even if I got rid of whatever Wilson had put in that pot, the smell would linger. But thinking of smells gave me an idea.

'Get down there and empty out whatever's in that pot,' I told Parshanti. 'There are sink holes everywhere. Just don't fall in. Clean up the pot as much as you can. I'll be back.'

'But the smell—'

'Leave it to me.'

I made it down to the Pang house faster than I'd thought possible, scrambling down the last part of the trail on my backside. My poor dress! But I didn't have time to regret it now. I didn't see Danny or Pang Tai, which was a pity – they would have understood what was happening faster.

Luckily Sissy and Girlie were used to following orders without question.

'Do you have *gula*? *Gula melaka*?'

'Yah, of course . . .'

'Only what we make ourselves, but yah.'

As I'd guessed, they made their own sugar using sap from the flowering buds on their palm trees. 'How much?'

'Quite a lot.'

'Bring everything you can carry. As fast as you can. Quick. And bring water too.'

Girlie and Sissy hurried into the house. 'And joss sticks,' I called after them. Every home has joss sticks for their ancestral altars. If my plan worked, the ancestors would forgive my borrowing some of their offerings to save the family. 'As many as you can find! Quickly, quickly, quickly! Bring them to the lorry track at the top of the Death Pool!'

When Wilson escorted Fahey – for once I was glad to see Fahey! – and five other police officers to the opium cooking site he'd 'found', Girlie, Sissy and I had pretty much done the 'cooking' I'd planned.

I waited in some dread for Wilson to pick on me, but he seemed not to recognise me and dismissed me, Girlie and Sissy as women who lived there and had come to see what was going on.

That surprised Fahey too, I saw. He looked curious but said nothing to me.

'You found another opium kitchen?' he said to Wilson.

Wilson had done this before?

131

'Don't call it false evidence before you've even seen it,' Wilson said. 'I'm providing you with evidence to document because you refuse to do anything without it. So here's your evidence. Do something about it, will you?'

Fahey looked into the pot that Wilson pointed to. The sugar had boiled down to a thick syrup. 'What is it?' he asked.

Wilson cleared his throat and delivered his lecture. 'The raw opium collected from the opium poppy pod has to be cooked before it's used. The raw opium was probably delivered from Indonesia in balls, covered with poppy leaves. Here, they would have broken up the balls and scooped the crude opium into this pot. Then it was boiled to the consistency of thick treacle, dried over charcoal and boiled again. This serves to remove impurities like twigs, earth, plant fragments and so on.'

Fahey went to peer into the pot. The contents didn't look anywhere near concentrated enough to be whipped up and dropped to set in lumps on banana leaves or pressed into bamboo tubes to solidify.

'And this is?' Fahey asked.

'Opium, obviously,' Wilson said.

Fahey sniffed. 'It smells like sugar. Sergeant Ong? Sergeant Quek?'

'Sugar, sir.'

'Smells like sugar, sir.'

Fahey leaned over and sniffed. 'Caramelised sugar,' he said. 'Reminds me of the toffee I used to get as a boy.'

'Opium smells of all kinds of stuff,' Wilson said. 'Depends on where they farmed it, really. Hey – I wouldn't do that if I were you. You really shouldn't . . .'

Fahey had stuck the end of a pencil into the dark brown sludge. He sniffed it, then touched his tongue to it, tentatively at first then again to confirm. 'Sweet,' he said.

'It tastes sweet?' Wilson asked. 'Opium is bitter when eaten raw. That's why they cook it. If it tastes sweet, I suppose that means it's been cooked enough,' He sounded as if he was quoting facts rather than speaking from experience.

'Sweet like toffee,' Fahey said. He stuck his pencil tip in again. 'Caramelised sugar with a hint of coconut. Quite delicious, actually.'

'I wouldn't if I were you.' Wilson looked worried. 'Highly addictive stuff. That's why it's such a scourge around here. The natives can't resist it.'

'It's *gula*!' I'd stuck in my own finger and sucked it. Despite everything they'd tried to teach us in domestic science classes, it's still the fastest way to taste something. 'They must have been making *gula melaka* here.'

Fahey nodded. He'd been in Singapore long enough to know palm sugar.

'What?' Jack Wilson hadn't.

My turn to show I could memorise botanical facts. 'Palm sugar. We boil down sap from flower buds of sugar palm or coconut palm trees to make *gula melaka*.'

Which was indeed what was in the pot on the fire.

There was nothing to show that the *gula* in the pot had just been dissolved in the hot water we'd mixed into it.

That's the beauty of chemistry. If you can extract water from something, you can also put it back.

'I was told it was opium!' Wilson blustered. 'That man cheated me!'

Had Wilson admitted to procuring the opium he had reported finding?

The police officers looked at each other and then at Fahey, who shook his head very slightly. I understood: wait and see what else he says.

'What's all this here for?' Wilson kicked at the joss sticks that the girls and I had lit and stuck into the ground around the sink hole into which Parshanti had dumped the original contents of the pot.

'It's smoking up the whole place – such a stink!'

I thought the sandalwood fragrance coming from the joss sticks masked the opium smell very well, though it was a little overwhelming. We'd lit most of the four packets Sissy and Girlie had found.

'You're trying to destroy evidence, aren't you?' Wilson peered into the rocks beyond the joss sticks. 'What are you trying to hide?'

'A man died up there,' I said.

'I know a man died here. I want to know which of you killed him and what you're trying to hide with this show. Don't just stand there, Detective! Do something!' Wilson turned on Fahey.

'It's for the dead man,' Fahey said. 'The people here believe that after a sudden death the spirit may not be ready to move on. The incense and sugar feed and comfort the spirit until it's ready to leave. And the smoke of the joss sticks purifies the space where the death occurred, though very likely it's the ritual that provides much of the comfort.'

Wilson and I stared at him. I don't know which of us was more taken aback that Fahey knew so much about local beliefs.

'You shouldn't be spouting all that superstitious mumbo-jumbo,' Wilson said.

'We have to know the people we're working for,' Fahey said.

'We're here to civilise and educate them, not indulge in their heathen superstitions! You'd better watch it or you'll go the same way as Le Froy. Now, take this hussy in or you'll be sorry.'

'Our main suspect is still on the run,' Fahey said. 'I see no reason to take Miss Chen in. We know where to find her should she be needed.'

'I know about you!' Wilson turned on me. 'I know all about you and the racket you and Le Froy have got going. You made sure Le Froy had the official licences cancelled and all opium equipment banned because your family wants the opium monopoly and money. That's how strong a hold you've got on him. Well, it's not going to last, I tell you. You're not going to have it all your way, missy!'

Wilson insisted on digging up some clay urns half buried in the ground, but when these proved to contain century eggs, he was horrified by the black gelatinous whites and mushy green-grey yolks. He thought the chickens that had laid them must have been cursed by the Devil.

*

After the men had left, Fahey insisting there was nothing to be done, there being no restrictions on home-made palm sugar, Parshanti and I went to down to the Pang house with Sissy and Girlie.

I wanted to explain to Pang Tai why I'd commandeered all her homemade sugar and several months' supply of joss sticks. Understandably, she was furious with Wilson.

I'd also hoped to persuade Mei Mei to tell me all that had gone on between her and Stinky. That wasn't so successful.

'Stinky wouldn't kill Ah Kok or anybody,' was all Mei Mei would say.

'Did Stinky give you that bruise on your face?' It was a new one, since I'd last seen her. Mei Mei shook her head but wouldn't look at me.'

'Stinky came back to see you,' I guessed, 'and when you asked why he killed Ah Kok he hit you.'

'No!' Mei Mei said. 'Me and Stinky never fight! He is good to me!'

I saw she was worried for Stinky, and rather scared of him. 'If you know where Stinky is, you must tell us. You must not sneak out to see him. Is he still in Singapore?'

'Mei Mei won't sneak out.' Pang Tai sounded as if she meant to make sure of it. A pity: I'd been thinking of suggesting the police watch and follow her if they wanted to find Stinky. But before I had a chance to ask Pang Tai if Mei Mei might lead us to Stinky she shouted at Parshanti: 'You! Don't touch that with your dirty hands!'

'Sorry!' Parshanti put them behind her back. I guessed she'd been examining the bowl of artificial oranges on the side table. I'd already noticed how dusty they were and was surprised, given how particular Pang Tai was about her own appearance.

'Your grandmother shouldn't let you mix with Indians,' Pang Tai said to me. 'If you're not careful, you'll end up smelling like them.'

Sissy and Girlie nodded gravely. I was torn between telling them Parshanti didn't smell (which was true) and if she hadn't driven me over, Wilson would have succeeded in framing them and I wished I'd let him (which was also true).

'We have to go,' I said instead. 'Parshanti, do you mind driving me back?'

Once we were in the car, I said, 'I'm sorry, Shanti.'

'Don't worry,' she said. 'It's nothing new. At least she saw me as your friend. I've met Wilson so many times when he came to the shop to talk to Dad, but he didn't even see me back there. I think he thought I was a worker or something.'

I was sorry also that I'd made her come with me. I'd not thought it through, just used her as the fastest way to get back here.

Sometimes I was so busy dealing with my own issues I forgot how much other people had on their plates.

Back at Chen Mansion

———◆———

'I should never have let you go out there,' Ah Ma said, when I got home, '*Hiyah*, just look at your poor dress! And why must you always find dead people?'

'It was Mei Mei who found the dead man, not me. Who told you what happened? Did Hakim come back?'

'I told you not to go to Bukit Batok.' Ah Ma didn't answer the question, confirming my suspicion. 'So dangerous! A crazy madman running around killing people! Did Pang Tai cook lunch for you?'

'No, Ah Ma.'

If I'd eaten lunch at the Pang house, that would have counted as another favour to be repaid. Ah Ma might be getting older and frailer but you wouldn't have guessed that from how she perked up at the news of a death – or how closely she kept track of social currency.

Had Ah Ma really forgotten to return Pang Tai's *tingkat*,

or had she intentionally tried to provoke a breach with the Pangs? An attempt I'd clumsily foiled?

'No. I was at Parshanti's house at lunchtime. Her ma sends her regards.' It was easier to let Ah Ma assume I'd lunched there than worry over me eating street-hawker *laksa* with Le Froy. 'Anyway, the police know who killed the man, and he's not in Bukit Batok any more.'

'Singapore island is so small. Where could he go?'

'Johor,' I said. 'Or Indonesia. His family is from Indonesia, so maybe he went back there to hide.'

'Indonesia? Not Chinese, *ah*? *Aiyah*, no wonder Pang Tai is so worried one of her girls will end up with him.'

I felt quite pleased to have given Ah Ma a nugget of information she hadn't known.

'From Indonesia you can also be Chinese.' Uncle Chen had come in with Little Ling. 'Anyway, some of our best workers are from Indonesia.'

'Pang Tai asked how you were,' I told Uncle Chen, 'and whether you had any girlfriends.'

Uncle Chen looked uncomfortable. 'Never again. I already got too many women in my life.'

'Why is Su Lin *jie*'s dress so dirty?' Little Ling asked. Though we were cousins, I liked it that she called me '*jie*' or 'older sister'. 'What happened to you, Su Lin *jie*?'

'Nothing happened to her. Go and change,' Ah Ma said to me, 'and put that dress to soak. It's no use giving you good things. Look how you treat them!'

Chen Mansion was shabby compared with Pang Tai's house. But as I made my way down the corridor to my bedroom, Little Ling's bed having replaced my mattress in the corner of Ah Ma's, I thought of how much more comfortable I was.

Of course, the parts of Chen Mansion that were intended to impress visitors were as uncomfortable as anything in the Pang house. They were filled with heavy teak furniture inset with ivory and mother of pearl and surrounded by jade and ivory vases, statues, altars with paintings and good-fortune calligraphy on the walls, but at least this was all old, gifts from people who would have been offended not to see their offerings on display.

And Ah Ma would never have let anything get as dusty as Pang Tai's decorations. She'd taught me that dust was where bad *chi*, or negative energy, was stored. As you cleared the dust out of your space, you also cleared out the bad luck.

The Pang house had been full of imported furniture and decorations. There had even been imported blue silk flowers tied to the good-luck bamboo, though in our climate flowers of all colours grew naturally and abundantly.

I wondered whether I'd have turned out more cultured and civilised if I'd grown up in a house like that, with someone like Pang Tai who knew how to make the most of her looks. On the other hand, I might have grown up prejudiced against Indians, which would have cost me at least two good friends.

'Su Lin *jie*? Come and eat.' Little Ling woke me for dinner at six. We ate early when it was just family. This way the servants could return to their quarters or go out while there was still some daylight.

I'd meant to help with dinner preparations as usual but had fallen asleep after I'd washed and changed.

'I wanted to play with you earlier,' Little Ling said, 'but Ah Ma said to let you sleep because you were tired. Are you sick?'

'No,' I said, 'just tired. Tell Ah Ma I'm coming now.'

It had been a long, stressful day, but the nap had done me good and I was ready for the simple dinner of rice with steamed egg and long beans fried with dried shrimp. The clear soup that night was *saan choy*, or slippery red spinach, one of my favourites. Little Ling very sweetly tried to give me a fishball out of her soup bowl because I was tired.

'I'm tired too,' Uncle Chen said. 'Why do you never give your baba fishballs?'

'Because you are bigger and stronger than Su Lin *jie*!' Little Ling said. 'And when you go to people's houses they always give you food!'

'Only when you come with me!'

When Uncle Chen visited colonial homes with curtain materials, pillows, pillowcases and sheets for sale, he sometimes took Little Ling with him. The British wives pressed fairy cakes and chocolate on her and Uncle Chen's sales went up so much when his daughter was with him that Ah Ma said, teasing, he ought to pay her.

Dinner was usually the most comfortable family time. The light was dim yellow – Ah Ma said because it attracted fewer insects, but I suspected those bulbs were cheaper – and, with no Shen Shen, Uncle Chen and I answered Little Ling's questions about school (she was starting at the Mission

Centre School next year), whether wasps were dangerous, whether ducks ate worms and how to tell when mangoes were ripe. Ah Ma would tell her old stories, with occasional corrections from Uncle Chen or me.

That evening, though, I felt restless and on edge.

'I want to be strong too!' Little Ling said.

'You will be strong,' Ah Ma said.

'You would have scolded me if I'd said that,' I reminded Ah Ma. 'You always told me not to talk so much!'

I was joking, but Uncle Chen chimed in, 'You think Ah Ma was strict with you? She was one hundred times stricter with me and your father. One hundred and fifty times stricter! We were like her slave boys, not her sons.'

He laughed, which made Little Ling laugh too.

'I had to make sure you boys were strong,' Ah Ma said. 'You had no father to protect you, so I knew you two had to be able to look after yourselves.'

That was probably what Pang Tai was trying to do with her children, I thought.

'The new government man, Wilson, tried to plant opium on the Pangs' property,' I said. 'It's not fair. They're just trying to keep the quarry going and he's trying to shut them down.'

Ah Ma and Uncle Chen didn't look shocked or even surprised.

'The Pangs are probably dealing opium,' Uncle Chen said. 'Not much money in granite nowadays.'

'They probably say the same thing about us,' I said. 'And Wilson probably thinks so too.'

Ah Ma nodded. 'Of course. Le Froy has already checked our business accounts but this man doesn't believe Le Froy. He will probably check again.'

'What?' I said. 'Why didn't you tell me?'

'You don't have much to do with the business. How is that old *pai kah ang moh*?'

That was an almost affectionate reference to Le Froy. But I noticed Ah Ma didn't ask me to invite him for a meal as she used to do. It wasn't as obvious as Ah Ma avoiding Pang Tai's overtures of friendship, but it was there and I should have noticed before now. What else hadn't I noticed? I didn't say anything until Uncle Chen took Little Ling outside to look for fireflies.

'Are you avoiding Le Froy because he's been investigating your businesses?' I asked Ah Ma.

'Who said I've been avoiding the man? Did he say so?'

'People say he's manipulating laws to benefit our family. No, wait, let me finish – I'm just telling you what people are saying. And they're saying Dr Shankar is trafficking opium and that he's being pressured by him to dispense "medical" opium. And now you're telling me the Pangs are selling opium. Don't you see it's just more of the crazy things people say?'

'All the Chinese business families are suspected, not just us,' Ah Ma said. 'That government man found opium-cooking equipment in the Au Yong house and the Lims' workshops.'

'Wilson set them up?' I was shocked.

'Of course. For sure they're dealing opium, but they're not so stupid to do it where he can find it.'

'We'd better be careful Wilson's men don't come and try it here,' I said, then noticed the look on my grandmother's face. 'What?'

'They tried already. But the gardener saw and chased them away. After that they were around two of the factories, but your uncle put extra guards. You can't expect people to be honest. You have to expect them to lie and try to *sabo* you. If they don't, you're lucky. If they do, you're prepared.'

Thinking of liars made me remember something else I needed to do.

'I'm going out for a while,' I said.

'Where are you off to?' Ah Ma called after me. 'Stay away from Bukit Batok.'

'I'll be next door, talking to Nasima.'

After years of living as neighbours, Nasima Mirza and I had become friends after the deaths of her father and sister during the Occupation. I'd been afraid she would move away afterwards, but instead she'd founded a school in her late father's house, in her late sister's name, and taught orphan girls English and numbers. The girls were registered as servants and paid a salary for their work in the house and garden, but the main reason for them to be there was to learn to read, write and manage accounts for their own households and businesses. It was very like the education Ah Ma's servant girls received, except Nasima's girls were from villages in Indonesia – which was why I wanted to see her.

The back door was open as usual and I was greeted by Rosmah, one of the girls.

'Is Miss Nasima at home? Can I see her?'

'Oh, yes! Please come in, Miss Su Lin! Miss Nasima is in the library.'

'Lovely to see you, Su Lin,' Nasima said. 'Social visit? Should I get the girls to bring tea? They've been practising and would love a chance to show off.'

'No need,' I said. 'I just wanted to ask you something. If someone ran away to Indonesia from here, where would he go?'

'Depends where he came from or if he has family,' Nasima said. 'Who are you trying to track down?'

'Just someone who disappeared from a quarry in Bukit Batok,' I said. The quiet room was starting to work its magic on me as it always did. Even though most of the books that lined its walls were in languages I couldn't read, I felt bolstered and safe, surrounded by so much knowledge. 'There was a murder, too.'

'Of course,' Nasima said. 'Are you a suspect? Again? Don't worry, Rosmah won't tell anyone she saw you here.' She smiled at Rosmah, who looked embarrassed and ran out of the room.

'No! It's nothing like that. I just happened to be there and . . .' Belatedly I realised she was teasing me.

'I heard about that,' Nasima said. 'Is it true the poor man's head was completely cut off? How did that happen?'

'They don't know. They haven't found the weapon.' I shivered, thinking of it. 'They said it must have been a very thin, very sharp blade or a very strong wire. But I don't know anything about that.' I shook my head to rid myself of the image.

'I think the possible killer was involved with a friend of mine, though she won't admit it. Now she says she doesn't know where he is or how to reach him, but I suspect she's lying. It would just be easier for everyone if she tells people what happened. The police have contacted the authorities in Indonesia, but so far there's been no response.'

'That's not surprising. There's a lot going on over there right now. Is the missing man Chinese?'

'Yes. Teo Shin Yi. But they call him Stinky.'

'Stinky?' Nasima wrinkled her nose. 'Because he . . . stinks?'

'I don't know.'

'That makes it harder. The Chinese are not popular in Indonesia. The locals and the foreign authorities distrust them. Even if his relations know where he is they might not tell them.'

Suddenly it felt like I was finding racism in all my friends. Or had I just been oblivious to it till now?

'And another thing. Be careful of an *ang moh* administrator named Jack Wilson if he turns up here. I think he's trying to set up my grandmother.'

'Jack Wilson,' Nasima said.

'You've heard of him?'

'In Indonesia. He was having a breakdown, crying in his sleep and drinking too much.'

'Guilty conscience,' I said. I didn't feel sorry for him.

'Excuse me.' Rosmah was back, breathless and excited. 'Aunty Next Door says the police phone for Miss Su Lin. They want her to go to town to the police station tomorrow.'

Helping With Investigations

———◆———

Next morning, Hakim was uncharacteristically quiet when he drove me into town. He knew I hadn't told Ah Ma about him giving Wilson a ride to Bukit Batok and I think he was wondering if it would come up.

I was more concerned with the upcoming interview and whether I had Wilson to thank for the summons. It had rained during the night so the roads were slick and muddy. The traffic was moving slowly, and rotting angsana flowers clogging the drains didn't help.

'Good luck,' Hakim said, when he dropped me off outside Police Headquarters.

'Over here, Miss Chen,' Fahey was at the doorway of the Detective Shack across the road, apparently having stepped out for coffee.

I knew better. His coffee was in a condensed-milk tin, the way locals drink it, which told me Le Froy had picked it up.

Even though I'd been telling myself I had nothing to worry about, it helped to know he was on the premises.

'Thanks for coming in, just a formality,' Fahey said. 'This is for you, by the way. John H. Wilson has made several accusations against you—'

'He's the one you should be accusing!' I said.

'—so I thought it was a good excuse for us to have a little chat.'

'You saw Wilson try to frame the Pangs with burned sugar. You know he's done it before to other Chinese families. Why aren't you doing something about him?'

Fahey ushered me in the direction of his office - formerly Le Froy's. 'Wilson is a separate issue. Anyway, it's not enough to follow the law, we have to be seen to be following the law.'

That was exactly what Le Froy used to say.

'I thought you might be able to tell us something about the Pangs and their foreman who was found dead yesterday. The Pangs say he must have been killed by one of the workers, but there's no sign of any of them being anywhere near the place.'

'It can't have been the workers,' I said. 'They're all locked up in dorms behind barbed wire left over from Japanese time.'

Fahey nodded. Not news to him, then. 'Even the locks?'

'What?' I'd been wondering whether Le Froy was in the Archive Room, also known as the Dungeon, next to the Detective Shack. I knew Fahey had given him that space to work in.

Before we'd turned it into the Archive Room it had been where the drunks were locked up until they came to their

senses. I just hoped the same thing wasn't being applied to
Le Froy . . .

In spite of everything I had against Fahey – that he was
inexperienced, incompetent, naive, didn't understand locals
and local ways, had been parachuted into his position by
a governor who couldn't get Le Froy to close his eyes to
illegalities – I wasn't afraid of him. That was enough for him
to score top marks with me where *ang moh* administrators
were concerned. I didn't like him questioning me, but I wasn't
afraid he would try to assault or frame me. And I knew
Fahey appreciated Le Froy's years of experience and his
understanding of how locals and Europeans worked.

'If you know what Wilson is trying to do, why are you
letting him get away with it? Is it the connections in London
he's always talking about?'

Fahey looked at the ceiling. 'Some might say that Mrs
Evans wants Wilson to get rid of Le Froy, and the people in
London want to get rid of Mrs Evans. She refuses to rejoin
her husband here while Le Froy remains on the island. But
the official complaint from Whitehall is that Le Froy has been
inciting local business owners to unrest.'

'Are you talking about the upset over your people selling
opium licences, then banning the processing and sale of
opium? And you're surprised locals are angry?'

'Sorry about that.' Le Froy's voice behind me made me
jump. 'But banning uncontrolled opioid use is one thing the
Japanese got right.'

It was so good to see him. I didn't realise I was smiling until he smiled back at me. 'Why are you sorry? You're not involved in foreign policy.'

'I might have reminded the governor of certain previous agreements.'

'Le Froy seems to think you can tell us about the Pang family,' Fahey put in. 'He said you seemed worried about the oldest girl, Pang Mei Mei?'

'He told you that?' Le Froy hadn't seemed to pay much attention when I'd talked about Mei Mei. And if he thought I might know something useful, why hadn't he asked me himself? 'I'm not really concerned for Mei Mei – it's more that I think she's hiding something and her family's covering for her.' I turned to Le Froy. 'I told you that!'

'He thought I should hear directly from you,' Fahey said. 'He seems to think you can provide me with better notes than any shorthand typist could, which is why no one else is sitting in on this meeting – if you're all right with that?'

'I thought it was Wilson who wanted me questioned.'

'He wanted to question you himself. But given he stressed how important it was, I thought it better not to leave it to a civilian.'

'He's an administrative investigator who reports directly to the Home Office,' Le Froy said.

'A civilian administrative investigator who is not involved in criminal investigations. We'll inform him of anything relevant to his work,' Fahey added.

In other words, I could say what I wanted to him – and whether it went on or off the record was up to me. It reminded me of how Le Froy would gather information on everyone and everything involved: he believed that once you built up a complete picture, the truth would be obvious.

'You're trying to do what Le Froy would do?'

It was a plus but also the main reason I couldn't stand that man. All those notes he was taking about Le Froy's systems and working methods, he sounded as if he wanted to write up his cases as though he was some kind of Sherlock Holmes.

And not only that. 'It reminds me of one of your cases, sir,' Fahey said to Le Froy. 'I've been reading the reports on some. Unorthodox but remarkable.'

'What?' I said.

Le Froy looked awkward. He always did when someone tried to talk about what he'd achieved.

Fahey turned to me. 'He blocked more than a few corrupt deals – morally if not legally corrupt – which made him an enemy of rich and powerful people. They wanted him out of Malaya, but he wants to stay. He resisted all attempts to pension him off and insisted on coming back in any capacity.'

I couldn't tell if he was implying that I was part of the reason Le Froy had insisted on staying out east. I leaped with glee inside but managed to keep an earnest expression on my face.

'I wrote up most of those reports, you know,' I said. Was he trying to play Watson to Le Froy's Sherlock Holmes? If anyone was to be Le Froy's Watson it should have been me.

'I know,' Fahey said. 'Tell me more about the Death Pool. Yes, I've heard the stories. Tell me again.'

I told him most of what I'd heard about the Death Pool and the Pang family. Nothing he couldn't have learned from anyone else. Of course I meant to keep my speculations to myself, but I might have said more than I intended, things I hadn't realised I believed until I tried to make sense of different observations and heard them coming out of my mouth.

Like saying Mei Mei had to have been involved, had to have gone up there to meet someone, or why would she have been beside a quarry pond that had been closed down years ago? And that Danny was unlikely to have been involved with anything like opium processing that risked getting the quarry shut down: his whole focus was on keeping the quarries open since it was the only way he had of earning money for his family.

'Are the Pangs having money problems?' Le Froy asked.

I thought of the dark, grand house full of expensive but dusty objects. 'I don't think so. Everyone's having money problems, but the Pangs own the land, the quarry rights and that house.'

'Danny Pang's known to have quite a temper,' Fahey said. 'Even before the war there were reports of him abusing workers.'

'Danny wasn't running the quarry before the war,' I said. 'The reports must have been made about his father. Can't you see Danny is the last person in the world to have done anything to Ah Kok? He needed him at the quarry. They were boyhood friends, the two of them and Stinky. At least until—'

I remembered the withered stalk and blooms Mei Mei had so carefully preserved, the angsana seeds she'd put away with them.

'What?' Le Froy asked.

'You need to find Stinky. If anyone knows where he is it's Mei Mei. I think Pang Tai suspects, but Mei Mei won't tell her anything. If Stinky is half as attached to Mei Mei as she is to him, he won't have run away to Indonesia. He'll be hiding somewhere around the quarry, looking for a chance to get in touch with her. Unless he was stringing her along. In that case he might be hanging around waiting for a chance to get rid of her.'

I noticed Fahey was scribbling notes as he listened to me. That had been my job in the old days when Le Froy conducted interviews. Well, this was what they got for not trusting locals.

'Pang Tai's hoping that if she closes her eyes the problem will go away, but it won't. What if it was Danny the killer was after? I thought it was Danny lying on the ground at first. Like Mei Mei thought it was Stinky. The three of them – Danny, Stinky and Ah Kok – were about the same height, so the killer might have made a mistake. And there would be more reason to attack Danny because he's the boss.'

It had been some time since anyone had listened to me in the way Fahey did. He made notes here and there and asked the occasional question, needing me to clarify rather than challenging me. It felt like talking to Parshanti in the old days, when we'd made up stories about our teachers and the lives they might have had if their beaux hadn't all died in the Great War . . . It sounds naive now, but when we were children, we'd all – including the lady Mission teachers – believed there would never again be a war like the last one.

'If Khoo Kheng Kok was killed because of mistaken identity it's unlikely the killer was his old friend,' Le Froy said. 'A stranger might make that mistake, not someone he'd worked with.'

'So maybe it wasn't mistaken identity. What if Mei Mei told Stinky she was in love with Ah Kok and not him? No. Scratch that. She wasn't.'

I'd seen Mei Mei with Ah Kok's body. She'd been shocked and devastated, but I was certain she'd not just lost the man she loved.

'The missing man. She was afraid he was the one who'd been killed. If Mei Mei was in love with anyone, it was him. The faster you find the missing Stinky and get his side of the story, the sooner the Pang quarry can get back to work.'

'According to the Pangs, the missing man wasn't Miss Pang's boyfriend,' Fahey said. 'They say he was Danny Pang's friend who used to live with her family.'

'The family may not know,' I said. 'Families don't know everything. Maybe they kept it quiet because Danny's mother and Danny himself would never have let Mei Mei marry Stinky because he was Indonesian.'

'And because Teo Shin Yi's mother was a bar-girl,' Fahey said, to my surprise. He nodded. 'But Mr Teo was accepted into the Pang household as a friend of the brother. A brother's friends are generally considered acceptable husbands. And most families come round, given time.'

I wondered whether he – or anyone else – really believed that. My own parents had married against family wishes but hadn't lived long enough for their families to come round. Would Ah Ma have accepted their marriage if my parents hadn't died in that epidemic?

'We've people watching the ferries, but . . .' Fahey shook his head. There were too many ways off an island. 'It's especially hard to monitor the waters at the moment with all those damned dragon boats out on the water all the time.'

'Practising for the Dragon Boat Festival,' I said. 'It's just bad timing. But the original dragon boats were searching for the poet's body in the water–' That triggered a memory. What if we were looking for a body?

I remembered the flies in the shack by the Death Pool. Sometimes it's not ghosts that make us uncomfortable in certain places but clues left by Nature that we unconsciously pick up. And I remembered Mei Mei's reaction when I'd told her I'd found the string of angsana seeds on the rocks by the Death Pool. Was she afraid Stinky had fallen in? But I remembered Danny had pushed Mei Mei into the Death Pool, and she had managed to climb out. If Stinky had fallen in, why hadn't he just climbed out?

'I think there's something in the Death Pool,' I said. 'The dead man's hands and clothes were wet, as if he'd been trying to push something into the water. What if he did?'

'Exactly what I was saying,' Le Froy observed.

'Dredge the Death Pool?' Fahey was doubtful. 'When you consider the cost, the manpower and the equipment needed–'

'It's a working quarry,' I said. 'They'll have the equipment. And if they've been shut down they won't be doing anything else. If anyone was trying to hide anything, isn't the Death Pool the obvious place?'

'Bingo!' Le Froy sounded pleased.

Fahey was shaking his head wryly.

'What? You think it'll be a waste of time?' I asked.

'Le Froy said yesterday we should search the Death Pool,' Fahey said. 'He talked about the dragon boats too. I don't get the connection.'

'The dead man's clothes and hands were wet,' Le Froy said, 'suggesting he was submerged or was trying to retrieve something from the pool.'

'I was going to look into it,' Fahey said, 'until that pompous ass Wilson tried to pull one of his set-ups. He's still fuming because we can't make arrests based on burned sugar. I told him if I was bringing anyone in over that fiasco it would be him.'

Dredging the Death Pool

The Death Pool quarry had been abandoned after at least two men had died there. 'At least' because, especially in the old days, deaths often went unreported, especially when the bodies could not be retrieved. Since digging had gone below the water table, it had filled rapidly once operations had shut down.

The rock walls were still unstable and there were still occasional shifts and rockslides.

The only reason the plateau had remained stable was likely the three angsana trees, whose roots reached out as far and deep underground as their branches did above.

'There are rumours that the Japanese put bodies in there,' Danny Pang said. 'Those stupid police want to look for what? Even if they find dead bodies, so what? Chase the Japanese and make them come back to confess?'

Danny had protested desperately against having the Death

Pool searched. 'The longer the police search here, the longer the quarry will be shut down. What am I supposed to do?'

But I could tell it was more than the quarry. Was he worried about disturbing the spirits of war victims? Despite Danny's bravado I could tell he was superstitious and scared. Or was he afraid the police would find whatever Ah Kok – or Mei Mei – had tried to hide in the pool?

At least I could try to dismiss the superstitious fears.

'The Japanese wouldn't bother to transport bodies all the way up here to dispose of them,' I said, 'when they could just throw them into the sea.'

Surely open water was much more effective. Singapore was a very small island, a diamond shape about thirty miles from east to west and seventeen from north to south. You couldn't walk very far in any direction without reaching a coast. The Japanese had taken full advantage of this, tying people together and marching them into the sea before shooting them.

But Danny didn't seem reassured. Maybe if you grew up close to an ominous pool of black water it became the receptacle for all your worst imaginings.

The police had cordoned off the area and were supervising, but the quarry workers did the dredging.

'It's what they would do if they were looking for a worker who had fallen in.' George Peters, the tall dark man from the fire station, seemed to know what was going on. He'd offered ladders and the use of the station jeep. Apparently the fire station wasn't operational yet and his main role was to monitor the fire alarms and summon help from one of the other fire stations until funds were raised for a fire engine based here.

I wanted to ask him what Wilson had asked him to do – or had told him about what he was setting up, but I didn't get a chance. It would probably be better if Fahey talked to him. If Fahey assured Peters he wouldn't be penalised for believing the lies Wilson had told him, he might be more willing to talk.

In the meantime, I watched the dredging alone. Danny had gone off in a huff after I wouldn't even try to stop the police as he'd wanted me to. I stayed under the shade of the angsana trees. Thanks to the ants and the elements, there was hardly any trace of the body that had been there.

Two workers went in at a time, ropes looped around their waists and three men bracing each of them on a pulley system. It was clear none of them was happy to be there. They threw dirty looks in my direction – had Danny blamed me for instigating the search?

They started systematically from the far side of the pool instead of the area nearest the rocks where Ah Kok's body had been found. That was where I'd suggested they should look first, which had probably made them avoid the area as long as they could. The dragonflies that darted over the water's surface were far more industrious.

Clearly the men were more interested in following their system than getting results, or they were hoping the police would give up and call off the operation before they found anything. But since I wasn't the one scrabbling in the mud at the bottom I had nothing to say.

There were rocks, of course.

It was almost four in the afternoon when one man yanked his rope urgently, indicating he had found something. He came up spluttering and babbling in Hokkien and Malay – something down there, no, not a body, he wasn't sure, but too heavy to lift.

As it turned out, it was a body. And that was only the first.

Altogether they found the remains of at least three humans.

'Of course, decomposition and putrefaction typically proceed more slowly in water, and taking predation into consideration, I really can't say yet.' Dr Leask had arrived soon after the first skull was found, but would not hazard a guess as to how long the bodies had been in the Death Pool.

'How was he killed?' Sergeant Gomez demanded. He was a tall, thin man who stood up to drunken brawlers of twice his girth without hesitating, but he was clearly discomfited by Dr Leask's careful probing of tiny broken yellow bones encrusted with slime. 'Was it the same as with the man who was found over there?'

'He wasn't killed at the same time or in the same way,' Dr Leask said. 'Even the most voracious turtles and snakehead fish could not have reduced him so completely and so quickly.

'The body is too far gone to identify it or what killed the victim. But you can see from the pelvic bones here and this partial skull that these are from another body. A very much younger one. Look, you can see from its size that this jawbone came from a child, possibly around three or four years old, probably less – and this? Unlikely to be from the same child because it's another jaw, even smaller.'

'Don't talk about them like that.'

Dr Leask looked up at him and stopped. Sergeant Gomez had raised and poised his rifle, almost as though he was going to bring down the butt on Dr Leask. He was also shaking slightly.

I knew what he was feeling because I felt it too. I was wanting desperately to tell Dr Leask he was wrong, that these couldn't be the bones of children, who'd not only died but apparently died unmissed and unmourned. It was frightening, and it was easier to hate and attack than to crumble and weep.

And it was easy to turn that anger on Dr Leask: why wasn't he more upset by what was in front of him?

'Hey,' he said. He'd slipped into what I thought of as his doctor mode. 'Look for yourself. Nothing can hurt them any more now.'

'Who were they?' Sergeant Gomez seemed to remember where he was and who he was talking to. He lowered his rifle and leaned on it, much as I was leaning on my stick. 'Who killed them? Is it from the Japanese time?'

'Possibly,' Dr Leask said, 'Or even earlier. They might not even have been killed. Workers use the quarry pools to get water for cooking and washing, and the rocks here are unstable. That was why they closed this quarry. The children might have been playing around here and fallen in. We can't tell.'

'Why would children have been playing here?'

The workers were muttering among themselves. I couldn't hear what they were saying but guessed they were talking about other workers who'd gone missing, who'd been dismissed as runaways. They weren't as upset as Sergeant Gomez over the children's remains. After all, children often became sick and died. They were more interested in the adults who had disappeared into the depths of the Death Pool. I hoped they might have had a gentler death here than at the hands of power-hungry Japanese or drunken British.

One of the divers signalled they had found something else.

This last discovery gave them the most trouble. Everyone was crowding around now as both divers went down together and many hands reached down to grab the bundle, wrapped in sacking, they raised to the surface. Even before they managed to ease its sodden weight onto the rocks the sickening stench of rotten meat was overwhelming. Like a dead rat stuck in a drain, only a hundred times worse. When they cut the ties and pulled away the wet cloth I glimpsed a formerly white singlet and bluish green flesh peeling off legs sticking out of dark shorts.

'There are rocks inside,' one man said, as the sacking material tore. 'It's just a sack of rocks. Why would anybody throw in a sack of rocks?'

'It really stinks. There must be something else inside.'

It was a man's bloated, decaying body. If it hadn't been in the sack the turtles would have eaten it by now. As it was, it was still impossible to make out any features due to the swelling and discoloration. The smell was horrible. My mind teetered on the edge of a joke but I pulled back from it. If this was the body of Teo Shin Yi, he hadn't been in hiding until he could get in touch with Mei Mei or run away to Indonesia. He'd been here, and dead, all this time.

Danny identified the clothes as 'something like' Stinky usually wore. Then, 'It's Stinky,' he said, 'for sure.' But he wouldn't or couldn't elaborate on why he was so certain. In contrast to his bravado after his other friend was found dead, Danny had to go off the trail to throw up. He was the one in shock now. Had Stinky been a closer friend?

Or was he just reacting to the smell?

'Obviously it's that woman. The one who says she found the body,' Wilson said. As he had ordered work halted at the quarry, he seemed to think he was in charge. 'There's always a woman behind it. Clearly she was leading both men on. She got one to kill the other, then slit his throat. She would have dumped him in the pool too, if someone hadn't come along and caught her in the act.'

That was me Wilson was talking about – or Sissy, Girlie and me. I'd not believed Mei Mei capable of such a thing before now, but I had never known her very well. And if she'd known Stinky was already dead, that would explain her outpouring of grief.

I caught the look Fahey and Gomez exchanged before Gomez stepped back and gave Wilson free rein to harangue the workers and the Pangs. It had nothing to do with 'Leave it to the experts' and was closer to 'Give him enough rope

and he'll hang himself,' while they began to pack and tag the
sad remains and arrange transport.

The divers returned to the water, and everyone else to
bagging what was handed up.

Dead Main Suspect

'I knew he was dead.' Mei Mei wept. 'When he didn't come back to see me, I knew he was dead.'

She fell apart completely. Part of me had wondered if she'd put on an act when Ah Kok was found, but now I didn't think so. I didn't believe anyone could act such crazed hysteria. She was like a cat that had just come upon her drowned kittens, claws slashing and snarling at anyone who came too close.

'It's my fault!' Mei Mei moaned. 'It's all my fault.'

The police wanted to take her into Police Headquarters for questioning, but were persuaded to let her stay with her family until she had calmed down.

'Won't be much good trying to talk to her now,' Fahey said. 'We can bring her in once we have the post-mortem results.'

'You should take her into custody!' Wilson snapped. He had been sick too, but had recovered faster than Danny and was trying to make up for it. 'And keep her under lock and

165

OVIDIA YU

key until we get proof. That woman's likely the murderer of
two men. You can't leave the main suspect at large.'

'We're putting a police officer on guard here,' Fahey said.
'She'll be all right, provided she doesn't leave the house.' He
insisted I ride back into town with him. I wasn't sorry.

Mercifully, Mei Mei hadn't seen the sad, sodden corpse.
Whatever she had lost, she could at least remember her
precious Romeo as she had last seen him.

Though I knew it was irrational, I felt guilty. If I'd not said
anything, Mei Mei need never have known. She could have
gone on hoping. Why did I always ask questions? Ah Ma
had warned that it would get me into trouble. But just then
another question came to me.

Did Mei Mei kill Stinky because he had accused her of
killing Ah Kok and wanted to tell Danny, his good friend?
Or had it happened the other way around?

'Which of them died first?' I asked. 'There must be some
way to tell. Could A have killed B before A was killed, and
could B have killed A?'

Fahey kept his eyes on the road but even in profile I
could tell he was struggling to hold back a laugh.

'It's all right,' I said. 'Dr Shankar says it's natural to want
to laugh after a shock. It's your body checking that it's still
alive and all systems are still working. But the thing is, even
if Stinky killed Ah Kok, he couldn't have wrapped himself
in sacking and weighted himself down and drowned, could
he? The writer Mrs Virginia Woolf walked into a river after

166

weighing down her pockets with stones so she would sink. I mean he could have, if he drowned, but how did Stinky die?'

'I'm not laughing at what happened,' Fahey said. 'Le Froy once told me that if I wanted to get the right answers, I had to learn to ask the right questions.'

'Why's that so funny?' I asked. 'I think he was right.'

'So do I. But he also said you taught him that.'

'Me?'

'He said listening to you taught him to question things he'd taken for granted all his life. In this case I'll pass on your question to the pathologist.'

I was surprised Le Froy hadn't been at the Death Pool but very happy to find him waiting for me in Fahey's office.

The body in the sack was identified as Teo Shin Yi after Dr Leask's examination found evidence of a previously broken left wrist and left ankle. Remnants of an accident years ago, soon after he'd come to live with the Pangs. As Danny said, that accident had also involved a fall into the Death Pool, with less serious consequences.

'We've found our main suspect, sir,' Fahey said.

'Or, rather, we've lost the main suspect,' Le Froy said.

'What I said, sir.'

'Why did you think the body would be there?' Le Froy asked me. 'What made you even think there was a body to be found? And why there?'

If Wilson or anyone else had asked me those questions, I would have been sure they were trying to get me to admit I either knew who had put it there or had put it there myself.

But it had been Le Froy and, especially after what Fahey had told me in the car, I tried to answer.

It isn't always easy knowing how you know things. When I was growing up, I'd know it was going to rain or that someone would try to steal something from Uncle Chen's shop without being able to say how I knew. I realised later that I'd unconsciously picked up signals, for example from birds and insects when it came to predicting the weather. Birds tend to quieten when rain is coming, even if the storm clouds are still too far away to see, while the insects are really noisy, especially the cicadas, which sing loudly and urinate at the same time. A warning: if it's a really hot day and you hear cicadas in the trees, then feel a cool spray on your head, that means it'll rain soon (but not yet) and you've just been peed on by a cicada.

As for humans stealing things, that was easier: they gave themselves away by either being nervous and secretive, or aggressively asking for something that wasn't in the shop, then storming off, picking up something on the way out and leaving without paying.

I didn't want to believe it of Mei Mei, but she had looked devastated when I found her with Ah Kok's body – but it hadn't been Ah Kok's death that she was so upset about. While she was covered with Ah Kok's blood, Mei Mei had been genuinely relieved it wasn't Stinky's.

Except, of course, now it was.

'It was Mei Mei who made me think so,' I said. 'She was really worried about Stinky, worried that something had happened to him, only she didn't know what. I think she'd arranged to meet him at the Death Pool and must have expected him to be there. Otherwise why would she immediately think of him when she saw the body? And why didn't she go for help? I think she was afraid Stinky's body was in the pool even if she couldn't bear to think it. Which also makes me think she didn't kill him. She was hoping against hope that he wasn't dead.'

Neither Fahey nor Le Froy objected to this.

'There's still the possibility that Teo Shin Yi killed Khoo Kheng Kok and another male adult and dumped the second victim in the Death Pool,' Fahey said. 'The clothes, the injuries, either a coincidence or Danny Pang is in it with him. They were friends, after all.'

'Mei Mei doesn't speak much English,' I said. 'Can I help translate when you're interviewing her?'

'Wilson won't like that,' Le Froy said.

'Given your experience in translation and shorthand, I believe it's a very good idea,' Fahey said. 'Let me just get the temporary employment forms.'

He left the room. I wondered if he was tactfully giving us time together alone.

'Fahey tried to talk to Pang Mei Mei too. After the last body was found. With a translator,' Le Froy said. 'She wouldn't say anything.'

'She might now,' I said. 'Now she knows it's no use trying to protect him. Fahey's maybe not so bad after all.'

'Colonial superiority isn't doing him any favours, but that isn't his fault. He's young and was brought up to worship the Empire as a member of the Church of England,' Le Froy said.

'Not everything about you colonials is bad,' I said. 'Like when you're making *kueh bangkit* and your old mould is rotten so you need a new one . . . but the ingredients – the tapioca flour and egg yolks and coconut cream – they're still good. You just need to put them in a new mould. At least Fahey doesn't believe what Wilson's saying about you.'

'What worries me,' Le Froy said, 'is that I know exactly what you mean. Has Chen Tai been making *kueh bangkit*? At this time of year?'

'Ah Ma didn't make it for Chinese New Year, so she thought why not? I'm sure she has a batch set aside for you, only . . .'

Only Ah Ma hadn't known I would see Le Froy that day.

We all knew he was fond of the little white cookies. They were favourites with me too – not over-sweet, they melted into light creamy deliciousness on your tongue with no chewing required. I could have done with a few right then. But though they were touted as suitable for any occasion, I didn't think that included witnessing the dredging up of dead bodies.

'Don't you think there's something funny about that man Wilson just turning up at the Pang Quarry, claiming he was there to see Danny Pang, whom he'd met before?' I mused. 'Then he said it was Ah Kok he'd met, and that Ah Kok was killed for talking to him.'

'Could it have been your friend Danny Pang Wilson met?' Le Froy asked.

I felt impatient. It wasn't like him to miss the point. 'Not Danny. Wilson says the man he met spoke good basic

English. Danny's English is . . . poor, and he would have been too embarrassed to talk English to a stranger.'

'Did Ah Kok speak English?'

'Not much. But Stinky did. He could read English too,'

It was almost comical that Wilson pushed the door open then, saying, 'Fahey! That body they found in the water, that's the man I talked to before. He was the man I was going to meet that morning. That was why they killed him, don't you see? They found out he was meeting me and they silenced him.' He closed the door behind him before he took in who he was talking to. 'You! And you! What are you doing here? What have you done with Senior Detective Fahey?'

'You said that about the first dead body we found,' Fahey said, opening the door and coming in behind him. 'What makes you so sure this time?'

'This is a confidential matter,' Wilson said to Le Froy and me.

I moved to the door, but Fahey was blocking my way out. 'I still need your signature on the employment contract,' he said.

'You're employing her? I warned you of who she is!'

'And you told me you had a meeting with the first victim, that you'd met him before and recognised him as Danny Pang.'

'I didn't get a good look at the first body. There was so much going on, so many people – and I knew he was going to be there so of course I assumed it was him. But this time I'm sure. The man they fished out of the water in that sack with rocks. He's the man I met in town. He's the man I was going to meet that day. That's why they killed him too.'

Could anyone believe him? However many dead bodies turned up, there was Jack Wilson saying he'd met them and that was why they were killed.

'There was no face left on that body,' I said. 'How can you be sure he's the man you met?'

'You said you met Ah Kok. The dead man by the pool,' Fahey repeated yet again.

'I only met him once. And—'

'And all Chinese men look the same to you?'

'And I didn't really look at the body,' Wilson said.

'You didn't see dead bodies when you were a soldier?'

'I still see them. All the time,' he said. 'I didn't want to add to the number.'

He looked so miserable that I almost felt sorry for him. Probably not sorry enough to give up to him any motor-car seat, front or back, but enough to pull up a stool and say, 'Sit down,' because he looked as if he was about to collapse.

'If you didn't look at the dead man, you can't say he's Stinky now any more than you should have said he was Ah Kok then,' I said.

'You.' Wilson pointed at me. 'I know who you are. She's from a rival family and she's been spending a lot of time at the quarry. Why? She's set this up, I tell you. There's something big going on here. Ask her what she's up to, what she's hiding. You should be questioning her, not hiring her.'

'It's like playing a game,' Le Froy said. 'Similar to the situation in Indonesia. The first thing you must do is decide who you want on your team.'

Best Offer You'll Get

I wasn't surprised to be told to report to the Detective Unit two days later. I was surprised when I learned it was for Danny Pang's interview – he had requested me as a translator if I was willing. Of course I was.

What was surprising was to find Danny and I were to be questioned by Jack Wilson in the Detective Shack where I'd once worked.

'This is not an official police interview,' Sergeant Gomez said. 'Mr Wilson requested the use of this room to speak with you, so you are free to decline if you wish. I will be taking notes.'

'This is private business. You don't need to be here,' Wilson said.

'This is Interview Room One B,' Sergeant Gomez said. 'All interviews are transcribed. It's routine.'

'Oh, and when you give Le Froy the use of your rooms here, do you have someone spying on him all the time too?'

'Retired Chief Inspector Le Froy has been assisting in the recovery of records pertaining to his work that were lost over the past three years,' Sergeant Gomez said properly and politely.

'Where's Fahey?' Wilson left the room.

'Make yourselves comfortable,' Sergeant Gomez said, not unkindly, then followed him. Apparently he wasn't obliged to document conversations between suspects – or between suspects and their translators.

'How's Mei Mei?' I took the chance to ask Danny.

'Like that, *lor*. They asked her to come too, but she didn't want to. She's just staying in her room and crying. You know these *ang mohs*, yes? My ma said you work with them. What do they want? Two of my friends *kenah* killed. Why are they questioning me?'

'I don't know. I'm not working with them now.'

Danny shook his head. 'They are always like that one. When they can use you, they're very good to you. When you're no use, they throw you to one side.'

'Right. Looks like we're ready.' Wilson returned, with artificial bonhomie and without Sergeant Gomez. That was a pity. I'd liked Sergeant Gomez better than Wilson. Something about Wilson made me uncomfortable. Maybe it was that he showed too many teeth when he smiled, just as a boy unfamiliar with football forces himself to kick too hard – or because he seemed ill at ease with everyone, including himself. I remembered what Nasima had said about his breakdown in Indonesia and drinking too much. At least he didn't seem to be drinking here.

'You are Danny Pang?'

Danny nodded.

'Let's begin by agreeing you're not the Mr Pang I met in town last week,' Wilson said.

'He says he met somebody who told him he was Mr Pang,' I advised Danny in Cantonese.

'Maybe he met the ghost of my dead father,' Danny said.

'He agrees it was not him you met,' I told Wilson in English.

'I also asked to see your sister Pang Mei Mei. Why isn't Pang Mei Mei here?'

'She is Pang Mei Mei,' Danny said, nodding at me.

Wilson peered at me. I expected him to roar at the attempted deception and kick me out, but he didn't. 'You?'

'Just say yes to whatever he asks you,' Danny said in Cantonese.

'No,' I said. 'I am not Pang Mei Mei.'

Yes, I'd agreed to help Danny Pang and I meant to try to, but impersonating a possible murderess was going too far. What if Wilson had me arrested for Ah Kok's death and the bodies found in the Death Pool?

'Shut your stupid mouth!' Danny snapped. 'Do as I tell you!' He was still speaking in Cantonese but the meaning was probably clear, even to Wilson. 'This *ang moh* fool's eyes are very bad. He can't tell who is who. I told her it wouldn't work but at least I tried. You are the one who wouldn't try. Just tell him Mei Mei is too sick to leave the house.'

I told Wilson that Pang Mei Mei was too sick to leave her home.

As though Wilson could mistake me for Mei Mei . . . which he almost did. I wondered if that explained his identifying first Ah Kok, then Stinky as the Mr Pang he'd apparently met. Anyone could have bad eyesight. The problem with Wilson was that his poor vision was paired with absolute certainty.

'If you are covering for somebody, this is the time to come clean,' Wilson said. 'This is your last chance, Mr Pang.'

'Tell him the workers are all criminals,' Danny said. 'They should question all the workers. And don't believe anything they say.'

I didn't want to, but I acted as a dutiful translator.

'We know none of the workers could have done it,' Wilson said. 'They are being kept under prison conditions. They are treated like PoWs in a concentration camp. Are they? Are they war prisoners? Japanese or collaborators? That's one of the reasons we might be shutting down the quarry for good.'

'You can't do that,' I said, forgetting to translate.

'Of course I can. I represent the Foreign Office and my responsibilities include overseeing management of local property and businesses,' Wilson said. 'If I'm not satisfied that a business is being run legitimately, I can't allow oper-ations to continue.'

'Are you threatening to close them down?'

'Workers all crooks and criminals,' Danny said in English, 'Indians and Indonesians. Got to be locked up.'

Having given away how much English he did understand, Danny looked sullen and stopped answering.

'Look here, Miss Chen,' Wilson lowered his voice, with a pointed look at Danny, 'it's nothing to me, but everyone knows Le Froy has a soft spot for you, so I'm warning you for his sake. You should be more careful. Clearly there's a madman behind this. A madman who's familiar with the quarry area.' He looked at Danny. 'You should use your common sense and stay away from the main suspects.'

I felt dizzy with rage. I'd always thought 'thine eyes shoot daggers at that man' was an English-literature cliché, but at that moment I felt daggers collecting behind my eyeballs just waiting to be fired at the pompous fool.

I turned to Danny. 'Danny?' Luckily Danny's English wasn't the best and Wilson had been speaking fast and low, so he probably hadn't understood what the man had said.

'Yah?'

'This guy *siao*,' I switched to Singlish, '*tolong lah*, let's go. He is not police. He cannot stop us.' I got to my feet and Danny did too.

'No,' Wilson said. 'Miss Chen? You stay. I have more to say to you.'

'Come, I drive you home,' Danny said.

I hesitated.

'Miss Chen, you'll want to hear what I have to say.'

Since he called me 'Miss Chen', instead of 'You, girl', I wanted to hear whatever it was.

'You don't have to drive me home,' I told Danny. 'You go.'

Danny frowned. 'Is that man trying to *kacau* you, ah?' *Kacau* means 'mix' in Malay, but in common usage it also means 'to bother' or 'try to seduce'.

'No, *lah*. But I want to see if I can persuade him to let you reopen the quarry.'

Danny accepted this. 'It's not just our family,' he said. 'It's all the workers too. They depend on the quarry. Otherwise what are they going to do?'

But Danny didn't get very far. 'This way, sir,' a policeman outside the interview room said. Was he eavesdropping? 'I'm to bring you to wait for your next interview. The one with the police. It is scheduled for eleven thirty but is running late because we're bringing over a Cantonese interpreter.'

I wondered how Wilson felt at being used as a waiting room.

'Of course your family's criminal connections are on record,' Wilson said, 'as well as the long-term business rivalry the Chens have with the Pangs.'

'The two families have been working together for years,' I said. 'That should be on record too.'

It was tedious but nothing new. I suspected some of his questions were based on old smuggling, drug and triad information Le Froy had compiled on the Chens long before I met him.

'What are they working on together now?'

'I don't know,' I said. 'All I know is that the Pangs are granite and gravel suppliers. Aside from that, I don't know anything about the family business.'

It felt like a complete waste of time and I was regretting not having made my escape when Wilson leaned across the table separating us and said, 'But ultimately all this can be wiped from your record if you give us evidence that Le Froy is being paid by the Chen family to leak classified government material. Then all of this will go away. All you

have to do is come up with a contract, a verbal agreement . . .
I can understand your reluctance, but we will not prosecute
your family or Le Froy. We just need to find out what's been
happening and stop it.'

I leaned away from him.

'Miss Chen, I don't think you realise how dangerous your
people are. Their rivalry with the Pang family goes a long way
back and they know all of each other's secrets. And once they
found someone from the Pang family was willing to speak
to me about their connection with Le Froy that man ended
up dead.'

It wasn't just Le Froy's job at stake. If Wilson was trying
to persuade locals to turn on each other he would tear our
society apart – even more so than collaboration with the
Japanese had done.

'I don't blame you. You were born into this mess. You just
did as you were told. You never meant to break the law or
do any harm. A case could be made for that. But you have to
give us something to show that you mean it.'

I'd seen for myself that Wilson was crazy enough to plant
opium to try to 'document' what he was so certain of. Was he
crazy enough to commit murder? Maybe to his mind killing
locals didn't count as murder.

'In exchange for helping me, I can get you out of here,'
Wilson said.

'You're asking me to betray my family in exchange for the
chance to go to England with Le Froy? What makes you think
I want to go to England?'

Wilson didn't bother to answer that. I suspect that, to his mind, all that we Singaporeans dreamed of was a chance to go to England and pretend to be English.

'I don't know what Le Froy might have led you to believe, but otherwise you wouldn't be allowed in. Not even as a visitor.'

'He's never led me to believe anything,' I said, feeling a sad pang that that was true.

'I know more about how things work here than you realise. Having taken a Caucasian lover, you'll never find a husband. And Le Froy isn't all you think he is.'

What did he imagine I thought Le Froy was?

An *ang moh* who symbolised power?

If Le Froy was exactly as he was, but Chinese, Indian or Malay, would I feel the same way about him? I couldn't say, because then he wouldn't have been who he was.

For a long time, while I was working for him, I hadn't allowed myself to acknowledge any kind of attraction. I didn't want to be lumped with the dance hostesses who made it their goal to snare a man, who might have a wife and family waiting for him back home, then wheedle him into renting rooms – or even a house – and moving in with them. That was considered a win – money, status and protection . . . at least until he left for home.

'I don't have to listen to this.' I stood up. Whoever Sergeant Gomez had been instructed to take me to next couldn't be worse than Wilson.

'And think what it would do to his reputation if it came out that you are half Japanese,' he continued, as though I'd not spoken. 'An enemy alien infiltrating British soil. You wouldn't want Le Froy to have his years of service and career struck off the record because of you?'

Le Froy always said, 'If you live in Singapore you are Singaporean,' because no one had roots here in the same way that the British trace back from Anglo-Saxon, Celtic and Nordic ancestors. And even they had come in from elsewhere, Great Britain being an island like ours.

To him, his version was better than what had actually happened so why not go with it? That was what drove people to either madness or greatness: belief that their version was better than the truth and revising the truth in their image.

'I have connections – important connections – in London who want Le Froy out for good. He has a bad reputation in the higher circles. He thinks locals are capable of taking over and running things themselves. He speaks as a local now. He's been corrupted. The current British regime isn't sure what to do with him. He's been offered a very decent pension to retire home, but he's still out here. You must agree that that alone is suspicious.'

'Not really. I've heard things are pretty grim in London,' Fahey said from the doorway. He sounded as though he'd been listening to the conversation all along. He probably had, given we were in a police interview room where subtle monitoring was sometimes needed.

'Even before the war able-bodied men were standing on street corners holding signs saying "desperate for any work". You can't blame a man for pinching something to feed his children. And it's probably worse now, with men returning from the war to starve at home.'

'Do you mind? This is a private conversation,' Wilson said. 'We're just coming to an agreement.'

'No, we're not,' I said.

'Your time's up,' Fahey said. 'Sorry, we need this room.'

'Who do you think you are?' Wilson said. 'I know who gave you your position and I can have it taken away.'

'You should go now,' Fahey said to me. Then, as I walked past him, he added, 'Keep safe. And stay away from the Pang quarry.'

To my surprise, though, it wasn't Wilson's diatribe against Le Froy that left me unsettled. Rather, it was something Danny had said about Mei Mei. I tried to think back.

Danny had surprised and irritated me by ordering me to tell Wilson that I was Mei Mei. How could he think I'd go along with it or that we'd get away with it? And yet – given Wilson's inability to tell locals apart – it might have worked if I'd played along. But what had Danny said about telling her it wouldn't work but saying it anyway?

If Mei Mei had told him to lie and persuade me to lie, she had fooled me completely. She must have fooled even the police guard who'd been sent to watch the house, or why else hadn't she been brought into town with Danny? For once I agreed with Wilson: regardless of how hysterical Mei Mei had appeared, Fahey should have taken her into custody and kept her under lock and key. And who was Mei Mei covering for? She couldn't have killed two men and disposed of one without help. Which meant that whoever had killed Danny's two best friends was still on the loose.

But the first thing I had to do was find out if Mei Mei was still at the quarry.

What Friends Are For

———◆———

'I have to go back to the Pang quarry,' I told Parshanti. I didn't want to wait for Danny. 'Can you drive me? Please? I know Pang Tai was horrible to you last time, but you don't have to talk to her. I just want to make sure Mei Mei's really there.'

'Why not?' Parshanti said. 'It's not like I have anything else to do with my life.'

I stopped and looked at her. 'What's wrong?'

'Nothing. Just Leasky's stupid cousin getting on my nerves. What's the hurry?'

'I think Mei Mei might be manipulating Danny and her family. She tried to get Danny to lie to the police for her, and wanted me to lie too. What if she was working with whoever killed Ah Kok and Stinky? Because if the angsana seeds I found on the rocks are hers, they show she was there when the body was put into the Death Pool.'

'You said she was so upset and so broken-hearted she couldn't have done anything,' Parshanti said. 'Or maybe she's a really good actress – like Ingrid Bergman in *Casablanca*. Even when you know you shouldn't trust her you end up doing what she wants.'

'No,' I said. I didn't know as much about films as Parshanti did, but I was talking about real life. 'I thought she was hysterical. Even Dr Leask thought she was – that's why he sedated her and she wasn't taken in for questioning. But what if it was all an act? Danny says she's too sick to leave her room, but I just want to check she's really still there. Can you drive me, please?'

Otherwise I would have to go to the *kopitiam* where Hakim went between passengers, but if he'd driven someone to Johor it might be hours before he got back.

'What if that overdressed racist asks why you're there?' Parshanti asked. 'I mean, are you going to say, "I think your daughter helped murder two men and is faking being in shock"?' I'd already started walking and she hurried to catch up with me. 'Where are you going?'

'To see if Hakim is at the *kopitiam*. I really shouldn't have asked you–'

'Of course I'll drive you there. What are friends for? Tell you what, we'll pick up some rice, sweet potatoes and dried fish for the workers. If Mei Mei's out of action they'll have to let them make food for themselves and anybody can cook that stuff.'

Parshanti was right, and I felt better even though I knew she was just humouring me. Once we were heading west out of the town, I asked, 'What did Dr Leask's cousin do?'

'Nothing.'

'You wouldn't be upset if it were nothing,' I said. I knew her too well to let her get away with that. 'Spit it out.'

'I love Leasky. He loves me. I'm not worrying about that. It's just that I'm realising that marrying him is marrying into his family. What if the rest of his family is all like that horrible cousin, Larry? I mean, he joined the Church just to get out of fighting without looking bad. Can you believe that?'

'Larry won't be here for long,' I said. 'At least you don't have to live with a whole extended family. Maybe give it some time.' I sounded lame, even to me.

'It's a lifetime of having them as in-laws. It was different when we thought we might die at any time. And we were talking about what would be the fastest way to kill ourselves and each other if the Japanese found us. Because, really, the things they did to people . . . Never mind. Anyway, once you've talked about stuff like that, once you've been that close and shared moments like that, even if you ended up never having to slit each other's jugular, you're kind of bonded for ever. The only alternative is never to see each other again. How could you form any kind of happy relationship with anyone else when someone is looking on who knows you from the inside out?'

I knew what she meant. That was how I felt about Le Froy.

'And I keep thinking of Kenneth.'

'Kenneth Mulliner?'

He had been Parshanti's first serious boyfriend and fiancé. He'd asked Dr and Mrs Shankar for their daughter's hand in marriage, which had been tearfully and joyfully granted. If he'd been alive . . .

'Of course! Who else? I was thinking, if it came to a choice between Andrew and Kenneth, I don't know which of them I would choose.'

'You don't have to decide. Kenneth isn't here. Leasky is. There's no point you wearing black and mourning Kenneth in gloom and doom for forty years, like Queen Victoria. It won't do Kenneth any good, won't do you any good and would be jolly unfair to Leasky. Do you really want to give him up in exchange for a ghost?'

'I don't want to be unfair to Leasky. And if I can't say he's the one and only—'

'You're looking for excuses.'

'He doesn't believe me,' Parshanti said. 'I told Leasky what Cousin Larry's like when I'm on my own but he just shrugged it off. He thinks I'm imagining stuff or making it up because, I don't know, because I'm jealous of his family or something. And I don't want to keep on at him because I know he's happy that someone from his family is here for our wedding.'

We turned on to Jurong Road and passed a jeep going in the opposite direction. It looked like the one that had driven Wilson to the quarry. Was the driver spying on the Pangs for Wilson? Was he going to try to set them up again? I should warn Danny and his mother. But first Mei Mei.

I was surprised not to see a policeman outside the Pang house.

'They said no need. The guard at the fire station is keeping watch for us, since the only road to get here goes past the fire station from Upper Bukit Timah Road,' Pang Tai said. That was only true if you were in a motor-car and afraid of driving across the old trails.

'But what are you doing here?' Pang Tai asked, staring over my shoulder at Parshanti. 'Where's Danny? I thought you and he were talking to the police today.'

'He's still there being questioned. He said Mei Mei was too sick to leave the house. I came to check she's all right.'

'Mei Mei is in her room. Safe. For her own good,' Pang Tai said.

'I think I saw George Peters from the fire station driving along the road away from here,' I said. 'Did he come to see you? He drove Wilson here the day that first body was found – and I'm sure he helped Wilson to try to make it look as though you were cooking opium here.'

'What?' Pang Tai looked angry. 'Who said we make opium here?'

I wanted to shake her. That's the problem with women who put so much effort into decorating themselves, whitening their faces and blackening their hair: it takes so much energy that their brain cells starve to death.

'Wilson tried to make it look like you were producing opium illegally.' Hadn't I explained to her why I'd taken all her *gula* and joss sticks? 'I think Peters helped him. We just saw him driving away from the house. He might be trying to contact Mei Mei.' I took her arm as a terrible new thought struck me. 'You must tell Danny to be careful! Please warn him that George Peters is sneaking around here. If he killed Ah Kok and Stinky, he might be after Danny next.'

Pang Tai finally seemed to get the urgency. Her eyes opened wide and she lowered her voice. 'I cannot tell anybody, only you, and you must not tell anybody else. I think Ah Kok and Stinky were doing opium trafficking. Maybe they wanted to take more money so the dealers killed them. Hey, you!' This to Parshanti, who'd been unloading the boot of the car. 'What's all that?'

'Food,' Parshanti said. 'For your workers. Su Lin said the supplies were running low.'

'Good of you, but the workers don't cook for themselves. We cook for them,' Pang Tai said. 'Sissy, Girlie, say thank you for the food, then take it and put it in the kitchen.'

The sack of rice and bundles of sweet potatoes and fish must have reminded Pang Tai that we were visitors and, as before, she disappeared.

Parshanti and I helped Sissy and Girlie carry the food around the house to the kitchen. Though Sissy and Girlie were older than we were, they acted more like children, afraid of being overheard by a fierce teacher.

'Is Mei Mei in your room?'

'Mei Mei won't talk to anyone,' Girlie said. 'She just cries and shouts.'

'She shouts at us, even,' Sissy said.

'Mei Mei liked Stinky. That's why she's sad,' Girlie said.

'Stinky liked Mei Mei, too. Stinky is dead,' Sissy said.

I couldn't help wondering: if Stinky loved Mei Mei, why hadn't he taken her to live with his family in Indonesia? Because she'd refused to go with him? Because Stinky was just one of the pawns she'd been manoeuvring?

'Can I see Mei Mei?' I asked.

Sissy and Girlie shook their heads.

'We came all the way here to see her so we should at least talk to her,' Parshanti said stubbornly. 'Which room is hers?' She headed into the main house from the kitchen.

'We can't just barge into her room,' I said.

'Why not? They already don't like me.' Parshanti had a point there.

When we reached the room the girls shared, the door was locked. 'Open up!' Parshanti called. 'We're not the police!'

'Now only Mei Mei sleeps there,' Sissy said.

'Mei Mei sleeps alone there. We sleep in the kitchen,' Girlie said.

I put my ear to the door and listened. I could hear laboured breathing. There was definitely someone in the room but I couldn't swear it was Mei Mei.

'Do you think Mei Mei wants to run away?'

Sissy and Girlie looked at each other, then shook their heads.

'Run away and go where?'

'She's got no money, nowhere to go.'

I had two dollars in Malayan coins in my cloth purse. I held it out. 'Can you give this to Mei Mei? Quietly?'

OVIDIA YU

'Quietly' was the euphemism we'd understood as children to mean 'without letting any grown-ups know'. I hoped it would still work, even though I wasn't a child any more.

Sissy and Girlie looked at each other. Something must have passed wordlessly between them because they turned back to me and nodded simultaneously.

'And tell her to come and see me if she can.'

Again they nodded.

'What's to stop them keeping your money for themselves?' Parshanti asked.

But the two women were already crouched in front of the door, sliding the coins underneath it. They got most of them under before we heard Pang Tai's door close and her footsteps approaching.

'For so long, Chen Tai and I wanted to get you and Danny together,' Pang Tai said. She didn't comment on my standing in front of her daughter's room, but took my arm and propelled me back to the uncomfortably fancy and dusty front room. Sissy and Girlie had scuttled off before she reached us, Parshanti with them.

'Your grandmother always said, "Don't say anything to Su Lin. She is so stubborn that even if she likes your son Danny she will jilt him just to show us that we were wrong for trying to arrange it." Why do you think your Ah Ma always sends you here to visit us? She has to keep quiet because she's afraid of making your *ang moh* boyfriend angry. But I'm not like your Ah Ma. I don't like doing things behind people's backs. I will tell you what I think even if you don't like it.'

Pang Tai had clearly prepared her speech while she was dressing.

'Thank you,' I said.

'Be careful, *ah*,' Pang Tai said. 'Your old Ah Ma is reaching the age at which she doesn't know how much she doesn't know. If you are not careful she will destroy everything your grandfather built up before any of you realises it.'

A car horn sounded outside. Thank goodness for Parshanti!

'I must go now,' I said.

'You be careful with beautiful girls like that Indian one,' Pang Tai said. 'They think they're better than anyone else. That one will make use of you until you are useless and she will poison your life.'

I was taken aback. 'She's not so bad,' I said. After all, Parshanti had driven me all the way out here to check that Mei Mei was still in the house. 'I have to go now,' I said again, and left as fast as I could.

We started on the bumpy lorry track in the direction of town. 'Oh, that was a grand old waste of time,' Parshanti said. 'Look, there's that tall, dark, handsome fireman again.' She waved out of the window at George Peters, whose jeep was coming towards us in the opposite direction. He looked behind him, then waved back, which made her laugh.

'Do you think he's sneaking up to see Mei Mei or one of the younger girls? Sorry, but I can't tell them apart. It must be deadly dull being posted out here.'

'Not likely,' I said, 'given their mother's prejudice against Indians.'

'Mothers don't know everything,' Parshanti said. 'Anyway, George Peters isn't Indian, he's Eurasian. You know, what the Brits call "others". Like Deirdre Rozario, who was at school a few years ahead of us – have you heard she's working as Governor Evans's personal assistant, with the emphasis on "personal"? She's even got her own suite of rooms in Government House.'

'It's a job,' I said. I knew people must have spread the same kind of stories about me when I went to work for Le Froy and the previous governor.

'Hey! He's pulled to the side of the road. Do you think he's changed his mind? Or maybe he wants to talk to us. He might be able to tell us something about what's happening around here.' She was already slowing down.

'Don't stop!' I said. 'You just want to flirt because he's good-looking. If we've wasted so much time, why are you trying to waste more? Can't we just get to the hospital?'

Parshanti pressed down on the accelerator and shifted up a gear. 'Why are you in such a temper? I thought he looked lonely. And he's good-looking, don't you think? I might be engaged but I'm not blind.'

'He looks suspicious,' I said. 'I don't trust him.'

Later I realised that if only we'd stopped and talked to him we might have saved a life.

Flowers in the Mortuary

'Nature has answers to everything,' Dr Leask said. 'If we only knew where to look. But sometimes Nature makes it easy for us.'

'Go on,' Parshanti said, 'in plain English. You found out something horrible and disgusting about how someone died, right?'

Dr Leask looked as if she'd just revealed the ending to a favourite story – and dismissed it. 'All in a day's work, my dear,' he said. 'How was your day? Larry said you girls went for a drive in the car.'

If it had been anyone else, I'd have said Dr Leask mentioned his cousin because he knew Parshanti didn't like him and wanted to annoy her. But I suspect he genuinely didn't know how much she loathed Larry. Sometimes the smartest people have the biggest blind spots.

'You found out about the body in the sack?' I asked. Parshanti rolled her eyes but she was interested too.

'The body in the sack that they took out of the abandoned quarry pool? That man died before the first body we found, likely up to twenty-four hours before.'

But the story was still worth telling.

Instead of dropping me off at the mortuary, Parshanti parked and came in with me. I could tell she wasn't sorry for a chance to spend some time with her Leasky, as long as it didn't look as though it was her idea – and as long as Larry wasn't around.

Dr Leask hadn't finished sorting all the bones and other material that had been found. Bones were laid out in four piles – three babies and parts yet to be identified, I guessed.

'I would say we're looking at what looks like the remains of newborns, originally in weighted sacks now disintegrated. All girls.'

Parshanti winced and my insides twisted. I didn't know if it was a problem outside Asia, but here all too many female infants and children were abandoned or had 'accidents'. When times were difficult, the top priority was to save the boys.

'Female infanticide?' I asked. 'How long ago did this happen?'

'Hard to say,' Dr Leask said, 'to both questions. I'm guessing at least ten years for the infants. Most likely more. And they weren't all left at the same time. There are remnants of clothing mixed in with one set of bones, but it's impossible to tell whether the others . . . Poor wee mites.

'The other bodies are of adult males. Two had been in the pool for more than a year since skeletonisation is complete. From what remains of their clothes I'd say death had come as the result of sickness or a workplace accident, and around the same time. It would be cheaper to put the bodies in the water than to bury them.'

'Could it have happened during the Occupation?' I asked.

'Very possible,' Dr Leask said. 'But the adult male body in sacking,' this was the one that interested him most, 'was the most recent death. Despite being underwater, which can speed up the process, it was still in the process of putrefaction – you can tell by the smell.'

Indeed. Even though the body had been placed in the mortuary refrigerator, the stench lingered under the powerful odour of protective bleach.

'Interestingly, he was killed in the same way as the first body we found. His neck was also cut almost completely through. There were marks on the spine where the blade had nicked it. We know he didn't drown because if the lungs were full of water there would have been no need for the stones.'

'Did you find the blade?' I asked. If the murder weapon had been recovered with the second body, it would help explain what had happened to the first.

'No. But what was really interesting, there was a stalk of angsana flowers almost eight inches long inside a cloth bag that he had tucked inside his shirt. And two angsana seeds. They look as if they had been threaded on a string that had decomposed in the water.'

Or that had been ripped apart before he was wrapped in sacking and put into the water. I remembered the three threaded angsana seeds that Mei Mei had claimed. Had she been wearing the necklace of angsana seeds? And had Stinky ripped it off her as he fought for his life, leaving part of the strand on the rocks and taking the other to his watery grave?

'The flowers were on the stalk?' I said.

'On the stalk,' Dr Leask said. 'Tucked into a cloth pouch inside his shirt. Because he was underwater it's difficult to assess the time of death, but the flowers show—'

'Time of death!' I said. 'He died when the blossoms were on the stalk, before they fell.'

'Precisely!' Dr Leask grinned.

Parshanti looked exasperated. 'You two, a man – several men are dead. Could you not look so thrilled?'

Sprays of angsana flowers can be anything from six inches to almost a foot long. Because the greenish flower buds develop high on the trees, they're seldom noticed until weather conditions trigger all of the trees on the island to burst into flower simultaneously for one glorious day. Once it's over, the area around the trees is covered with a thick, fragrant carpet of yellow blossom.

We don't know what makes them all bloom at the same time. Maybe if scientists studied why they do so instead of ways to kill people more efficiently we'd all be happier.

'I'm not thrilled,' I said. 'It's just that this means the body in the Death Pool – Stinky's – was killed first, before Ah Kok's body was found. The flowers on the stalk show he was put into the water while the blossom was still on the trees. That means he was killed on Friday. The day before Ah Kok.'

I hoped I wouldn't always associate yellow carpets of angsana with death.

'Yes,' Dr Leask said.

'Were they killed in the same way?' Parshanti asked. 'By the same person?'

'Yes and no. They were both strangled and almost beheaded with a thin garrotte that cut deep enough to mark the bone. There's a mark on Stinky's skull that suggests he was struck on the back of the head first,' Dr Leask said. 'But I can't say for sure how long before death that blow was struck.'

'Could it have been revenge?' I asked. 'If someone knew how Ah Kok killed Stinky and threw his body into the pool, could they have killed in the same way in revenge?' I shook my head. 'No. At least, I wouldn't do it.'

'No?' Dr Leask was amused, despite the gruesome topic.

'Not likely. You might kill to defend yourself or to make money, but to kill for revenge just isn't worth it. Much better to take your time and poison your victim later when he's forgotten about it and isn't expecting it.'

'Remind me not to make you angry,' Dr Leask murmured.

'Stinky was hit on the head and strangled, right? The strangling was just to finish the job,' Parshanti said. 'Could a woman have done it?'

Was she thinking of Mei Mei too? Could Mei Mei's hysteria have been the result of just having killed a second man?

'I'd say a man,' Dr Leask said, 'because even if a woman could have sliced through the throat, she wouldn't have had the strength to put Stinky's body into that sack and push it into the quarry pond, weighted with rocks.'

'But maybe two women could have,' I said. 'Or a woman and a man?' I felt a woman's brain had worked it all out. Men tend to attack and kill more directly, and conceal more clumsily. 'But what were they killed with?' I asked, still unable to visualise the weapon.

'Like I said, the closest thing I can think of is the huge wire cheese-cutters I grew up with. I've seen a woman cut through a two-foot truckle of cheese with those. Compared to that, a man's throat is nothing. But I doubt one woman could have put him in the sack with rocks and tipped him into the water. I'd guess that took at least two fairly muscular people.'

Or three weak ones, I thought. Could Sissy and Girlie have followed Mei Mei's instructions to dispose of a body? Somehow I didn't think so.

'But the human body under duress is capable of incredible feats of strength,' Dr Leask said. 'My cousin Larry was telling me he'd seen a woman lift a motor-car off a—'

'Forget it,' Parshanti said. 'I wish you could spend fifteen minutes with me without talking about dead bodies.'

Dr Leask looked confused. 'Her child survived. Somehow, incredibly, she saved him. That was the point Larry was trying to make. He said that—'

'I'm sick of his stories!' Parshanti headed out of the lab.

'What did I say?' Dr Leask said.

'Maybe you should talk to her,' I said. I wasn't going to be caught between the two of them.

'I try to.' Dr Leask sighed. 'Even I can see that it's Larry. He tried to talk to her but he doesn't know her like I do. He must have said something wrong. He knows it and I know it but we can't figure out what's making her so angry. It's like she hates him. He keeps trying to make it up to her but it's just getting worse. When we were growing up, Larry was always the popular one, the one the girls looked up to and the teachers liked. I used to wish I was more like him. It was only after I met Parshanti that someone preferred me to him.'

After Dr Leask was called away to examine another accident scene I went in search of Parshanti. I suspected she would be nearby, waiting to hear what Dr Leask had said after she stormed off. But before I got out of the hospital car park my way was blocked by Wilson. Clearly he'd been watching out for me.

'Miss Chen, I've been waiting for you to get back to me.'

'I told you! I can't tell you anything because I don't know anything.'

'Miss Chen, I just need you to read through some statements and sign them for me.' He held the door open. 'They're in my office.'

It would be most undignified, especially given I couldn't run very fast, but I was seriously thinking of making a run for it when my other arm was grabbed. Larry Leask said, 'About time. You're late. Come on!'

'Hey,' Wilson said, 'we're in the middle of a meeting.'

But Larry yanked me from his grasp and out of the building.

'Thanks for saving my life,' I said, only half joking. 'Were you looking for Dr Leask?'

'I was looking for you, actually,' he said.

'Me?'

'I saw Wilson skulking around in ambush and decided you might need rescuing. I should have worked out a fee for my services.' He pouted exaggeratedly and I couldn't help laughing.

I could see why Parshanti said he was too forward, but he was also funny. And chaplains were like pastors and priests, weren't they, keeping watch over their flocks? And, besides, this was Dr Leask's cousin, which made him practically family to Parshanti.

'I could buy you a drink as a thank-you,' I offered. 'Actually I'm looking for Parshanti. Have you seen her?'

'I wouldn't get a chance to if she saw me first,' he said.

He was right. Parshanti had made clear she wanted as little to do with him as possible, but most people would have pretended not to notice that.

I couldn't see what Parshanti had against the man. Larry Leask had a gift for putting people at ease. He was disarming and charming, the kind of man women fell for and men could talk to.

He was very like Parshanti. Maybe that was the problem.

Talking to Larry Leask

◆

'I've been wanting to talk to you,' Larry Leask said, once we were seated on wooden stools with our ice-cold *bandung*, rose-flavoured milk. 'I think I got off on the wrong foot with your friend Parshanti. Gordon says she won't listen to him, but he also said you know her better than anyone else and maybe you can suggest how I can patch things up and start again. Please?'

He looked a little desperate and very handsome. I liked him for bringing up the situation with Parshanti. Most men might have pretended not to have noticed anything was wrong – after all, he could escape the island and the situation with his new cousin-in-law once the wedding was over.

'You should talk to her,' I said. 'Say to her what you just said to me.'

'I come across a bit too strongly when I'm nervous,' he said. 'I didn't want to be seen as this uptight chaplain here to pass the family's judgement on Gordon's wife to be. Yes,

I said I was coming to have a look at her and report back, but that was a joke. Some of the family members aren't too happy about him marrying someone –' Larry stopped and cleared his throat. I could tell he was mentally editing and censoring what he'd been told by his relatives. '– someone none of them had met. So I was going to meet her, then go back and tell them how happy Gordon and she are together. I'm sure you can understand that.'

Families were the same all over the world. Of course I understood that. 'Dr Leask said his family was so happy he'd survived the war that nothing he did now could upset them.' That was what he had told Parshanti.

Dr Leask had written to tell his father and stepmother, who'd brought him up after his mother died before he was ten, as soon as he and Parshanti had told her parents they were getting married. His parents had written back, suggesting he shouldn't rush into anything but should return home for a long visit to recover from living in the equatorial jungle for more than two years.

It wasn't the warmest welcome into their family, but Parshanti and I had agreed it could have been much worse. His family hadn't tried to stop the wedding, though they hadn't been as supportive as her parents. But Parshanti had a lifetime to win them over, and if she didn't? Well, they lived half a world away and how they felt about her wouldn't really make any difference to her and the doctor's marriage.

That had changed with the arrival of Cousin Larry.

'That was how my aunt and uncle felt at first, of course. After the terrible time when they didn't know where he was, just to have him returned from the dead was a miracle. But after that, well, they wanted him to go home. They wanted to see him and have him close by. That was why they wanted me to tell him they'd managed to find him a position in an Edinburgh hospital where he can recover his health and help with the returning soldiers while thinking things over. Marriage isn't something to rush into.'

'Parshanti might have thought you were supposed to get him home so that he would forget about her.'

'His parents just wanted to see him for themselves. They weren't thinking much further ahead than that. That was why they asked him to bring her over to meet them and suggested she take on a nursing post at the same hospital.'

'Dr Leask never told Parshanti that.' Or if he had, she hadn't told me.

Larry looked embarrassed, 'I think she was offended that I'd assumed she was a nurse. I thought she was. Gordon had talked about how efficient and cool-headed she was, how quickly she picked up how to assist him on procedures. It was meant as a compliment.'

'Maybe she thought you were overdoing it,' I said.

'I was only trying to show her I liked her and that Gordon was a lucky man. But I don't know how to talk to girls, and I was making an effort.'

'She might have thought you were flirting with her,' I said. That was putting it mildly. Parshanti had complained that Larry had been doing exactly that whenever there was no one to see. She said he looked at her as if she was a cheap bar-girl. 'Were you?'

'If I'd been flirting I would have been talking about flowers and poetry.' He reached over and took my hand. He held on when I automatically jerked away, then turned it over and traced a petal shape on my palm. 'Flowers have so many different meanings. What matters is that he who gives the flowers and she who receives them agree on the meaning.'

I pulled my hand away and he laughed. 'Now that's flirting.'

Was he flirting with me?

'I'm not comfortable with that,' I said. I could always blame female propriety or fear of gossip. I could see the girl behind the *kopitiam* counter watching us – more likely watching Lawrence Leask – with undisguised interest.

'See?' Larry said. 'You tell me you're uncomfortable. I tell you I'm sorry – I'm sorry,' he bowed towards me, touching his fingers to his forehead, 'and I won't do it again. No more talking about flowers. But you're not going to avoid me, give me dirty looks and complain to your lover about me, are you?'

His talk about flowers had triggered a new thought for me. I remembered the withered stalk of large yellow papery angsana blossoms Mei Mei had preserved so carefully. They had clearly signified something to her. And on Stinky's body, Dr Leask had found a stalk of angsana flowers too. One from him to her and one from her to him? So no: Mei Mei might have been in league with Stinky, but I didn't think she'd known about his death until his body was found.

'Sorry.' I jumped up. 'I just thought of something. I have to go.' I wondered if Dr Leask could tell whether the flower stalk he'd found on Stinky had been fresh or dried before it had gone into the water. If the latter, it couldn't help pinpoint the time of his death but it showed an understanding between Stinky and Mei Mei.

'No!' Suddenly Parshanti was behind me. 'It's too late to run off. What are you doing sitting in public with him?'

'What?' I said blankly. 'What's wrong with you?' My thoughts were still with Mei Mei and Stinky.

'Su Lin was trying to help me work out what I've done to make you so angry with me,' Larry said.

'How dare you? Oh, you're hopeless! Both of you!' Parshanti stormed off.

'Oh dear,' said Larry. 'How very dramatic.'

'Excuse me,' I said, 'I have to go.'

He said something but I didn't hear what exactly as I dashed after Parshanti, only turning to call, 'Thanks for the *bandung*!' over my shoulder.

'You of all people! How can you not believe me?' Parshanti was waiting for me just outside.

'Not believe what? Why are you angry that I had a drink with Leasky's cousin?'

'You were talking about me behind my back with that worm! What about Le Froy?'

'What's Le Froy got to do with anything?' Suddenly something clicked for me.

Most of Parshanti's annoying girlish, flirty actions had disappeared after her time in the jungle. Until now. I'd not realised how little I missed them till they returned. And they'd returned since Larry Leask's arrival.

'Are you jealous of Larry?'

'Oh, we're calling him Larry now, are we?'

'Only to distinguish him from your Leasky!'

'Don't call him "Leasky"!'

'Why? Because only you are allowed to? Okay. I can't talk to your Leasky or your Larry either. You find Larry Leask attractive, don't you?' Maybe I could have put that better, but Parshanti had had so many romantic crushes during our schooldays that I thought this was just another.

Parshanti almost slapped me. I saw her arm come up and grabbed her wrist to stop her. She was easily strong enough to push me over but she didn't. I suspected she was glad I'd stopped her.

'What's wrong with you?' I said, not finding it funny any more.

'That's what he said.'

'What?'

'When Larry molested me, he said he could tell I fancied him and he was just giving me what I wanted.'

I stared at her. In the old days I would have dragged her off to tell her parents or my grandmother but now? 'Have you told Dr Leask?'

'Of course! Leasky was angry and confronted him, but Larry apologised and said I must have misunderstood. He said he was just trying to be friendly and he would never do such a thing. He made it a huge joke and said maybe if he'd been drunk but he didn't drink any more. He made me a huge fake apology and treated me as if I was some idiot making a fuss to get attention. I could see Leasky thinking maybe he was right. How can I marry a man who thinks I would say I was molested to gain attention?'

'Could you have misunderstood?' I asked carefully. 'I'm not saying he didn't do whatever it was, but maybe it means something different to him. Like – like Japanese slurping noodles loudly to be polite and us thinking it's rude. You know, some cultural misunderstanding.'

'Now you're being stupid! Why can't you just believe me? And why do you have to bring food into everything? That's all you ever think about! Food and your precious Le Froy! Why don't you take up with Cousin Larry instead, since you're so keen on him? At least he's got two feet and isn't a cripple.'

Now I was angry too. 'Why don't I just believe you? Because I've seen you flirting! You told me yourself it's just a game, just practice, when you smile at them and tease them.'

'Never!'

'You used to come to the Detective Shack to flirt with Sergeant Pillay and Sergeant de Souza, pretending you'd come to see me but spending all your time leaning over their desks, hinting to each of them that he was your favourite, but to keep it secret, trying to get them to fight over you. You even tried it on Le Froy, but he kicked you out of his office. We all knew what you were up to and used to laugh at you when you weren't around.'

That was an exaggeration. Prakesh and Ferdie had teased each other about Parshanti – Prakesh had had a noticeable crush on her – but they'd accepted her as my good friend.

And, yes, Parshanti was my good friend, my best friend, so why were we fighting like this over a man who didn't matter to either of us?

'Look,' I said, 'whatever happened between you and Larry—'

But Parshanti's blood was up and I was her new target. 'You're the one imagining things! You're the one dragging up stuff from the past because you can't let it go! You're jealous, aren't you? Jealous because you were with them day and night and none of them ever gave you a second glance!'

But I wasn't going to quarrel with her, however much she wanted to fight – though I did too.

'Look, the only reason I was with Larry is he asked me to help him work out how to get on better with you.'

'Do you call him "Larry dear" or "Larry darling"?'

Parshanti could be so needling when she wanted to. I would have found it so satisfying to smack her and storm off.

'I can't call him Mr Leask because of your Leasky,' I said. I thought I'd managed to sound calm and rational.

'Why not? My Leasky's Dr Leask, remember?'

At least she was still calling him her Leasky. That was the most important thing, wasn't it? The same thought must have struck Parshanti because she grimaced.

'I just don't see why you believe him over me.' She pouted, sticking out her lower lip like she used to do when we were at school and she knew she was in the wrong but hoped to get out of trouble. 'Nobody believes me any more.'

'Of course I believe you,' I said. This wasn't a court of law: I wasn't sworn in to tell the truth. Parshanti was asking whether I was still on her side and, of course, I was.

'Then why would you talk to that man after I warned you about his atrocious behaviour?'

I didn't want to trigger her again by reminding her that her own behaviour was the reason I'd been talking to Lawrence Leask.

'No man should put his hands on you,' I said. 'I'm sorry that happened to you, but I don't understand why you're so angry with Dr Leask. He didn't do anything, right?'

'There are unpleasant men all over the world and I can handle them. I'm just upset that the man I'm going to marry is closely related to one and, worse, that he believes him rather than me about what happened. But what do you care? Go on, run to your beloved Le Froy and continue believing that a white man can do no wrong. I don't have time to waste talking to you.'

But I could tell the fight had gone out of her. We would have made up in two seconds (even if we still didn't agree with each other) but we were interrupted: 'Miss Chen, are you all right?'

It was Hakim Harez, the pirate taxi driver.

'Mr Hakim, yes, everything is fine. Why?'

I glanced about and saw that a small crowd, including Larry Leask, was watching us screaming at each other in the middle of the street. Parshanti patted her hair and refused to meet my eyes.

'I'm going back to the east side. Come, I drive you? For free. Quick get in. Afterwards *mata-mata* come.'

Mata-mata – literally 'eyes' in Malay – meant the police in Singlish.

'Quick, Miss Chen. Otherwise I *kenah* fined for stopping in the middle of the road.'

'Don't worry. Once the *mata-mata* see you're with the big *mata-mata*'s darling they won't fine you!' Parshanti said nastily, and stalked off.

I got into the back of Hakim's pirate taxi. I'd always thought nothing could ever come between me and Parshanti, but Parshanti had changed. We both had.

Scaring the Pirate Taxi Driver

———◆———

Hakim Harez drove without saying anything till we were away from the worst of the city traffic and trishaws.

'Did Ah Ma send you to follow me?'

'No *lah*, miss. I need to talk to you. But I can drive you back if you want. Otherwise after I talk to you, I can just drop you back where you like, back to the same place.'

'So talk.' I settled back in my seat.

People were always asking my grandmother for favours. Most often it had to do with money they owed her or that they wanted to borrow from her, but sometimes it was to ask for jobs or introductions to people. I liked Hakim, even though he'd abandoned me and Ah Ma's *bak zhangs* at the Pang quarry, and was happy to present his case to Ah Ma as best I could.

At least it would be a light diversion from Parshanti's mess. Or so I thought.

'Miss, I need you to tell Chen Tai something.'

'Hakim, why are you calling me "miss"? You always call me Su Lin.'

'Now Miss is grown-up, Hakim must show respect.'

'Then call me Su Lin,' I said. 'If you call me miss, I will call you *encik*, okay or not, Hakim?' '*Encik*' meant 'sir' in Malay.

I saw Hakim smile in the rear-view mirror. 'Okay, Su Lin.'

'What do you want to tell Chen Tai?'

Hakim wanted to tell my grandmother that Jack Wilson had asked him for information on me, my grandmother and all of the Chen family. Wilson had pretty much accused him of transporting illegal or untaxed goods. The penalty for the latter was especially severe. He had demanded records of trips Hakim had made for the Chens and evidence of bribes handed to Le Froy to persuade the police to turn a blind eye.

When Hakim protested he was just a chicken farmer and market gardener who drove friends around as a favour (a pirate taxi driver), Wilson threatened that he could have Hakim's car and property confiscated. He and his wife would be jailed, his children left to starve.

'He said he will give me statements to sign. I told him I cannot read English. He said I have no need to read, just sign my name the same as on my identification papers.'

That was pretty much what Wilson had tried to get me to do.

'I want you to tell Chen Tai I'm not going to drive her any more.'

'You should tell the police, Hakim. Tell them Jack Wilson is threatening you and trying to blackmail you.'

'Hah! Tell the police for what? He said he is working with the police. Anyway, they probably all *pakat* with him.'

In the original Malay, *pakat* means 'to discuss', but in Singlish it's come to mean a conspiracy.

'You heard what happened in Indonesia? British soldiers dammed the rivers to cause flooding in the villages. Then they went to shoot the people trying to escape and the Indonesian soldiers trying to rescue them. Some of the Indian soldiers in the British Army tried to tell people what had happened but the British court-martialled and shot them!'

That story had certainly evolved since I'd first heard it. I wanted to say that even if British troops had fired on villagers trying to save themselves and their belongings, it was unlikely they'd deliberately caused the floods. But I hadn't been there. If someone like Wilson had been in charge, Hakim's version might have been correct, and I was believing the British lies I'd been told. I didn't know any more.

'Did you know that Pang Tai from the Pang quarries has been going around saying your Ah Ma is trying to turn people against her to put her out of business?'

'Why would Ah Ma do that?' Would she do such a thing? She would have needed a very good reason before she exerted so much energy.

'That's what people don't know. But whenever people don't do what Pang Tai wants, she is sure that somebody is conspiring against her. Because that is how she conspires against other people.'

Hakim laughed and thumped his wheel. He seemed to have cheered up now that he'd told me about Wilson's attempt at coercion.

'When did Wilson say those things to you?' I thought it might be good to get a timeline on record. 'How did he get hold of you?'

'Since that first time, he calls me quite often to drive him out to that fire station in Upper Bukit Timah.'

'Really?' After his clumsy opium set-up had failed I couldn't think why Wilson would still be spending time there. Surely even he wouldn't be fool enough to try it again.

'He's friends with George Peters,' Hakim said. 'George Peters was posted there but the building is still under construction, there are no fire-fighting machines yet and he's only got one jeep. He's supposed to be supervising the area, which means he's a security guard. He can play guitar and sing, you know. Before the war he was an entertainer. Then during the Occupation he lost his wife. Now his sons are with his mother in Selangor. Once he's made enough money here, he says, he'll go back to Selangor for good.'

I remembered seeing George Peters leaving the Pangs' place. There were very few other properties and quarries in the area and most were owned or run by the Pang family. I wondered what Peters would be willing to do to save enough money to retire to Selangor.

'No need to pay,' Hakim said, when he stopped the car at the gate outside Chen Mansion. 'I will deduct it from your grandmother's account when I pay her the rest. Remember to tell her what I told you, *ah*. Tell her I have no choice. I must leave.'

'You must park, come in and tell Ah Ma what you told me,' I said. I wanted her to hear it from him. I hoped she could come up with a solution for the poor man, whom Wilson had managed to frighten so badly.

'No. I shouldn't even be talking to you. If somebody sees me and tells him, I won't be safe even in Johore. You tell her from me that I will make payments for the car from . . .'

I stayed in the car, afraid he would drive off once I got out to call to my grandmother.

Hakim broke off and I saw he was staring at Nasima, one of our neighbours, who was outside showing two of her girls how to trim the butterfly-pea vines that hung over the hedge into the storm drain.

Nasima Mirza was a beauty. Not like Parshanti, whose liveliness and manner were at least half of her charm. Nasima might have stepped out of a work of art whether eastern or western. Yet she was refreshingly down to earth and practical.

'You want some?' Nasima waved a pannier of the purplish blue flowers. Butterfly-pea tea was reputed to help with women's cycles as well as keeping our skin firm and free of wrinkles.

'Can you open the gates for us?' I called to her.

'Of course!' Nasima and the girls ran to open them. As Hakim drove through, I signalled to Nasima to close them and she did. I would thank her and explain later.

Luckily my grandmother was at home and ready to listen.

'So. Are you just going to run away?' Ah Ma asked him.

'Yes,' Hakim said. 'I don't want to drive here any more. I want to go up-country because England says Malaya can be independent, but they are keeping Singapore.'

'You want to run away because you are scared of Wilson,' Ah Ma said.

'That's also true,' Hakim agreed.

'*Hiyah*, why are you so stupid, Hakim? What does your wife say? Does she want to leave her house and her chickens?'

Hakim looked shifty.

'You haven't told her yet.'

'My wife is not well. I don't want to worry her.'

'Oh, no. Instead you're going to tell her, "*Sayang*, darling, we are leaving the house and going to Johore." And what about the children's schooling? And your parents? *Hiyah*, you're so stupid. Do you really want to leave Singapore?'

Hakim shook his head. 'But that man Wilson will chase me. He knows where to find my car.'

'So you switch cars!'

Ah Ma called Uncle Chen to tell the men at the garage to find Hakim an open-back truck with benches. 'Better for you to transport goods to market. Maybe you shouldn't drive people for a while.'

'I can transport live chickens with this.' Hakim sounded relieved. 'No need to transport people.'

'Give your wife my regards, and I have some *bak zhang* for her. Vegetarian, with chestnuts and mushrooms. Next time people threaten you, come and tell me before you decide to run away.'

'That Wilson is crazy. Crazy people are dangerous, like mad dogs. But the one he's really after is Le Froy. He wanted to have Le Froy arrested and all his files confiscated, but the detective chief said he couldn't because Le Froy is his external consultant and there might be confidential material in his files.'

Another point in Fahey's favour, I thought. 'How do you know all this?'

'I drive people around, I hear them talk. People don't like him. But they say it's not him. It's not even Governor Evans. There are big shots in London chasing Wilson. Once he gets rid of Le Froy, they will let him leave Singapore and go home.'

I saw Ah Ma and Uncle Chen working hard that afternoon, sending out queries to track down others that Wilson might have tried to threaten or blackmail.

'That man is trying to make people think the Chens want to control the British administration and police force,' Uncle Chen said. '*Aiyoh*, people can be so stupid! To control my own small business is hard enough. Why would I want to control other people's?'

'I thought you weren't in touch with any of these people any more?' I said, seeing some of the characters who came in to make their reports . . . or, rather, who had decided to drop in for a cup of tea and *kueh*. Ah Ma preferred to deal 'friend-friend' style without anything on paper that the authorities could pin down.

'I thought you'd forgotten how to get in touch with them?'

'If I forget, then too bad, *lor*,' Ah Ma said lightly. 'I'm getting old but I won't forget. Managing business is better than playing mahjong for keeping the brain active. Plus you make more money from business than from mahjong.'

'Not all business!' I said. 'From what these people are saying, nobody can find money for new construction, I don't see how the Pang quarry can be breaking even when nobody can pay the Pangs, even before all this business got the quarry temporarily shut down. Wilson may be putting the final nail in their coffin with his accusations.'

Maybe that was what he meant to do. I was more and more certain that he was somehow involved with the deaths at the quarry. Did he get rid of men who refused to do what he wanted? And what was his connection with Mei Mei?

'You don't have to know anything about all this,' Ah Ma said. 'Better you don't. And what is happening at Pang quarry is also not your business.'

Time with Family

———◆———

It was raining heavily again. Dark sky, closed windows and the smell of damp in the air. The clean but not quite dry laundry had been moved indoors and I thought it must be what it was like to be on a ship surrounded by water. It made me want to curl up and sleep.

Even with everything that was going on, it was good to be at home. The simple pleasures of my own bed, my clothes folded on my shelf in the cupboard. And the smell coming from the hotpot in the back kitchen. So many people had lost much more than we had.

I had my own bedroom now. Little Ling was supposed to share it with me, but she preferred to sleep in Ah Ma's room, as I had done when I was her age.

Anyway, I had the room to myself now and I wasn't sorry. I could have the dim kerosene light on. It wasn't bright enough for me to read easily but it was oddly comforting.

Worries, like animal spirits and other *hantus*, grow stronger in darkness.

If I'd still had a job I would have used this time to work. Then I could have seen myself as hardworking rather than sleepless.

As it was, my thoughts went back to Le Froy. As long as I kept busy during the day I could keep them at bay. But whenever my guard was down they flooded in. A sign of weakness, I told myself. But I already knew I was weak so that didn't help.

Did we really have anything in common? I certainly felt close to him and he'd indicated that he felt the same. But what did we have in common other than the need to untangle complications and messes? That was hardly enough foundation for a life together.

Now we both knew each other better we'd stopped seeing the other from the outside. I remembered how at first Le Froy had been so cautious of hurting my Chinese maiden sensibilities, so careful to let me see that, despite my crooked hip and withered leg, he didn't see me as a cripple but as a competent assistant. I wondered about his family – if I would ever face the problems Parshanti was facing now.

Le Froy never liked revealing details of his past life and family. I had the impression they were wealthy and disgraced because of something that had happened years ago, around the time of the Great War. But that didn't matter. Why couldn't he see it? It was the cultures who placed importance on ancestors that made life hardest for their descendants.

That was the advantage of being in Singapore. It was so small that the whole island was an extension of the port and the airfield, and everyone was in transit. Even if you lived your whole life here, you were still in transit. But that was the great thing about a voyage. When you are between places you can remake yourself when you arrive. Or if you live in Singapore, which changes every day, or so it seems, you decide how you want to adapt to the changes. But that only supposed Le Froy was willing to stay on in Singapore . . .

I could hear Little Ling talking to herself as she ran down the corridor playing Run From the Tiger by herself. She had stopped asking where her mother was, but that didn't mean she didn't miss Shen Shen.

I tried to spend more time with her, and for a while she'd been keen to play Going to School, which involved me sitting down as the student while she stood in front of me as the teacher and fired questions at me. To my surprise, playing school with Little Ling had become one of my favourite things to do at home. I tried to answer her honestly, not brush her off, as I had been brushed off while I was growing up – 'Why do you talk so much?' or 'Why do you ask so many questions?' or simply 'Mind your own business!'

Little Ling came into my room now. 'Your friends cannot come to see you during school time,' she announced.

'What's that, *sayang*?'

Little Ling was everyone's *sayang*. Though Shen Shen had assumed I would be jealous of Little Ling, I wasn't. I'd realised it wasn't just Little Ling but also the child I'd once been whom I was nurturing when I spent time with her. Most of the time, we enjoyed our time together.

'I said, you must tell your friends they cannot come to see you during school time.'

Today, though, I was just too tired to play with her. Even if the murders at the Pang quarry were not my business, I still had to decide what to do about Parshanti. Of course I was on her side and would support her no matter what happened. But, as a true friend, ought I to support her even if I believed she was wrong? And what about her relationship with Dr Leask, if she insisted on him cutting off his cousin?

I stretched out on my bed and turned my back on *my* cousin.

Of course, the Leask cousins might be able to work something out between them, but what if Parshanti turned on more of Dr Leask's family?

'Su Lin-*jie*!' Little Ling crossed her arms and scolded me. 'Sit up properly and pay attention. I told you, your friends cannot come to see you during school time.'

'I don't have any friends,' I said, thinking of Parshanti, who, unfairly, hated me just then.

'I'll tell him to go away, then.'

What?

I rolled off my bed and went after Little Ling, whose feet were heading towards the kitchen at the back of the house.

The Chen Mansion kitchen was in a separate building, across a small courtyard. This was where the back gate led to, so that deliveries of charcoal and disposal of rubbish didn't have to go through the main house. It was also a way to sneak into the house without coming up the front driveway.

I admit that my first thought was that Le Froy needed to see me without anyone knowing. Maybe someone was watching our front gate. Of course Little Ling would have recognised Le Froy, but if she was playing 'school'?

But it wasn't Le Froy. It was Danny Pang, who was wet despite the huge umbrella he was holding. Thanks to the rain drumming down, it was unlikely anyone in the house had heard him arrive.

'Please,' he said, 'Su Lin, you are our only hope. You must tell me what the police are trying to do to us.'

'I don't know anything, Danny,' I said. 'You talked to the police - to Senior Detective Fahey, what did he say?'

Danny ignored my question. 'You must tell them to let us go back to work in the quarry. We've got contracts. If we cannot deliver, the business will crash. They are trying to destroy our business!'

Business couldn't have been good anyway, from what I'd learned. But I could understand Danny feeling desperate and wanting to do all he could.

'Somebody killed two of your employees. They just want to catch who did it.'

'That's what they keep saying! I know! Two of my friends are dead! Maybe they died because of me! But if we cannot work, we'll have no money so we cannot buy rice and all the workers, all my sisters, we all will die! I might as well throw them into the water. They'd die faster then, which is better than starving to death. Please, Su Lin, I beg you. Tell the police to let us go back to work.'

'I'm sorry, Danny, but there's nothing I can do.'

I felt bad for him and would have helped if there was anything I could do. At least until he said, 'My ma said, if you ask your friend Le Froy, he would help us.'

'That's not true,' I said.

'The other man, Wilson, said that Le Froy is trying to make trouble for me. He said he is jealous of me and wants to get rid of me because you and I are supposed to get married.'

'What? That's rubbish!'

'You're talking rubbish!' Little Ling said gleefully. I'd forgotten she was there.

'Go inside the house!' I snapped. 'Now!'

I was sorry when Little Ling ran off tearfully, but I'd make it up to her later. I had to sort out what Danny had told me, and I didn't want Little Ling around to hear what I had to say to him.

'It's not rubbish,' Danny said. 'You know that our families wanted us to get married until you got mixed up with that *ang moh*.'

'My family has said no such thing.' I barely managed to stop myself telling him what my family thought of the Pangs.

'Of course they want you to marry a Chinese man instead of some foreign devil! I said our families arranged for us to get married when we were children.'

'That's a lie! You're crazy! Why did you say that?'

'That's what they wanted me to say,' Danny said. 'The translator told me that if I wanted to go home faster I should just agree with them, so I did. You must go and tell them the same thing.'

'Agree with them about what?' Ah Ma asked.

She was standing at the top of the back stairs. Little Ling, who'd twined herself around the railing, looked tearful and triumphant.

'Tell him you never arranged with his parents for us to get married,' I said.

Ah Ma looked at Danny. 'Your mother wants you and Su Lin to get married?'

'No!' Danny said. 'My ma said – my ma never said–' He turned and left, plunging through the back gate, not even pausing to open his umbrella against the rain. I heard his truck grumble to life in the side alley, then rumble into the distance.

'Why did he come here to talk to you?' Ah Ma asked.

'I think he's just desperate about the quarry,' I said. Of course he must be upset about his friends too, even if he couldn't articulate it. I didn't know what I would do if my friends were killed. Maybe I'd try to distract myself by focusing on my work – which was what Danny was doing, only he couldn't work because the quarry was at a standstill.

My grandmother slipped a small hand into the crook of my arm, so that I was supporting her. 'We can leave it to them. Come, Su Lin, help me make *kueh bangkit*,' she said.

'Ah Ma? I thought you'd just made *kueh bangkit*?'

'So many people wanted them I gave them all away.' She looked at me – slyly, I thought. 'Don't you want some to give to your Le Froy?'

It was her way of saying she'd heard what Danny had said about foreign devils and contradicting it. Sometimes people can't put things into words. But if you know them well enough, you hear what they're saying anyway.

'I'll help you,' I said. 'Do you want me to make coconut cream first?'

Cracking open coconuts, while visualising Wilson's skull, and grating them might make me feel better.

'That's already done,' Ah Ma said, smiling at her kitchen army.

There were more people in there than usual. I recognised some of Nasima's girls and guessed they had come over to learn kitchen skills. Nasima preferred books to cooking, but made arrangements for them to learn what they needed to know.

'Miss Su Lin?' It was Rosmah. 'Miss Nasima asked me to tell you what I told her about my brother flying kites at home.'

I thought I was hearing things. 'Not now, Rosmah,' I said. 'Don't let me disturb you from your cooking lesson.'

'Oh, no, Miss Su Lin. I must go back. Miss Nasima asked me to come over to tell you about my brother flying kites but then I saw you are making *kueh* here and I wanted to learn how because I want to make them myself and sell . . .' She looked guilty.

Ah Ma shrugged. 'It's raining so heavily. If the girls can't work in the garden, they might as well learn to cook.'

'What about your brother's kites?' I asked, wondering what Nasima was up to.

'Back home, when they are fighting kites, they use fishing line for the kite strings. And they glue on glass powder so that they can cut the strings of other kites. They are very sharp and very strong. When they get caught in trees the kite strings can cut branches off.'

'Wait! How can a kite string cut off the branch of a tree?'

'Fishing line is very strong. And the glass powder makes it very sharp. Can cut off your fingers, even! Birds and animals and motorcyclists that run into the kite string can die because the string can cut through flesh and bone.'

Fighting Kite Strings

———◆———

Had anyone thought of deadly kite strings? It was unlikely any of the British detectives or doctors had ever flown fighting kites ...

I'd thrown propriety to the winds and hurried back to town despite the rain.

'Why not wait until the rain stops?' Ah Ma asked. 'What can be so important? The bus stop will be flooded and the buses won't wait.'

'I don't know if it's important,' I said, 'but it might be. And the rain may not stop for days.'

'But how will you get anywhere? You want to swim?'

The family car had been sold after Uncle Chen's late wife had damaged it. It could probably have been repaired but I don't think Uncle Chen wanted to be reminded of Shen Shen every time he drove it. Now he had a van to transport the household goods he sold.

'Uncle Chen, can you lend me your van to go to the hospital?'

'You know how to drive, *meh*?'

Ah Ma knew very well I didn't. But why hadn't I learned? I'd always meant to. Parshanti had her driving licence, and so did Nancy Drew, the American girl detective in *The Secret of the Old Clock*. Once I'd told Dr Leask and Le Froy what I'd learned about deadly fishing line, and once the rain stopped, I would take driving lessons.

'You spend so little time at home now. You can't even stay at home one afternoon. Why not wait until the rain stops?'

I couldn't explain the urgency I felt or explain it to Ah Ma without alarming her.

'Uncle Chen? Please – I want to tell them what Nasima's girl told me.'

Uncle Chen looked at Little Ling. 'Want to go for a car ride in the rain?'

'Yes, Papa!'

So Uncle Chen drove me to town, with Little Ling along for a ride. And I promised myself again that I would take driving lessons.

I found Le Froy with Dr Leask in the hospital canteen.

'Everything all right?' Le Froy said.

'Slow day,' Dr Leask said. 'The rush will start as soon as the roads are clear.'

'Have you thought of kite strings?' I asked Dr Leask. 'The injury to Ah Kok – the first body we found, could it have

231

been caused by a fighting-kite string, fishing line with glass powder glued to it?'

Dr Leask looked as if he didn't understand my question. 'Why and how would someone glue glass powder to a fishing line?'

'Fighting kites,' Le Froy said. 'I've heard about kite fighting. Haven't seen it here though. In India they coat the strings with crushed glass and rice glue. It's very dangerous. The strings are razor sharp and when people get tangled in dangling kite strings they're injured and even killed.'

'I'll look into it. I tested the powder for metal deposits but hadn't thought of glass. I can test glass containers for hydrolytic resistance, but to test for glass, non-crystalline, amorphous, non-reactive . . .' Dr Leask stood and walked out of the canteen, leaving his half-eaten bowl of sweet red bean soup.

I sat on the bench he'd vacated, across the table from Le Froy. 'Hello,' I said to him, wondering how to bring up the *kueh bangkit* Ah Ma was making to signal her acceptance of him.

'Used like a garrotte, then,' Le Froy said.

The *kueh bangkit* would have to wait.

Dr Leask would be back once he'd proved or disproved the presence of glass. It was no use going after him now. But that didn't stop Le Froy theorising. 'A garrotte primed with glass and metal glued to it would slice through skin and muscle. The victim would be strangled if he didn't bleed to death first. The problem is, there wouldn't be any way to tighten it around your victim's neck . . .' he mimed the action '. . . without getting your fingers cut off. What made you come up with this?'

'A neighbour's helper told me her brother in Indonesia used to fly fighting kites and coated the kite strings with crushed glass. And I remembered the cuts I saw on the trunks of the angsana trees by the Death Pool. Those might also have been made by glass-coated fishing line. If someone was using one to cut through tree bark and Ah Kok turned up . . .'

I didn't want to name Mei Mei. But I would need to warn Pang Tai and Danny of what might have happened.

'Indonesia,' said Le Froy. 'The other victim, Stinky, he had family in Indonesia. Did he grow up there?'

'Wilson was posted to Indonesia before he came here, wasn't he?' I said. 'He could well have learned about coating kite strings there,' and he might have been working with Mei Mei. I couldn't see that but, then, I couldn't see what Ah Kok and Stinky saw in her either. Mei Mei was either a good actress or I was very bad at picking up what attracted men to women.

'I'll be back soon.' Le Froy got up too. I suspected he was going to telephone Fahey and wished I could make sure he mentioned Wilson's Indonesia connections as well as Stinky's.

I was sitting with their half-drunk glasses of tea, wondering whether to get myself a snack to justify my occupying the table, when Larry Leask came over and sat down.

'Waiting for me, sweetheart?'

'Hello. No. Dr Leask and Mr Le Froy will be back soon.'

Larry raised his eyebrows. 'Bolted off together, did they? They should know better than to leave a lovely young lady alone.'

He sat uncomfortably close to me on the bench. I edged away.

'Have you had a chance to discuss me with your friend Parshanti?' He leaned in to whisper in my ear, and I smelt an unpleasant combination of beer and poor digestion on his breath. Was he drunk so early in the day? And why was his hand squeezing my thigh?

I pushed it away. 'Stop that!' I said, loudly enough for the canteen staff to look over. But I didn't care. If anyone was going to be embarrassed it should be him.

'There are enough corpses here. Don't be another!' Larry's hand was behind me now, groping my buttock through the thin fabric of my dress. 'I'll show you what you're missing with that old fellow. Come on. I'll teach you a couple of tricks you can use on him. It's as easy as eating a banana – hey! My trousers! You little minx!'

Dr Leask and Le Froy came in together and the canteen staff, who'd started towards our table, looked relieved and returned to their stations without clearing up the mess of red bean soup dripping from Larry Leask's trousers onto the floor.

Le Froy picked up the mood in the room immediately and looked at me with eyebrows raised. I gave him a smile that said, *Everything's okay – well, not okay but not worth going into*, and he nodded.

Dr Leask had come back in with a fishing line. 'It's tough, too tough for a fifty-pound fish to break, and even without powdered glass, it can cut through a stick of sugar cane. And if it can cut through sugar cane it'll definitely cut through a human throat.' He sounded pleased. Then, looking at the red mess on his cousin's trousers and the floor, 'What's up?'

Larry laughed nastily. Or maybe he just laughed and gave me a dirty look. 'Nothing much. I was just trying to teach her something helpful. Your girl already knows all the best tricks but this one . . .'

Dr Leask looked blank.

Larry grabbed a banana from the giant bunch that hung on the wall hook by the table and peeled it. Then he started pushing it into and out of his mouth suggestively. He was watching me as he did it. Which was why he didn't see Dr Leask's expression until he hit him.

Dr Leask hit him? Dr Leask?

No, I hadn't imagined it. Larry ended up on the floor against the wall. He rolled his eyes towards Dr Leask, looking as shocked as I felt. 'Gordon, hey, a joke's a joke but this is enough. You'd better hope I don't press charges for assault. What are you doing?'

Those last words were directed to Le Froy, who'd walked over in his usual gracefully swift but unhurried manner – no one would have guessed he had an artificial foot – as though to help him up. Larry held up a hand to him. Le Froy ignored it and lifted him by the front of his shirt instead.

Larry tried to laugh, but Le Froy tightened his grip and it came out as a choked 'Hey!'

Le Froy was stronger than he looked. I'd always known that but I'd never seen him pin a man by his neck to the wall. Larry's heels kicked maybe two inches off the floor as his hands scrabbled at Le Froy's fingers around his neck.

'Gordon!' squawked Larry. 'Do something! Help me!'

'I'll write it up as an accidental death if you finish him off,' Dr Leask said. 'Do you need help?'

'Don't,' I said to Le Froy. 'He's not worth it.'

Le Froy held on for a moment longer before dropping him. 'No, he's not.'

'But thank you,' I said.

'You'll pay for this!' Larry leaned against the wall, holding his throat. 'I'm an army chaplain, a representative of British forces. You can't go around strangling people for nothing. Wilson's right. You're a madman!'

'You always hated your cousin Gordon, didn't you?' Le Froy said. 'I suspect largely because he never got angry or even seemed to notice he was being made fun of. You couldn't upset him as you did most other people. And, of course, it didn't help that your cousin was doing so much better at school, at college, in his profession. Because, unlike you, he worked. And he was always his grandmother's favourite, wasn't he? That was why she left him her old house and twenty thousand pounds . . . that you're hoping will come to you if you make him too angry ever to go home.'

The Leasks looked at Le Froy.

'Granny is dead?' Dr Leask said. He looked at his cousin.

'You can't know that,' Larry said. 'You're guessing. You don't know anything.'

'I have my sources too,' Le Froy said.

'I'm a really bad judge of character, aren't I?' I said. I'd liked Larry Leask until a little while ago, despite everything Parshanti had said.

'You're not the only one,' Dr Leask said. 'We could put him in the Death Pool with the rest of the bodies in there. Unidentified and not missed.'

'You mean the quarry workers' bodies you found?' I said. 'They might be unidentified but that doesn't mean they're not missed. There could be people somewhere still hoping they'll return some day.' I knew how the Shankars had never given up hope that Parshanti's brother would come back.

'Except they weren't quarry workers,' Dr Leask said. 'Extremely unlikely, anyway. I'd say they were Chinese or Malay men, fairly tall – from the dimensions of their femurs – and in their late fifties at least. Better fed, taller and older than most quarry workers, who seldom last that long. Like miners, you know. Dangerous work in terrible conditions for very little pay . . . Those who aren't injured or killed in their twenties tend to die of lung and gut problems, not to mention overwork, in their thirties . . . and the Pang quarry men are mostly not local. They were brought over by the Japanese to work in the quarries after the Pangs' own quarry workers were encouraged by the previous boss to go up-country and fight the Japanese.'

'The Japanese killed a lot of Chinese men,' I said.

'The Japanese never bothered to hide the bodies of men they killed,' Dr Leask said. 'They broadcast their killings. That was the whole point, wasn't it? To intimidate. You can't intimidate with missing bodies.'

I could see why Parshanti found him so exasperating sometimes. I find facts fascinating, but there are times when you have to pay attention to the people who are right there in front of you.

'Are you really a chaplain?' I asked Larry Leask. 'Or is that just an excuse to proposition women?'

'I'm good at my job,' Larry said. 'I told you, this was a favour for the family. They asked me because I can talk to anybody, not just women. It's true. I've helped a lot of people by getting them to talk to me when they won't talk to anybody else.'

Maybe so, but that gift wasn't apparent at the moment.

'I need to apologise to Parshanti,' I said.

'So do I,' Dr Leask said. 'Hurts, doesn't it?' He grimaced. 'I'm glad, though. Best resolution possible.'

Dr Leask was a good man. And he knew as well as I did that Parshanti wasn't going to let us off easily. 'Should have listened to her from the start. I certainly earned it, though!'

So had I. I was glad now, though.

Making-up Dinner

———◆———

'I'm sorry,' I said to Parshanti. 'Larry Leask is a no-good snake through and through, and I should never have disbelieved anything you said, but I still think you should marry his cousin.'

We'd ended up at the Shankars' where I sneaked upstairs and told Parshanti what Dr Leask had said – and done – to his cousin. Not surprisingly she was delighted.

Of course, being Parshanti, she had to pretend she wasn't. 'Why did he believe you and not me? And he hit him for you, not me!'

'He did it for you because he realised he should have believed you all along. That's what made him so mad. I wish you'd seen him whack Larry!' That made her smile.

'Me too. Once in a lifetime for Leasky and I wasn't even there!' Parshanti moaned. 'I wish I'd seen it.'

'I wish you had too. You're the only thing he thinks worth getting worked up over.'

'Su, you're talking rubbish,' Parshanti said. But she was smiling.

When we went downstairs, Dr Leask was in the kitchen making his grandmother's beef meatloaf. Parshanti laid her fingers on the inflamed knuckles of his right hand. 'You didn't believe me,' she said to him. 'Why believe Su Lin?'

'I believe you now,' Dr Leask said. 'Su Lin has a way of presenting evidence.'

'What I don't get,' Parshanti said, 'is what he's still doing here.'

'I was only trying to help.' Larry's throat was an angry red and he was going to have a black eye to go with the bruise on his cheek by tomorrow. 'Your father,' he nodded to Dr Leask, 'settled my accounts and paid my passage here to help you sort things out. It was just an assignment.'

'"Sort things out" as in ruin my life?' Dr Leask's quiet, quizzical voice held menace.

'It's not like that. They were afraid you'd been ensnared and brainwashed.'

'How? With what?'

Larry shrugged. 'Maybe voodoo and black magic. Maybe she told you she was having your baby. Your father just wanted to make sure you weren't tangled in something you couldn't get out of. Come on, what was anyone supposed to think? You disappeared into the jungle in enemy territory letting them think you were dead – you could have been tortured or gone mad.'

'I wrote to them. I told them all about Parshanti.'

'Of course you did. "I'm going to marry a girl named Parshanti Shankar. She's very nice. I hope you'll like her."' Larry mimicked Dr Leask's voice. He had regained some of his composure in the presence of Parshanti's parents, who had heard a censored version – no simulated sex or physical violence – of what had happened.

Mrs Shankar was of the opinion that family was family, no matter what. She could understand what Dr Leask's father had done, though she couldn't approve of it, and had urged the cousins to shake hands on it. 'I don't know what went on between you and I don't need to know. You're all alive and that's what matters. We'll have dinner together, all of us, and a good evening.'

Mrs Shankar reached over and squeezed Parshanti's arm. 'Are you all right, my dove?'

'I'm not upset,' Parshanti said. But the baby name softened her and she allowed her mother to pull her into a proper hug.

'There's friction in all families,' Mrs Shankar said. 'That's how you wear down the rough parts and fit together. After the last few years we all have a lot of friction to catch up on. I had my share of problems getting used to being married to my man.' She smiled at her husband. 'I can't say I've never looked at another man . . .'

'Excuse me, my dear?' Dr Shankar said. 'I can't say I've never looked at another woman either. I've looked a lot at their insides and outsides. I've just never seen any other woman whose insides and outsides measure up to yours.'

'I looked, but I knew you were the only man for me. I knew it deep in my bones and blood. I couldn't get my family to open their eyes enough to see that, but I knew, and I swore no one would put my own children through that. Not me and not anyone else.'

She smiled at me. 'I consider you one of mine too.'

'I know,' I said.

'Ten minutes to dinner,' Dr Leask called from the kitchen. 'It's out of the oven, but it needs to rest to reabsorb its juices for the best flavour. Like we should rest our muscles after exercising.'

A heavenly smell was wafting out of the kitchen.

'Meatloaf smells good,' I said.

'And it is good, despite all the weird stuff in it,' Parshanti said.

'What's wrong with bread and cheese? Or sugar? Or carrots?'

I noticed Dr Leask didn't mention the American tomato ketchup I'd seen him add to the mix.

'You should add some century eggs, just in case Wilson turns up,' I said. I was happy to see Le Froy laugh at that.

'What's wrong with century eggs?' Parshanti asked.

I told them that Wilson had been horrified, imagining that the eggs pickling in the Pangs' backyard had been laid like that by some bizarre chickens.

'My mother used to rub butter on the outside of the eggs – when we had enough eggs and enough butter,' Dr Leask said. 'She did it when the eggs were fresh laid and still warm. She rolled them in her buttery palms.' He demonstrated with half a bread roll. 'The butter coated, strengthened and sealed the shells. They stayed good all winter in the shed and, as a bonus, tasted richer because of the butterfat.'

'I remember that too,' Larry said. He was more subdued now. 'Better century eggs than rotten ones.'

'We'll make something of you yet,' Dr Leask said. 'But the real test will come in the durian season if you're still around.'

'I still don't trust him,' Parshanti whispered to me.

'Not as much as I don't trust Jack Wilson,' I said.

'Where's Fahey?' I asked Le Froy. 'Did you tell him about Wilson being in Indonesia and probably knowing all about preparing strings for fighting kites?'

'I didn't see Fahey. He was out at Bukit Batok – it was a fire this time, not at any of the quarries but at the fire station, believe it or not.'

'One body was brought in,' Dr Shankar said. 'Almost impossible to identify, of course. But there was only one fireman posted at the Upper Bukit Timah fire station so it has to be him. It looks like he got drunk, knocked himself out and set the fire station ablaze. The place is still under construction so it was mostly wood and went up in flames as if it was made of straw. I haven't looked at the remains yet but it's obvious what happened there. The poor man.'

'So why is Fahey out there?' Dr Leask asked. He and Le Froy looked at Dr Shankar.

'What's interesting is that they found the remains of what looked to be opium-processing equipment in empty garages. That's not surprising, given how many licences were sold to that part of the island before they were revoked.' He looked at Le Froy as he spoke, but Le Froy said nothing. 'There was no record of it being confiscated property.'

'It was an ideal place for a small opium-processing operation. He was all alone there. There were also the remains of wrappers that raw opium balls come in. They're pretty distinctive.'

'We saw George Peters earlier,' I said. 'He was probably supplying Wilson with the opium he used to frame the opium processors. Was it a joint operation?'

'Nothing the Fire Department knows about.'

What if we had stopped to talk to him, as Parshanti had suggested? He might have let slip something about what was going on. Parshanti was good at getting people to talk. George Peters might still have been alive now . . . or Parshanti and I might also be dead.

'Wilson couldn't tell opium from sugar,' I said. 'What if he thought George Peters cheated him by using sugar instead of opium?'

'You mean this was revenge for the *gula melaka*?' Parshanti asked.

If it had been, we were indirectly responsible for George Peters's death.

'The police believe it was an accident,' Dr Shankar said. 'Flammable substances in a wooden building. Nobody's to say anything about the opium traces.'

But I was sure George Peters had been deliberately killed. If not because Wilson thought he'd double-crossed him, then why? Had he been frightened by the deaths of Stinky and

Ah Kok? Or had he been killed in revenge because he'd murdered Stinky and Ah Kok? Or because he'd known or guessed who had killed them? And who else had he been working so closely with but Jack Wilson?

After dinner I watched Parshanti and Dr Leask talking with their heads close together. Larry Leask sat alone, ostentatiously close to the open window so he could smoke. Mrs Shankar didn't allow smoking indoors because the smell got into her ladies' fine fabrics. We had all officially made up but that didn't mean I trusted him. Like a treaty signed after battle, it was just an agreement not to kill each other in the immediate future.

In this case, everyone was in a state of goodwill, having eaten far too much together. Perhaps that's why Asians serve far too much food whenever extended families get together.

'I forgot to send a trishaw messenger to Chen Mansion to tell my grandmother I wouldn't be back for dinner,' I remembered.

'Her telephone line has been restored, has it?' Le Froy asked, suddenly concerned.

We'd had a phone line at Chen Mansion, but during the Occupation much of the communications infrastructure had been damaged or deliberately destroyed. Before the war, it had been possible to call long distance from Singapore's Malaya Tribune office to London. Now we couldn't even be sure of calling the hospital or the fire station.

'Yah. But the phone lines must be down again. They're always going down. I tried calling earlier but couldn't get through.'

Le Froy took out his notebook and turned away. I saw him scribbling and knew he was making a note to get someone to check the telegraph poles out east. Some people blamed the frequent collapses on the unhappy spirits of those who had been beaten to death tied to them, but I thought it more likely that they hadn't been designed to hold up more than copper wires and the occasional bird. Whatever the cause, Le Froy would see to it that they were fixed. For a practical person, you can't get more romantic than that.

But his gesture proved unnecessary as the Shankars' telephone rang. It was Uncle Chen, calling for me.

'You must come home straight away,' he said, but wouldn't say why. Only 'I'll come to pick you up. Don't worry. Nothing is wrong. Everybody here is all right. I phoned the hospital but you weren't there. I'm coming now. And don't say anything to the police.'

'I'll get a trishaw back,' I said. 'By the time you get here I can already be home.' I didn't know what was wrong, but Uncle Chen wasn't the sort to make up things for effect.

'I'll drive you,' Parshanti said at once.

'No,' Le Froy said. 'I'll drive you back. Tell your uncle.'

He spoke loudly, and Uncle Chen must have heard him because he said, 'No police.'

'I'm not police,' Le Froy said. He took the receiver from me. 'I won't come in. I won't interfere. But I'll drive Su Lin back fast and safely.'

Uncle Chen must have agreed because Le Froy put down the phone. 'Do you know what's happening there?' he asked me.

I shook my head, already hurrying to get my things together.

'I won't come in with you, but I'll be outside until you give me the all-clear.'

'Thank you,' I said.

Parshanti gave me a quick hug before I left, and her mother put her arms around us both. 'My girls,' she said. She'd noticed that we'd cleared up whatever was wrong between us. But I couldn't think about that then.

What had happened? Uncle Chen said there was nothing wrong, but something had to be. Had Wilson decided to move in on my family? What else could have made Uncle Chen summon me home like that?

Mei Mei Turns Up

———◆———

'You said I could come to see you,' Mei Mei said.
    She was in Ah Ma's room, sitting next to Ah Ma
on the padded bench at the foot of the bed, bruised and
clearly terrified.

'What happened?' I asked.

'She ran away from home,' Ah Ma said, 'because she
wanted to tell you that Stinky wouldn't have killed anyone.'

I knew Ah Ma was telling me what she'd been told, not
necessarily what she believed.

'He didn't,' Mei Mei said. 'He wouldn't.'

And what did I believe? I'd built up Mei Mei in my mind
as a conniving manipulator, but looking at her now I found
that hard to believe. She had a black eye that looked several
days old, and both eyes were red from lack of sleep. Her
hair was unpinned and unwashed and there was a crust of
dried blood at the corner of her mouth. There were other
bruises too, recent and older, but her feet were the worst –

scraped and bleeding, as though she'd been walking on gravel without shoes.

I squatted in front of her. 'How did you get here?' I asked.

'I had to run away. Ma and Danny don't want me to talk to anybody. They say don't get involved, don't get into trouble.'

I nodded, understanding. Protective families were all the same. They wanted you to hide like a turtle in the sand and hope whatever was happening in the world would pass you by. Sometimes it might, but other times you ended up as soup.

'They let me out to use the WC. Once I was outside I hid in the back of Danny's pickup. I knew he was going to town because he'd started the engine to warm up. Then when he stopped at the Bukit Timah Road junction and got down, I was scared if he collected something he would put it in the back and see me, so I climbed down and started walking.'

'You walked all the way here? From the Upper Bukit Timah Road?'

'I was scared Danny would see me so I didn't dare to walk too close to the road, but I followed it to Beauty World. From there I took a trolleybus with the money you gave me under the door.'

Ah Ma threw me a surprised look – any mention of money always caught her attention.

'I'm glad you had it,' I said. I would tell Ah Ma what Parshanti and I had done later. 'Ah Ma, where are you going?'

'I'm going to send a girl to ask Nasima to come over,' she said, moving to the door. 'Tell me if you hear anything interesting.'

'Nasima? Why?' I called after her, but my grandmother didn't answer.

'You and Stinky were very close.' I took Ah Ma's place next to Mei Mei.

'Yes. We grew up together. Ma adopted Stinky after his pa died. My pa always said that Stinky was his second son. That's why Stinky was so upset when Pa got killed – he said he was the second father he'd lost. My pa was proud of Stinky because he could read contracts and check accounts. My pa and the other boys couldn't read English, but Stinky taught himself.'

'You talked to Stinky a lot?' I prompted, wishing I could take notes.

Mei Mei nodded. 'Stinky used to meet me under the old angsana trees by the Death Pool. We went to talk there because we couldn't talk in the house.'

'Your ma didn't like you talking to Stinky?'

'My ma didn't like anybody talking except to her.'

'But why up there?'

'Because of the trees. I needed to get the red sap for my mother's poultices. And Stinky liked the trees. He said in Indonesia they call them *sono kembang* and it's good luck to be near them.'

I wasn't surprised. In Singapore's Taoist, Buddhist and animism beliefs, angsana trees are said to symbolise and confer strength, health and prosperity.

'We met there the day before he disappeared. I remember the trees were starting to bloom again that day. Stinky climbed up and cut a stalk of flower buds for me. He said that by the time the angsana's winged fruit fell we would be far away. Like the angsana seeds, we would fly and float to Indonesia and we would set down roots there and grow our own family. But I told him to keep the stalk because I still had the one he cut down for me last year. I dried it and kept it.'

That was the dried stalk I'd seen in her drawer, when she'd put away the angsana seeds I'd found on the rocks.

'And the angsana seeds on a string?'

'I made those. I used to make angsana seed necklaces when we were children. Stinky told me I gave him one when he first came to live with us and he kept it for years.' Mei Mei smiled at the memory. 'After that I made new necklaces for us every year. Until now.'

She looked as if she was going to start crying again.

'And then that night Stinky asked me to to meet him there again. At the angsana trees,' Mei Mei said. 'Quite late, when the flowers were dropping. I knew that something was wrong, but he didn't tell me what. He just said he was going to talk to Danny about something. And once that was settled, he would tell Danny he wanted to marry me. He said he would go on working for Danny if Danny wanted, or he would take me back to stay with his family in Indonesia. He had got in touch with some of his mother's relatives there and they would welcome us.'

The Indonesian connection again, I thought.

'Why didn't you say any of this that day when we found Ah Kok's body?'

'They told me Stinky killed Ah Kok because of me,' Mei Mei said. 'They warned me not to say anything to anybody for my own good. I just wanted Stinky to come back and explain what had happened.'

'Did you know about the opium cooking?'

'Of course! Ma was making and selling opium before the war. Pa didn't know about it. He said opium was a curse on the Chinese people. Opium was bringing in more money than granite. Stinky and Ah Kok were helping her. They were in charge of the workers making opium. It wasn't against the law at that time. After they'd extracted what she could sell, they gave the rest to the workers to keep them quiet and eating less.'

'Did Ah Kok also stay with your family?'

'No. He and his father had a hut outside the workers' dormitories. His father was my pa's foreman and Ah Kok worked with him.'

'Ah Kok's father wasn't married?'

'No,' Mei Mei said. 'Uncle Khoo had a sworn wife back in China. He was hoping to earn enough money to bring her out. That was why he wouldn't even look at me or my sisters or any of the girls Ma introduced to him. Even when she got angry with him he wouldn't. Ma told Pa to fire him for being useless, but Pa wouldn't. He said Uncle Khoo was like a brother to him. That was the only time I remember Ma not getting her way.'

'But she didn't send Ah Kok and Stinky away after your pa and uncle died?'

'No. By that time she needed Stinky because he was the only one who could read the letters from the bank. Stinky was trying to teach me to read too. He tried to teach Danny, but Danny said he was trying to make him look stupid and got so angry that he had to stop. Danny just couldn't read. Please don't tell him I told you. He hates people knowing because they'll think he's stupid.'

'It doesn't mean he is,' I said automatically. After recovering from a stroke, one of our teachers at the Mission Centre had found herself unable to read, though she had no problem talking. She could recognise individual alphabets, but once they were put together into words they got jumbled into incomprehensible patterns. Her doctors said it was 'word blindness', that the part of her brain responsible for reading had been damaged in the stroke.

'Has Danny ever had a head injury?' I asked.

Mei Mei stared at me. 'Danny's not stupid,' she said, showing she was brighter than I'd given her credit for.

I had to remember that.

'It was Stinky who met that man Wilson, not Danny,' Mei Mei said. 'Wilson had sent letters about shutting down businesses that had been set up by the Japanese and Stinky read them to us. Danny told Stinky to meet Wilson and tell him that the quarry was set up by our father, before the Japanese time. The only reason it was on Japanese records was because after our father disappeared the Japanese let Danny take over.'

'Why didn't Danny tell Wilson himself? I'm sure they would have found a translator.'

Mei Mei looked awkward. 'In case it was a trap or some funny business.'

'So Stinky would *kenah* instead of Danny?'

Mei Mei nodded. She seemed to accept that Danny had to be protected at all costs. I could understand if he'd been the king of a country or even the headman of a village . . . Ah Ma returned with Nasima before I could arrange my thoughts into speaking order.

'Come, sister. Let me look at you,' Nasima said, in Malay. She was in full medical nurse mode.

After one panicked look around for a way out, Mei Mei let Nasima examine her face and arms.

'Can we have a moment of privacy?' Nasima asked.

Ah Ma and I got up to leave, but Mei Mei said to me, 'Please stay,' and Nasima nodded.

Under the rough blue cotton shirt, the bruises and slashes on Mei Mei's back were much worse than those on her face and shoulders. Nasima's face was a mask of professional concern, but she spoke soothingly as she worked and her hands were sure and gentle. I could see Mei Mei relaxing even though she winced as Nasima cleaned and treated her injuries.

'She'll be all right,' Nasima said to me softly, after making Mei Mei stretch out, face down, on Ah Ma's bed to let the soothing balms take effect. 'She needs to eat more, but she's healthy. Who did this to her? She's one of the Pang girls, yes? Daughters of your grandmother's best friend?'

Ha. Nasima knew Pang Tai was no friend of Ah Ma. She had a way of knowing everything, thanks to her network of girls who went out to work as cleaners and were trained to say little and listen to everything.

'If she's the oldest Pang girl I heard she had a Japanese officer lover. The family was spared thanks to that.'

'The family wasn't spared,' I said. 'Their father was taken away and probably killed.'

Nasima was probably right about Mei Mei's Japanese lover, but that didn't mean anything. Women had done what they must to save their families. I could believe Mei Mei had loved only Stinky all along, but maybe this explained why she was so afraid of angering her family or leaving home. Was this the big secret she didn't want exposed? Anybody could see it wasn't her fault.

Was that why Stinky had wanted to take her to Indonesia? Away from all the bad memories of the war?

'Let me know what else I can do to help,' Nasima said, as she left.

'You'd better stay here for a while,' I told Mei Mei. 'Do you want to send word to tell your ma you're safe?'

Mei Mei shook her head.

'Or Danny? Wait – you said that Danny went to the Bukit Timah fire station? Did everything look normal when you were there?'

Mei Mei nodded. She didn't seem to know there had been a fire.

'What time was that?'

'Morning. I walked very slowly because I was hiding and then because my feet were very painful.'

255

I remembered Dr Shankar saying it was impossible to identify the body that had been found in the Bukit Timah fire-station blaze. They had assumed it was George Peters because he'd been the only officer posted there. But if Danny Pang had been there too . . .

I was suddenly terrified Danny's might be the body at the Bukit Batok fire station. What if George Peters and Wilson had killed Danny? The last of the Lucky Three friends who'd survived the war might not have lived much longer than the others.

'We have to tell the police about Danny going to the Bukit Timah fire station,' I said.

'No! Cannot—'

'We must. There was a big fire there this afternoon. They found a man's body, but they don't know whose it is yet.'

'Not Danny?'

'I don't know. I hope not. But we must tell them.'

'How are we going to get there?' Mei Mei looked scared. 'I can give you back your money that I didn't use.'

I opened Ah Ma's bedroom door and found her – unsurprisingly – in the corridor outside. 'Where's Uncle Chen?' I asked. He'd already driven me into town once that day, petrol wasn't cheap and he liked to be around at Little Ling's bedtime . . . but I really needed to get to the police station in town. I could have telephoned, but the officer on graveyard duty wouldn't take seriously the information that Danny Pang was at the fire station. He would just make a note of it to be attended to tomorrow and for some reason this felt very urgent.

'Your uncle Chen is standing outside in the rain talking to your *ang moh mata-mata*,' Ah Ma said.

'What?'

It struck me I hadn't given Le Froy the all-clear signal I'd promised. I would apologise another time. For now: 'Come on, Mei Mei, Le Froy will know what to do.'

It's Not Proof

———◆———

'It wasn't Danny Pang,' Dr Shankar said.

By the time we went out, Le Froy already knew, thanks to Uncle Chen, about our visitor. He had grasped the situation immediately and said the best person to speak to was Dr Shankar, so we headed back to the Shankars' shophouse.

'How can you be so sure?' I asked Dr Shankar. 'I thought you couldn't identify the body because it was too burned?'

Beside me, Mei Mei caught her breath. I could have been more tactful, but I just wanted to find out whether or not her brother was dead.

'I couldn't identify the body,' Dr Shankar said, 'but there was enough left to show it was an Indian or Indian-Eurasian male.'

The victim was George Peters, then. If Dr Shankar had mentioned it at dinner, I needn't have put Mei Mei into a panic over her brother and rushed her back to town. Though now that I had her here, wanting to clear Stinky's name . . .

'Can you tell Detective Fahey that Mei Mei says Stinky talked to Wilson for Danny Pang?' I said to Le Froy. 'Wilson was trying to take over the quarry as a Japanese-created business, even though it was Danny's father who started it. Wilson showed Stinky official papers. Stinky could read English. What if he saw those papers were forgeries and threatened to expose Wilson? That would explain why Wilson killed him.'

'It's not proof,' Le Froy said.

Blast the man. Watching him listen to me, I'd known what he would say. Why couldn't he surprise me for once and say something like 'That's enough to go on,' or 'Makes sense. I'll get Fahey to dig out the proof'?

'I didn't say I had proof. It's a theory, a possible explanation. The proof will be in Wilson's office.'

I was in a heightened state of tension. Ever since I'd learned of the fire and George Peters's death, I'd felt that in my refusal to let Parshanti stop to talk to him, I'd somehow been responsible, even though I'd no idea what had happened.

No. Correction: I was certain Jack Wilson had killed him or had had him killed. I just didn't know why. But I might have found out if I'd taken the time to try to talk to him instead of refusing because I'd assumed he was working with Wilson.

'As I said, it's not proof, but it's worth talking to Wilson and seeing what he has to say about this,' Le Froy said slowly. 'Fahey should be the one to do the talking. I think he'll want to hear this. And I think he would like to see you, Miss Pang.'

Dr Shankar was already on the phone to Fahey.

'Parshanti will be sorry to have missed you.' Mrs Shankar, sewing as usual, smiled at me. I was just glad Larry Leask wasn't around either. She stage-whispered to me, 'There's some of Leasky's meatloaf left over from dinner and this one looks like she could use a mouthful.'

I'd wondered if Mei Mei ate beef. Many Buddhists and Hindus believe the cow is a gift from the gods and an object of reverence rather than an ingredient, but the Pangs hadn't struck me as religious. Also, there was the cheese . . . but when I warmed some meatloaf and put it in front of Mei Mei she demurred only briefly before plunging in. Mrs Shankar was right, Mei Mei ate like one starved.

Mei Mei was looking much better by the time Fahey arrived. He, Dr Shankar and Le Froy had a brief exchange of words before Fahey came and sat down across the table from Mei Mei.

Dr Shankar ushered Mrs Shankar upstairs – even though she was protesting that she must ask Fahey if he'd had dinner yet.

'How do you feel?' Fahey asked Mei Mei, Le Froy translating for him.

'A bit funny.'

She looked funny, not just because of the discoloration from the bruising and the soothing pastes Nasima had applied to her skin.

'She's been through a lot,' I said. I don't know why I felt defensive. As though Fahey was criticising her for how she looked at a time like this, only he wasn't.

Le Froy gave me a small smile, as though to say he understood – and that I should let Mei Mei speak for herself. At least we understood each other again. I kept my mouth shut. So did the two men. I realised they had interviewed people together before.

Finally Mei Mei spoke. 'I feel like a ghost,' she said. 'I'm inside my body, looking out, but perhaps it's not really my body,'

'Did you take anything? Like any medication? Did you smoke or chew anything?'

'Ma gave me something because my head was really painful and I couldn't get up to cook,' Mei Mei said. 'I think it was the same stuff they give the workers when they are sick but need to work.'

'"They" meaning Danny?' I couldn't help asking.

Mei Mei looked startled, as though my question had made her realise she'd been talking aloud. She shrugged, then nodded.

'I hear your friend Stinky was talking to Wilson. He spoke English?'

Mei Mei nodded.

'He was your boyfriend?'

'We wanted to get married.'

'How did he learn to read English?'

'Stinky's mother was dead, his father too. His parents spoke Javanese as well as Dutch, and his father spoke English too so he picked it up when he was growing up. They were Indonesian Chinese from Gassing. Stinky's father was a childhood friend of my pa. Stinky's ma was visiting

Singapore with Stinky when the war started. After she was killed, my pa said Stinky must stay with us. He called Stinky his second son. Stinky helped pa with the orders and accounts because Danny hated doing that.'

'Would Stinky have talked to Wilson on his own?' Fahey asked. 'Could he have given him information about the quarry operations that would have provided Wilson with an excuse to shut the quarry down?'

'Oh, no,' Mei Mei said. 'Stinky wouldn't do that. He hated the British. Oh!' She looked awkwardly at the men listening to her.

'That's okay,' Le Froy said. 'Sometimes I hate them too.'

'Same here,' Fahey said.

They laughed and so did I.

This seemed to give Mei Mei courage. 'Stinky talked to Wilson for Danny because Wilson spoke Bahasa Indonesia.' I was surprised and a little impressed. Bahasa Indonesia was close enough to Malay that I could understand bits of it, but not so close that I could speak it. 'But Stinky only said what Danny told him to say.'

How could she – or Danny – know that?

'After Stinky's body was found in the pool, they said the police wouldn't listen to me if I said anything.'

Again the two men waited in silence. I was dying to tell Mei Mei to spit it out, but they waited and I did too.

'Stinky was unhappy about the workers. They were mostly immigrants. Some were Indonesian. Most of them came because they couldn't get work at home. During Japanese time things changed – but after the war Danny wanted to keep the Japanese system. The quarry workers were locked up and not allowed to leave.'

'Was Stinky unhappy enough that he might have worked with Wilson to close down the quarry?' Fahey asked. But when Le Froy translated this Mei Mei just shook her head and couldn't or wouldn't answer.

'You know Danny Pang,' Fahey said to me. 'Could he have killed a friend he suspected of trying to get his quarry business closed down?'

I started to say, 'No,' automatically. It's human nature to assume anyone you've spent any amount of time with isn't a killer simply because you're still alive. But at least two people had spent more time with Danny Pang than I had and they were both dead so . . . 'No,' I said anyway. 'Of course Danny could kill someone. But he's the sort who would get into a fight and boast about it afterwards. I can't see him killing two friends – one being his sister's boyfriend – and not talking about it. Besides, if Danny was going to kill anybody, I think it would have been Wilson.'

'But why is Wilson so sure that something's going on at the quarry? Sure enough to plant evidence. Obviously because he has insider information he trusts. And that was coming from . . . George Peters. Who must have been supplying him with opium and information. He was Wilson's inside man. And George Peters is now dead.' None of them disagreed with me.

'But there must be some record of that. Wilson would have had to pay George Peters – and he would have kept records of meeting him and paying him to cover himself.

Because he wouldn't have had the money to pay him off. Whoever he got the money from would have been wanting an account from him,' Le Froy said.

I turned on Le Froy: 'You know Wilson's really here to compromise you, don't you? He's been going around town trying to dig up dirt on you and making up stuff when he can't find any.'

Fahey nodded, and I knew he'd been trying to get Le Froy to see that too.

'Wilson tried to persuade me to sign a statement saying you were being paid by my family to warn them about what the police were doing. He also went round my grandmother's tenants and business colleagues, people she'd worked with years ago, threatening them with fines for breaking laws they weren't aware of and saying they would be let off if they testified against you. I don't know how he found so many.' I thought of the stream of people who'd come to Chen Mansion after Ah Ma had sent messages asking who had been approached.

'The downside of keeping good records,' Fahey said.

'What?'

'Wilson had access to Le Froy's archives,' Fahey said. 'He had very detailed notes on the Chen family business dealings in the 1920s and 1930s.'

'What?' I was shocked. 'You were investigating my family?'

'I was investigating Singapore business and your family was part of it,' Le Froy said.

'And?'

'And I recorded what I found. Confidentially.'

I saw Le Froy was angrier than I was over Wilson's breach of privacy.

'I don't understand,' Mei Mei said.

'They have to talk to Wilson,' I told her, 'to find out what Stinky told him and if he told Stinky what he was going to do to the quarry.'

Le Froy translated this for Fahey, who cleared his throat, 'If that's all we have, I'm forced to say that—'

'I think we should refuse to submit to force,' Le Froy said. I'd never loved him more.

Fahey tensed, then took a breath and grinned. 'Yes, sir.'

I was even happy with that.

'You could also ask what he's been saying about the people he's been investigating,' I said. 'And blackmailing.'

'What reason would we have to do that?' Fahey sounded equable but I knew he was dismissing the suggestion.

'You're the police. You can ask to see things civilians can't.'

'We still need a reason,' Fahey said. 'We can't just go round demanding to see things.'

At the same time Le Froy said, 'You don't want him to know you're interested until you find what you're interested in.'

'How is that possible?' Fahey said.

'Have a conversation,' Le Froy said. 'If you let people talk long enough they usually tell you what you need to know.'

'Should I send for him?' Fahey looked more like a student challenged to provide the right answer than a member of the Straits Police Force upholding law and order. 'He's probably still in his office – your office, sir. He practically lives there.'

'In his office where all his papers and files should be,' Le Froy agreed.

'Maybe we should go there,' Fahey said. 'Beard him in his den. And I want you there to confirm everything in the reports is as it should be.'

Jack Wilson's Office

———◆———

'What do you want? What are you doing in here?'

Jack Wilson leaped to his feet when Le Froy knocked and pushed open the door. He looked panicked and bleary-eyed, as though he'd woken from a bad dream.

He'd definitely woken from a nap. There was an ink smear on his cheek.

'This office is my private space. These are all confidential papers. I must ask you to leave at once, or I will be obliged to summon the authorities.'

Wilson fell silent as Fahey – no better representative of authority – entered behind Le Froy and held open the door for Mei Mei and me.

The office Wilson now occupied had been Le Froy's until two months ago. It wasn't large, but the walls were panelled English-style in dark wood. The shelves on the wall were filled with books and file holders. I'd once thought of it as a little bit of England – the England of Jane Austen and

Anthony Trollope – but it felt very different and unwelcoming now. Three chairs still stood against the wall facing the desk but they were stacked with boxes and papers.

I coughed. Though it was stuffy with the windows closed, there was dust everywhere.

'The cleaner hasn't been in here today?' Le Froy said. The 'today' was polite. I'd have said no one had dusted for weeks. Le Froy sounded concerned, which surprised me. He liked order and organisation, but he was the last person in the world to worry about dust and dirt.

'I told her not to come any more,' Wilson said. 'I caught her spying on me. I couldn't risk it. It's not safe to allow locals in here.' He looked suspiciously at me and Mei Mei. 'If you have anything to discuss with me the women will have to wait outside.'

I resented being dismissed as anyone's woman, but Mei Mei flared up. 'Stinky met you. He said you showed him papers. He was supposed to meet you the day he disappeared. I think you met him and killed him! And you told Stinky that if Danny could prove he had the Japanese deed documents he could keep the quarry. Stinky took them to show you. Now they are missing so you must have them.'

I translated all this as quickly as I could, managing not to ask why Mei Mei hadn't mentioned till now that Stinky had given him documents.

'He showed me some papers,' Wilson said. 'He looked at the documents issued by the Japanese giving the surviving members of the Pang family permission to work the quarry – this was after the death of Danny Pang's father – and he told me the dates on them were wrong. I told him to show me the dates on his documents and he did. But he got worked up about some discrepancy that he wouldn't explain and he never turned up again. That's the only reason I went out to the Pang quarry. I thought Le Froy had told them to have nothing to do with me.'

'Why did you think I would do that?' Le Froy asked, as I whispered a translation to Mei Mei.

'Because I knew you'd been sending messengers to multiple businesses including the Pangs'.' Wilson grew more confident as he spoke. 'I intercepted your messages offering them bribes.'

'I don't remember any such messages,' Le Froy said. 'I wrote to local businesses asking about their financial situation and offering to discuss options. Copies of all the letters are in the Public Health Services Bureau fund files.'

'That was where I found them,' Wilson said smugly. 'It's obvious that "discuss" is a code for offering a bribe in exchange for favours.'

'It's not obvious to me,' Le Froy said.

'You know as well as I do that all these locals are crooked and not to be trusted. Even the so-called Danny Pang I met wasn't even the real Danny Pang, and probably ended up being murdered for impersonating him.

'And you,' he turned to me, 'you lied about not speaking English. You're clearly the messenger for Le Froy. And you went out to the Pangs' the day the first man was killed, which surely cannot be a coincidence. You're part of his plot to do me in.'

'Why,' Fahey asked quietly, 'would former Chief Inspector Le Froy wish to "do you in"?'

'Obviously he's found out I was assigned to collect evidence to get rid of him. He should have left a long time ago because he's no longer with the police. What right does he have to be in Singapore?'

'Singapore is a British colony and I'm a British citizen,' Le Froy said.

'Anyway, as Governor Evans says, you've outstayed your usefulness. And he refuses to allow his wife to return to the island and be subjected to your presence as long as you're here.'

'Governor Evans is relentlessly genial and generally useless,' Le Froy said. 'His wife had suffered from isolation out here in the east and he suffered from his wife. Yet I find it difficult to believe he said that.'

Fahey winced. 'Sir, that's the kind of thing that when reported—'

'You see why the man should not be allowed to continue?' Wilson jumped in.

'But some in the Home Office feel they owe a debt to Le Froy for recovering the funds *misplaced* by Governor Evans without scandal or public outcry,' Fahey said, 'but cannot acknowledge that. Perhaps you should ask your contact to make clear to Mrs Evans that if Le Froy is removed the story of her attempt to make off with the funds might be exposed.'

Fahey's voice was calm, but I saw for the first time the steel beneath the boyish surface.

Wilson seemed to feel it too. To his credit he seemed to register Fahey's words instead of trying to contradict him.

'What's your solution, sir,' I asked Jack Wilson, 'to the situation at the Pang quarry?'

Maybe it was 'sir' that made him answer me. Or maybe it was because this was a question he could answer, unlike Le Froy's.

'It should be shut down. They're treating their workers like prisoners in a concentration camp. And with the current prices for granite, there's no way they can be covering their costs, even if they work day and night and manage to sell everything they dig out at two or three times the current market rate. The quarry is dead. They should accept that, close it down and release their workers, after they've found out which of them killed the two foremen. Clearly the way those workers were treated gives them motive enough.'

'So you think the quarry workers killed Stinky and Ah Kok?'

'Of course. There's no one else. Those women in the house couldn't have done it.'

'Wouldn't the workers have run away if they'd killed their foremen?'

'Why do you think they have them locked up behind barbed wire?' Wilson said. He had clearly given the matter some thought.

'That's why we were investigating them too,' Le Froy said, surprising me.

'That's why *I* was investigating them,' Wilson said. 'You were going to hand them wads of public-health money.'

'What did the man who told you he was Danny Pang say was wrong with the Japanese records?' Le Froy asked.

'Something about the dates being incorrect. I couldn't see anything wrong. It was a con. The man was just waiting to be offered money.'

'I gave Stinky the papers to give you to see,' Mei Mei said. 'I gave him the papers from the box in the office. Danny told Stinky to talk to the new government people and tell them our family had been running the quarry business for more than thirty years. But the government people said that wasn't enough. They wanted to see papers.'

'Can we see the Pang quarry documents?'

'Without documentation,' Wilson said, 'anybody can claim anything. And I never said I've got the Pang quarry documents. Even if I did, I'm under no obligation to show them to you.' I saw him glancing at the shelf behind me and turned to look at the box files there. Wilson didn't like that.

'Your uncle is under investigation too,' Wilson said. 'We know Chen Tou Seng has been driving around the island bothering British officers' wives and spying on them. At least one of these women, Mrs Cooper, has been trying to track him down for some time since she returned to England. I'll have you know she's been pushing enquiries to the highest levels.' He drummed a finger on a yellow telegram on his desk. 'It's catching up with him. It's catching up with all of you!'

I was shaken. I wasn't worried about what Uncle Chen might have done, but if this Cooper woman was a friend of Mrs Evans, who knew what she would accuse him of? And then something even more shocking happened.

Wilson opened a drawer in his desk and took out a gun.

'You don't want to do that,' Le Froy said. He stretched out an arm – not towards Wilson but across Fahey's chest, blocking his arms. Fahey glared at him, but took his hand off his own holster.

'What I want is for all of you to get out of my office.' Wilson stormed to the door, still brandishing his gun, and stood by it, holding it open for us.

Le Froy nodded politely and walked through it. The rest of us followed. I heard the sound of the key turning in the lock.

'You should have let me take him.' Fahey sounded annoyed. 'Could have solved two murders and got rid of a cowardly snake at one shot.'

'He'll calm down and come round.' Le Froy sounded tired. 'He doesn't know what he's doing any more.'

'The situation's not good, sir,' Fahey said to Le Froy. 'There's not enough to go on. Any documents related to Japanese-assigned properties are confidential. We can't requisition them without reason and we can't come up with a reason without the documents.'

He spoke quietly, but not quietly enough.

Le Froy didn't answer. His eyes were on me. 'Where are you girls off to? Need a lift?'

'Oh, no,' I said. 'Mei Mei and I are going to the Shankars'.'

'The Shankars'?' Le Froy looked at Mei Mei. 'Both of you? Why?'

'Sewing,' I said. 'Mei Mei's good at sewing and Mrs Shankar said if I knew anyone who could sew—'

Fahey's hands were tied. Le Froy's position was already precarious. But I could do what neither of them could.

As the men had been threatening each other, I'd slipped a key-ring off the hook nailed to the wall just under the desk by the door. I wasn't really stealing. That had once been my desk. I'd sat there, hammered in the nail and hung those keys on it, and if I'd taken them home with me at any other time no one would have thought twice about it.

'Come,' I said to Mei Mei, and hurried her round the corner to the alley between the next two buildings. It smelt as if men came there to smoke and pee, but it was dark and we wouldn't be noticed unless Le Froy and Fahey looked for us, which was unlikely: I could hear them arguing as they walked in the opposite direction.

'What are we going to do?' Mei Mei's eyes were wide and terrified, but I noticed she'd said 'we', not 'you', and I gave her credit for that. 'The police officer said the situation is not good. Meaning he is going to let that man who killed Ah Kok and Stinky get away?'

'The situation is not good, meaning we have to change it,' I said.

'But if even the police cannot do anything?'

'Then we must do what the police cannot.'

I expected Mei Mei to object, but she closed her eyes for a moment, took a deep breath and nodded. I realised she had been living covertly for a long time.

'Danny and the others were making and selling opium during the Occupation. Danny said it was to help people when there was no medicine and not enough food. After the war Danny said it was easier to make big money with opium. Granite is so much work and nobody wants to pay. He borrowed money to bid for opium licences. He also bought licences under the names of the other quarries around here. He was going to manage the business and be a big tycoon. No more dynamiting rocks and breathing dust.'

'Then they made opium processing illegal.'

'Danny was so angry,' Mei Mei said. 'Was there something in the Japanese lease documents about the opium? Is that why Stinky said something is wrong?'

'We should get back the Pang quarry documents that Wilson was using to pressure Danny. Maybe after that Danny will tell us what's really happening.'

Documents and Danny Pang

———◆———

The only difficulty now was waiting for Wilson to leave his office. And – horrible thought – what if he didn't? The man looked like he'd been sleeping in there when we'd barged in. What if he just went back to sleep?

'Hey, Limpy.'

It was Larry Leask. 'Go away,' I said.

'And who's this?' He smiled at Mei Mei. 'I don't believe we've met.'

'No one who wants to have anything to do with you.'

'That's not very friendly.' Larry seemed to have got over being put down. 'I was only doing my job. No different from any soldier or spy. Now it's in the open, can't we start again?'

'What?' Mei Mei said. The English she'd picked up hadn't prepared her to deal with Chaplain Lawrence Leask but, to my surprise, she didn't seem intimidated by him.

'You say you're a real chaplain and can talk to anyone?' I had a sudden idea. 'Prove it. See if you can get Wilson out of his office, buy him a couple of drinks and find out what's been giving him nightmares.'

'What?'

'I heard in Indonesia he was drinking too much and having nightmares. Maybe if you can exorcise his demons he'll go home and stop plaguing us here.'

Larry shrugged. I could see that the idea of a challenge to redeem his reputation appealed. Or maybe it was just the prospect of having a drink in the line of duty. 'I live to serve,' he said. 'If the man's already a drinker, this will be a walk in the park.'

It didn't take more than ten minutes. Maybe the chaplain approach worked, or maybe Wilson had also been looking for an excuse. Mei Mei and I watched as he locked and tested the street door before following Larry in the direction of the Shackle Club on Beach Road.

'Come on,' I said to Mei Mei. 'Be quiet.'

I needn't have worried. Mei Mei was better at sneaking about than I was. I reminded myself to keep an eye on her. Her attachment to Stinky had seemed genuine – but there was no guarantee she wouldn't switch allegiance as easily as the weather changed.

At least the rain had stopped by the time we made our way to Wilson's office door.

But had the locks been changed since I'd last used my keys?

I sent up a general prayer to all the gods I could think of – Christian, Taoist, Muslim, Hindu – and one or more of them came through. The key turned and the door opened.

It was darker inside than it was on the street because the blinds were shut and blocked out the streetlamps. I thought of Wilson sitting there all by himself night after night and almost felt sorry for him. At least I knew Larry could be pleasant company when he wanted to be.

The office had an electric ceiling light, but I didn't want to turn it on in case brightness showed through cracks in the blinds and alerted Wilson on his way back. Though I hoped we'd be out of there with our evidence before then.

Luckily I had the little oil lamp I always carried. It was smaller than a water bottle and not much heavier than a packet of cigarettes and a lighter. Unlike a Western torch, it didn't require expensive batteries. I just had to unscrew the cap and click on the flame.

Mei Mei followed as I made straight for the cupboard Wilson had looked at. I felt sure I was close to finding out whatever Wilson was trying to hide, and that it had to do with the bodies at the Pang granite quarry as well as the confidential documents he wouldn't show to Fahey.

A folder marked 'Strictly Confidential' looked promising. But the telegrams it contained showed Wilson had been telling someone in London there was no evidence that Le Froy was misusing the public-health fund. The cables called him lazy, accused him of taking bribes from Le Froy and repeatedly demanded that he did not discuss the situation with Governor Evans, as Wilson seemed to want to do. He clearly believed that since he'd been assigned his project, through an intermediary, on Governor Evans's orders, it would be simpler to present his findings directly.

I couldn't believe what I was seeing. Had I got Wilson wrong?

There were also letters Wilson had written and apparently hadn't posted. They were very Christian in sentiment, showing he had been traumatised by the shooting of Indonesian military and civilians by the British. His seniors had told him he must stop demanding that the army officers involved apologise and pay compensation or he would be put up on charges of treason. This assignment in Singapore was his last chance to show he could obey orders.

'Have you found anything yet?' Mei Mei's quiet query brought me back to the matter at hand.

'Still looking.'

'There are papers on the floor next to the desk.' Mei Mei pointed to a folder. 'Pang quarry.'

'You can read?'

'Just a bit. Stinky was teaching me. He said once I could read and write it wouldn't matter if I wasn't very strong. I could still work.'

That was exactly what my grandmother had said when she'd sent me to school. I wished I'd had a chance to get to know Stinky.

Mei Mei and I looked at the documents inside the folder. Under the dim, flickering lamplight, everything looked all right to me. If only I'd studied law maybe errors would be leaping off the page, but as it was, it looked like a certificate accepting the transfer of the lease issued to Pang Choon Mong (deceased) to his son Pang Chee Meng (Danny).

'It's no use,' I said. 'I'll try to get someone who reads Japanese and knows about legal documents to look at these.'

The problem was that anyone who knew about legal documents would probably recognise the illegality of taking these papers out of Wilson's office without authorisation.

'We'd better get out of here,' I said.

'Wait.'

'What is it?'

Mei Mei put her finger under a signature at the bottom of one of the papers. 'That date is Pa's birthday.'

'I'm sorry,' I said, 'but I'm sure your father would want you to remember all the birthdays he had when he was still alive . . .'

I was trying to think of the fastest way to copy the information. I had a good memory, but not for legal matters: I knew the order in which the points and qualifiers were set out could make a world of difference.

'But my father was alive on his birthday that year,' Mei Mei said. 'My birthday is two weeks after and Pa wished many more birthdays for both of us. He said I must not be in a hurry to marry because he would miss me too much. He always said that. I remember wondering what Pa would say when Stinky told him about wanting us to get married. But he died before Stinky could tell him. And now Stinky is gone too.'

I looked at the document again. The Japanese date system, like the Chinese, starts with the year, followed by the month and the day. 'This is your pa's birthday? 1943 *nen*, three, *gatsu*, twenty-seven *nichi*, *ka-yō*,' which meant Tuesday, 27 March 1943.

'Yes,' Mei Mei said. 'The Japanese were here, we were all scared and there wasn't much food, but Pa said we should celebrate with birthday noodles as usual, because we were still together and we didn't know for how much longer we would be. But I never thought Pa and Uncle Khoo would *kenah*! Pa always said they were already old men so why would the Japanese waste bullets on them?'

'Your uncle Khoo – Ah Kok's father – he was still alive then, too? Are you sure?'

'Oh, yes!' Mei Mei sounded impatient. 'They were both there for Pa's birthday. It was his last birthday, so of course I remember. Why do you keep asking me that?'

'It's written here,' I pointed further up in the same document, 'that your brother was given the management rights of the Pang quarry because the joint owner-managers, Pang Choon Mong and Khoo Beng Kiat, deserted their posts three months before. "Sentenced to death for desertion".'

'Sentenced to death for desertion' was how the Japanese had reassigned property without proof of death.

If I'd expected shock or disbelief it fell flat. Mei Mei merely shrugged. 'People are always getting dates wrong. I know for sure that Pa and Uncle Khoo were alive on Pa's birthday because they were with us, Ah Kok and Stinky too. Pa joked that he couldn't remember how old he was. He said he was twenty-five years old instead of fifty-two. You can check with Ma if you don't believe me. She's very good with numbers and dates and she writes down everything.'

Of course it was possible the wrong date had been signed. It looked like Danny had signed the lease instead of getting Stinky to do it. The signature was crudely scrawled in a childish hand, but the date below was written clearly and precisely.

And the date on the official chop matched the date beneath the signatures.

Mei Mei was certain that her father and his foreman were alive then. Was this what Stinky had spotted when he'd told Wilson something was wrong?

Just then I heard something outside. I scrambled to turn down the oil lamp. No time to put the papers back as they were.

'It's not the front door,' I hissed to Mei Mei. 'Somebody's already inside!'

There were several offices in the building, but I could have sworn all the occupants had left. If one had come back to pick up something they'd forgotten, there was a chance they'd leave without noticing us.

We heard several doors opening and closing. Should we have made a run for it? Then footsteps approached and Wilson's door opened to reveal . . . Danny Pang.

'What are you doing here?' he said.

'We're trying to find the Pang quarry documents. Wilson is trying to blackmail you, saying he'll close down the quarry, isn't he? He's been threatening a lot of people.'

Danny squinted, as though he didn't understand me. He turned on his sister. 'Why did you run away? Ma is going to kill you!'

'What does Wilson have on you?' I asked. 'It might not be real. He's invented a lot of things. I know you sent Stinky to talk to him. What did he tell Stinky?'

'Poor old Stinky. Thought he was so clever. In the end he was more *goondu* than anybody else. He thought he could bargain with me. What does he know about bargaining?'

'For money?' I asked. That was unlikely, because Stinky would have known what Danny had – or didn't have.

'Nah! He wanted to marry Mei Mei and take her to Indonesia with him in exchange for him saying nothing. He didn't want money or a share of the business.'

'What?' Mei Mei said. 'Stinky said that?'

'That *goondu* wanted you!' Danny laughed at her. 'Blind as well as stupid.'

'I was stupid,' I said. 'I should have known something was wrong. When everybody was wondering where Stinky was hiding, you said they would never find him. That was because you knew he was already dead. Do you know who killed him? Was it Wilson? Did Wilson get George Peters to kill them?'

'Nobody would have found him if you hadn't made so much noise,' Danny retorted. 'Always the busybody, nosy parker, *kaypoh*. All this is your fault. Everything was going fine until you turned up.'

I hadn't meant to provoke him. Danny in a temper was dangerous to everyone, including himself. I remembered how one Chinese New Year he'd got into a fight with the lion dancers and tried to fight them. He even hit his father when he had tried to stop him. But that led me to another thought . . . Could Danny have killed Ah Kok and Stinky in a rage?

But Danny in a rage wouldn't have been capable of disposing of Stinky's body.

'Someone's coming!' Danny said. I couldn't see anything through the closed blinds. 'Wilson is coming back. We should go somewhere else to talk.' That made sense. I didn't want to explain things to Wilson . . . though seeing what he'd written about Le Froy made me rethink my opinion of him. There just wasn't time now.

'No!' Mei Mei didn't want to go but when Danny grabbed her arm and dragged her to the back door she didn't resist.

I followed. I wasn't ready to talk to Wilson and wanted to make sure Mei Mei was safe. The glass in the window by the back door had been knocked out. Danny must have done it, then reached through to unlock and unlatch it. This being a government building, he would be in serious trouble if he was reported – but I couldn't report him without getting into trouble myself. Now I was infected by Danny's urgency. Mei Mei and I would be in trouble if Wilson caught us here.

Danny's pickup was in the alley behind the building. He let down the back panel to form a ramp. 'Get inside.'

I considered making a dash for it. Even with my weak hip and leg I could get far enough to distract him while Mei Mei escaped and found help . . . but Mei Mei was already walking up the ramp to the back, Danny dragging her. That told me where her bruises had come from. I couldn't let her go home until I'd told Pang Tai what Danny was doing to his sister.

I followed her into the back of the pickup. There were wooden storage crates on both sides with only a narrow space between them. I guessed Mei Mei had hidden in one to get away from the quarry. I decided that when Danny went to the driver's cabin I would make Mei Mei climb out of the back with me. She'd escaped from the pickup once before, so it shouldn't be too difficult for her.

As for me? I wasn't much good at jumping. I just needed to land without hurting myself.

'Get into the box,' Danny said. 'Hurry up. People are waiting.'

'What?' Who was waiting?

He'd taken the wooden lid off one and Mei Mei was sitting in it, crying silently as Danny tied her wrists together. I should have run for it when I could. Maybe it wasn't too late. But what about Mei Mei?

'Get in.' Danny grabbed and lifted me, dumping me next to Mei Mei.

We'd sneaked in so successfully that no one knew where we were. When would Le Froy realise we'd not arrived at the Shankars'? Why hadn't Wilson come back? How much was Larry making him drink? Was someone in the alley between the two buildings? I thought I saw movement and peered into the night. 'Is anyone there?' I shouted. 'Help!'

'Shut your mouth!' Danny said. He glared into the darkness, but there was nothing. It had probably been a rat or a stray cat. Now that people had other sources of food, stray animals were reappearing on the streets.

Birthday and Death Day

———◆———

Even with the wooden lid over us, I knew we were in the Bukit Batok quarry area from the rattling of loose pebbles under the pickup's tyres as it climbed. It would have to stop after turning off the lorry track because Danny had to open the gate blocking the driveway leading to the house. It was our last chance. If only I could get my hands loose before Danny brought us to whichever part of the quarry he was heading for, to whoever was waiting for him.

Once loose I could crawl over the backboard and drop onto the road below – I struggled desperately, whispering to Mei Mei to free her hands if she could.

The pickup stopped. We heard the cab door open and slam shut, then footsteps retreating.

Mei Mei moaned. She'd probably been moaning the whole time but, with the engine noise, I'd not heard her till now.

'Can you get your hands loose?'

She didn't answer so I guessed that meant no. I'd been trying to twist myself free since Danny had started the engine so I couldn't blame her. But we had to do something fast because it would be even harder to get away when Danny's accomplice turned up. I grunted with effort. If only I still had my little oil lamp – but I had my cloth pouch, so . . . Yes! I manage to reach the little nail clipper that (thanks to Ah Ma) I always carried with me.

I managed to cut myself loose and set about freeing Mei Mei. She was whimpering and didn't seem to understand when I tried to tell her we needed to get off before Danny came back to the truck.

Because once he did it would be too late.

I tried to push the lid off the box but it was wedged on tightly and I got splinters in my hands. I swivelled as best I could and tried to kick it off – then shrieked when suddenly, without warning, it was yanked off.

'What are you playing at?' It was Larry. 'Don't I get a reward for a job well done? I bought Wilson two drinks, listened to his misery and packed him home to bed. Thought you'd still be turning over his office, but I saw you climbing in here and hiding instead. I know you're pulling something on Wilson. Come on, let me in on it. I won't tell.'

The man was a fool. But a very useful fool.

'Help us out of this box. How did you get here?'

'An old driver hanging around. "Follow that pickup!" I told him. The old swindler insisted on being paid up front.'

I wondered if Hakim had been watching me.

'Where is it? The car that brought you here?'

'Left me at the bottom of the track. He dropped me before the turn, said the stones would destroy his tyres. That suited me – I wanted to surprise you. Oh, there it is . . .'

We all heard the sound of the departing engine. The driver must have gone further up the track till he found a spot wide enough to turn in, and decided he wasn't waiting any longer in such a forsaken spot.

'I hope your friend will give me a lift back to town.'

Danny appeared. He was holding a gun. It looked like a Japanese Nambu pistol.

Larry looked at Danny. He looked at Danny's gun. 'This has nothing to do with me. I'll just get out of here.'

'Stay where you are,' Danny said. 'Mei Mei, tie him up.'

'I was only teasing them.'

'Danny, you killed Ah Kok, didn't you?' I said. Being rattled around in the dark in the back of the pickup had laid out everything wonderfully clearly to me.

'Ah Kok caught you pushing the sack into the Death Pool. He tried to stop you – that's why his feet were wet and there was pond dirt all over his hands.'

'What sack?' Larry asked.

'The sack he put Stinky's body in,' I said. 'You killed Stinky first and tried to hide his body.'

'You don't know what you're talking about,' Danny said. His eyes were darting around. I thought he was looking to see if Larry had brought anyone with him. If only he had!

'It had to be you. You're the only one who could have killed Ah Kok and Stinky,' I said. 'They would have been on guard against strangers or any of the workers, but they trusted you. Why did you kill Stinky? Because of Mei Mei? He wasn't treating her badly. They were going to get married.'

'Stinky accused me of killing my father and Ah Kok's father,' Danny said. 'He threatened me.'

Mei Mei wailed and screamed something at her brother in rapid-fire Cantonese. My dialect skills weren't good enough for me to follow what she was saying, but I could tell she wasn't happy.

'Look,' I nodded towards Larry, 'he doesn't know anything and he's not involved. Why not just let him go? By the time he walks back to the main road—'

'He's a fool. Sticking his nose in for nothing. Come on, Mei Mei.' Danny gestured with the gun. 'Get on with it!'

Right then Larry had a moment of bravery and lunged for Danny. 'Run, girls!' he shouted. 'Save yourselves! Help should be coming. Just keep clear of him until they get here.'

I hesitated. Where was I supposed to run to for help?

Danny whacked Larry in the face and lurched towards me. Larry grabbed his arm and held him back, despite the blood running down his face.

'Damn it, girl, go! I'm no hero but if I'm going to die anyway you may as well live!'

Danny swung round and punched him in the mouth. I wanted to help Larry but – damn my useless body – I was no fighter. I made the decision. Once Danny got him down it would be too late for us both.

'I'll come back for you,' I said rapidly in English, hoping Danny was too caught up in his own grunts and growls to make out my words. 'I promise. Try to hide. Tell him to go and chase me, then try to hide. I'll come back for you as soon as I can. And I will send help.'

I scrambled back the way we'd come, down the long gravel lorry track and round the bend where the taxi had dropped Larry. Now what? I didn't think Larry could hold Danny back for long. Danny was full of muscle while Larry – I hoped I would survive long enough to tell everyone how brave Larry had been when it came to the pinch.

It was almost a mile to Bukit Timah Road. That was where Danny would expect me to go for help, retracing the route towards Jurong Road and Upper Bukit Timah Road and back into town, stopping at the remains of the fire station in the hope of summoning help. They might have put someone else on duty there – or restored the telephone line. I doubted it.

And how far could I get before Danny caught up with me?

I couldn't find my way through semi-jungle in the dark, and the roads would leave me too exposed. At this time of night there would be no buses or trams, and no other vehicle would stop to give a lift to what might be a *pontianak* or some other demon. It would be easy for Danny to find me, if I stayed close to the main road. And it would be easier for me to get hopelessly lost if I didn't.

I would confound him, I decided. By taking to the undergrowth and retracing my steps. I would go around Danny and his pickup, in the opposite direction, to the Pang house. That was the last place he would look for me. I didn't hope to get to their telephone, if it had even been reconnected, but I might find a bicycle that would make my journey so much easier. Really, all I needed to do was evade

Danny till daylight came. Then I could make my way back to town and tell everyone what had happened.

Even if Danny found me, at least I could tell Pang Tai what her son had done and warn her to keep herself and her younger daughters away from him.

Pang Tai

I'd planned to go around to the back of the house, but
to my surprise the front door stood open. Had someone
just gone in – or come out? The living room was dark and
there was no sign of Pang Tai or Girlie and Sissy. But there
was a light coming from an open door further down the
corridor and I headed towards it.

It was the room I'd seen Pang Tai go into to change
and I quickly pushed my way in without knocking. In my
book, manners and modesty take second place to escaping
from murderers.

'Pang Tai? Are you here? Sorry, but this is very important . . .'

I stared around me. It was a large room, running the
length of the corridor on that side of the house. But it was
crammed so full of things – furniture, boxes, vases, paintings
– that it felt cramped and restricted despite the same high
ceiling as the rest of the place. I could tell the windows hadn't

been opened for a long time because the air smelt stale and heavy, with echoes of imported Western perfumes and Tiger Balm lotion.

'Su Lin?' I heard Pang Tai but couldn't see her. I made my way past a large Western-style white porcelain bath standing on black iron claw feet that contained several rolled-up carpets and several pairs of leather shoes – men's and women's – and found her in front of a standing mirror, behind a high-backed armoire. This space was more like a storeroom than a bedroom or dressing room.

'Su Lin?' Pang Tai didn't seem surprised to see me, even as she said, 'What are you doing here so late?' She was standing up close to the mirror and I saw she was applying 'Snow White' powder to her face with a puff that she shut into the tin when she saw me. She added a slash of lipstick before she turned to me and I saw she had over-plucked her eyebrows because there was only discoloured skin under the brown brow lines hurriedly and unevenly drawn in. Eyebrows, like tree branches, don't always grow back when they've been trimmed too harshly. No matter how much willpower you have, you can't control everything.

The joss sticks in a heavy ceramic urn beside her had burned down to ash – the pot was filled with it – that smelt of sandalwood and agarwood. I know incense is supposed to carry prayers to God, the gods or your ancestors, but I doubted prayers could find their way through the clutter here.

'It's Danny,' I said. 'He's gone crazy. He even attacked Mei Mei. You should get out of here before he turns on you.'

293

Pang Tai just stared at me. It was understandable, I suppose. Between her precious son and the woman who'd just barged into her boudoir without warning . . . 'Please,' I said again. 'If you don't want to come with us, can you lend me a vehicle so I can get Mei Mei away and find help? You must lock yourself away safely until we come back. Does your WC have a lock? A real lock?'

Most houses with indoor lavatories and children had no locks on the doors, just little hook latches that prevented accidental embarrassment but did nothing to block a determined intruder.

'If not, lock yourself inside here, if you can. Stay in your bedroom and keep the door closed and locked.'

Her eyes went from me to the door, which opened before I could move. Danny Pang had come in, half dragging and half carrying a sagging Larry Leask, with Mei Mei behind them.

'The Chen girl says you killed Stinky,' Pang Tai said, in a dreamy voice.

'I already told you. She went to the Chens.' Danny jerked his chin at Mei Mei. 'It's not my fault. She told them everything.'

'No, Ma!' Mei Mei cried. 'I only—'

'You shut up!' Pang Tai said.

Danny turned away from his mother. He let Larry slump to the floor and used his pistol to direct him to where Mei Mei and I were standing.

'Where are Sissy and Girlie?' Mei Mei asked Danny quietly.

'Ma locked them in your room,' Danny said. 'She couldn't find you and they couldn't tell her where you were.'

'Did she hurt them? Or you?'

Danny shrugged. After everything she'd gone through, Mei Mei was worried about her sisters . . . and Danny?

I wasn't the only one distracted. As Danny looked away from him, Larry used the side of the tub to lever himself off the ground and made a grab for Danny's gun . . . I moved in to help him, but before I reached the struggling pair, Larry collapsed. He was out cold this time.

Pang Tai had cracked the large ceramic urn on his head and was standing over him, holding it in both hands, in case he needed a second dose.

'No!' I shouted. 'Pang Tai, no! He's not attacking us! It's Danny! Danny's gone crazy!' I had to make her understand before Danny turned on her too.

'Useless,' Pang Tai said. 'Something so simple but you cannot do it yourself.'

'I'm doing it, Ma,' Danny said sullenly.

Pang Tai looked at me and sighed loudly. 'After all I've done for you, a grown man like you cannot even get rid of one *pai-kah* for me.'

'I never asked you to do anything.' Danny retrieved his gun, sounding like a sulky kid.

'You're useless! Worse than your sisters!'

Pang Tai was deliberately inciting her son. She knew Danny wasn't a cold-blooded killer, so she had to work him up until he lashed out.

'Don't talk to Danny like that,' I said. 'It's not his fault. He wants to do what you want. He always tries to do what you want.'

Danny didn't look at me, but he seemed to stand a little straighter. I was arguing in favour of my would-be murderer getting on with murdering me, but at that moment I didn't have any choice other than to try to calm him down. Better to be in your murderer's good books than the reverse.

Pang Tai turned on me. 'You're so stupid you still think you can make him like you. My Danny would never look at a *pai-kah* like you. Who would want dirty grandchildren from you?'

'Ma!' Danny looked a bit abashed. I wondered if he'd given his mother the impression he liked me.

'Shut up! You're such a numbskull, as bad as your stupid father.'

'Danny's father was a good man and a very good businessman,' I said. 'My grandmother and my uncle respected him.'

'He was a fool. He would have destroyed the business and got us all killed if I'd let him. He wanted to sell soft rock and limestone to the Japanese instead of granite and gravel so that their buildings and roads would collapse.'

'Ma? Did you get Pa killed?' It was the first thing I'd heard Mei Mei say to her mother.

'He got himself killed. He asked for it. The war was over, the Japanese were in charge. So the correct thing to do is work for the Japanese.'

Pang Tai was talking to me rather than to Mei Mei.

'But, oh, no. That stupid man says he cannot sell anything to the Japanese because they killed his relatives in China. Come on, *lah*, you want them to kill you too? He tells all

his workers to run away to the jungle up-country rather
than help the Japanese mine granite. And he and his equally
stupid foreman brought in dynamite to blow up our quarry
rather than produce granite and gravel for them.'

'So you told the Japanese what they were going to do?'

'When the British are in charge you support the British.
When the Japanese are in charge, you support the Japanese,
lor. That's the right thing to do. I was only trying to protect
my children.'

I'd been right about how easily Danny could be
manipulated. I'd just not realised it was his mother who'd
been pulling his strings.

'Anyway, that man only gave me daughters. And such
useless daughters! Anyway, everything was fine until this one
started telling everybody about it.'

'I never did!' Danny said. 'Stinky came and started
shouting rubbish about birthdays and dying days. He said
the dates were wrong. He was shouting like he was going to
attack me, so Ma hit him.'

'What?' Pang Tai, with her snooty genteel manners, hit
Stinky? It sounded crazy, but I'd just seen her cosh Larry on
the head with an urn. I hoped Larry was still alive.

'Stinky told me he saw the dates on the Japanese
document,' Mei Mei whispered. 'He said those dates were
wrong. He said the signatures on the papers were dated on
Pa's birthday, and Pa had been missing for three months
already. That was before my birthday.'

She laughed. Maybe insanity ran in their family.

'Before your birthday?' I played along.

'Yes! Because my father was alive on his birthday. He disappeared on my birthday, two weeks after his own. That morning he said he was going to come home early because it was my birthday. But he never came back. That was the day he disappeared. You must remember, Ma. We didn't know where you were and Pa had to go and look for you. And Uncle Khoo went with him. Then you came back and you said you hadn't seen them. And they never came back.'

Danny was surprisingly silent. He looked at Pang Tai who was shaking her head and saying, 'You're crazy, you're crazy.'

I remembered what Dr Leask had said about the two older bodies found in the Death Pool and felt dread twist, like a cold worm, in my guts. 'Were they were taken away by Japanese soldiers?' I asked.

'Of course!' Pang Tai said. 'What's the use of talking about such things? How can you come and blame the family if they were killed by Japanese soldiers? After all, they went outside after curfew. Everybody knows what those soldiers were like, but that stupid man had to go outside and ask for trouble.'

Maybe if Pang Tai hadn't said that . . .

'I remember that night,' Mei Mei said quietly. 'We were ready to sit down to eat. I had cooked and served dinner. Ah Kok and his father were eating with us because it was my birthday meal. Danny came and said our mother was tapping angsana sap by the Death Pool when she slipped, fell and got trapped. He couldn't get her out. Pa and Uncle Khoo rushed out. Stinky and Ah Kok were also going, but Danny made them stay in the house. He said he had something for them to do. A surprise present for me, and he needed their help to fix it. He said Pa and Uncle Khoo could take care of things. And he was quite fierce. So Ah Kok and Stinky went to the back of the house with Danny instead of going up to the Death Pool . . .'

'And then?' I asked.

'And then nothing. There was no surprise present. Pa and Uncle Khoo never came back.'

I wished I'd paid more attention to Dr Leask's questions about whose bodies had been in the Death Pool. I only hoped he would find out if I never got the chance to tell him.

'Ma came back later and said she didn't know what had happened to them. She hadn't seen Pa or Uncle Khoo. She managed eventually to climb out of the water and came home. She warned us never to talk about it because we weren't supposed to leave the house after curfew and she didn't want us to get into trouble with the *kempetai*.'

'But the *kempetai* didn't bother you after that, did they? In fact, they supported you in running the quarry. They provided you with prisoners and the guns to keep them in check.'

'We had to carry on at the quarry,' Danny said. 'We were just doing our work. We don't bother them, they don't bother us.'

'I saw the Japanese documents giving you and your mother the right to take over your dead father's business,' I said. 'They were signed two weeks before your father died. That was your doing, wasn't it?' I turned to Pang Tai. 'You didn't trust anyone, so you didn't have your husband and his foreman killed until after you got the documents from the Japanese soldiers who wanted your opium. Their bodies were found in the Death

Pool. And those poor bundles of baby bones, you put those in there too, didn't you? Because you didn't want to bring up more daughters.'

'Who are you to talk? They should have drowned you when you were born!'

Pang Tai lunged forward and smacked me hard on the side of the head. She was strong for such a small woman. But I had an advantage too. Like Pang Tai said, I was crippled. I lost my balance, falling heavily against her and bringing us both crashing down.

The advantage of not being very big is you have less bulk to lift off the floor. If I could just get to the door before she stopped me I could block it with something and lock her in till I could— But no. She grabbed something out of a box. It looked like a coil of shiny wire fixed to two bamboo handles.

'Danny made it for me to kill pigs,' Pang Tai said. It was the fishing-line garrotte, coated with glass powder.

'No, Ma! Stop!' Danny said. For a moment I thought he was defending me, but—

'Not here, Ma! Too messy. You know there's always so much blood.'

'You're useless!' Pang Tai said. 'Scared of blood, scared of killing people, always scared. Your old mother has to do everything.'

'I'm not scared,' Danny said. 'I don't want to clean up. I also don't want to carry so many bodies up to the pool.'

Pang Tai came to a decision. 'Make them go up to the Death Pool.'

Ending at the Death Pool

———————♦———————

Larry Leask was still unconscious.

'You two,' Danny said to Mei Mei and me, 'pick him up and carry him. Faster, move!'

'Don't be so stupid,' Pang Tai said. 'Tie his hands,' she ordered Mei Mei. 'Then put the rope around his legs, tight-tight, better make sure. Danny, you drag him up while they push. Come on, what are you waiting for?'

I knew that the track from the back of the Pang house to the Death Pool might be the last one I ever walked.

Climbing up the track in the dark was even harder than it was by day. Danny hauled on the rope tied around Larry's legs while Mei Mei and I did our best to protect his head from rocks on the path. In the clearing, the three huge angsana trees looked ominous against purple-grey clouds that foretold a rainstorm.

Insects whined and I saw spots of light from fireflies. Little Ling would have liked them, I thought. But I wouldn't have let her try to catch fireflies here, so close to the edge of the Death Pool. Too dangerous. But would I ever have a chance to protect her from anything after tonight?

'But why?' I asked. After all, what did I have to lose?

'They are cheating us,' Danny said. 'They charge us money for licences. We clear space in the old quarries for processing. We have buyers waiting. Everything is set up, and then they come and say we cannot go ahead. The money is waiting to be taken. Why should we let people spoil everything?'

'Don't talk so much,' Pang Tai said.

She was holding the handles fixed to the loop of shiny filament. I guessed she also used it to cut into the bark of the angsana trees to release sap and—

'You used that to kill Ah Kok and Stinky,' I said.

'I didn't know she was going to kill Stinky,' Danny said. He seemed to be appealing to Mei Mei. It made no difference. 'I didn't know until after—'

'Ha! Don't blame me!' Pang Tai said. 'Who came running to me going, "What shall I do, Ma? He knows, Ma! He's going to tell, Ma!" I was the only one who knew what to do. The rest of you? All useless!'

As I listened to that woman mocking her son, I saw I'd been wrong about Pang Tai thinking her son was precious and perfect. She'd been cultivating him to become useful to her.

If Danny was looking for excuses, Pang Tai was looking at all of us and she was grinning. It was horrible. She was enjoying herself. The look on her face was of exhilaration, an expression you'd imagine on the face of someone who'd seen God. She had killed and got away with it. Now she was anticipating doing it again.

'You killed George Peters too, didn't you?' I said.

'Who?'

'The man from the fire station. You started the fire there to cover up the murder. That was why nobody connected it with Ah Kok and Stinky being killed here.' It was really painful to say the next bit but I forced myself. 'That was really smart of you.'

'I started the fire so that people would think he got drunk and fell asleep!' Danny said. 'I'm cleverer than people think.'

'I see that now,' I said.

Danny preened.

'Stop talking nonsense!' Pang Tai yelled at him. 'You are such a *goondu* fool!'

'He's not stupid,' I said softly.

'I'm not stupid,' Danny said. 'I took care of that. Peters was stupid and greedy.'

'It's your fault that man ended up dead,' Pang Tai said to me. 'You got the police to check on where he was getting money when he wasn't working at the fire station. He was just there as a *jaga*.'

I hadn't asked the police to check George Peters, but I was glad to hear they had.

'That fool helped the *ang moh* busybody to set up the fake opium-cooking station because he was angry that I wouldn't bribe him to keep quiet. But he didn't know where the processing area was. Only that the product was brought down from the Death Pool track, so he took the *ang moh* up here. And after the bodies were found in the Death Pool he panicked. He came here and said too many people were asking too many questions. What could I do? All along he's asking for more money. Then you came and scared him so much he didn't even want money. I knew there was no hope for him. Sooner or later he'd go crying to the police.'

'So you killed him, then made Danny bring him back to the station and set fire to the place.' I filed away that nugget of information and hoped I would live long enough to use it.

'I have to protect my family. Everything was fine until you came along,' Pang Tai said. 'All of this is your fault.'

I gave the kind of snort that Ah Ma let loose when a market vendor tried to sell her substandard pork, impressing myself. 'Don't try to blame me. You didn't have to kill Stinky. He was willing to go away and not tell anybody anything that morning.'

'He was acting crazy!' Danny said. 'Accusing me of working with the Japanese to have my father killed! I never did! And Ma's the one that hit Stinky.'

Given what I'd seen Pang Tai do to Larry Leask I had no trouble believing him.

'Then the two of you put him into a sack with stones and pushed him into the Death Pool.'

'Ma told me to fetch the sack. Stinky was still alive when I left. When I came back, he was dead.' Danny sliced horizontally across his throat. He looked at Mei Mei. 'You two were so foolish, thinking nobody knew about you. Ma knew right from the start. Even Pa knew. He said, "Could be worse."'

'How could it be worse?' Pang Tai interrupted. 'The son of some bar-girl! Practically a prostitute, stinking of cheap perfume and sex.'

'Stinky probably asked Danny why the agreement between him and the Japanese was dated before his father was murdered.' I looked at Mei Mei. 'You said Stinky was going to meet someone but wouldn't tell you who. You thought he'd gone to meet Jack Wilson, but might he have been meeting your brother?'

'Maybe. Before work at the quarry started, he said,' Mei Mei murmured. 'He had to hurry because he wanted to talk before the quarry started blasting. I thought it was because of the noise.'

'So you were alone up here when Ah Kok came to look for Stinky?' I said to Danny. I wondered if Sissy and Girlie were around, if any of the workers could call the authorities if I managed to reach them. I suspected not.

'Ah Kok turned up when I was pushing the sack into the quarry. I'd got it almost over the edge when I heard him shouting for Stinky as he came up the trail so I hid behind the hut. Ah Kok saw the sack half in the water and went to try to pull it out. I came out and said, "What happened?" and Ah Kok said, "I think there's somebody inside. Help me get this out."'

'Ah Kok didn't know anything,' I said. 'He was pulling Stinky's body out of the pool when you came up behind him and killed him.'

'No, I didn't!' Danny cried. His bravado was gone. 'He was my friend! I only hit him to stop him. Then Ma sent me to the store to get another sack and more stones. So I went to get them and when I came back Ma was gone and Mei Mei was there making so much noise and I couldn't think – I just wanted her to shut up!'

'Where did your mother get that thing?' I asked.

'The pig killer? I made it for her,' Danny said. 'We had to kill our own pigs during the war. Fishing line, treated with powdered glass. Better than using a knife or *parang*.'

I stared at Danny. Was this madness or, worse, was it true?

'If my sister hadn't come and made so much noise, I would have put Ah Kok into the pool too. And everything would be all right now.'

Pang Tai turned to Mei Mei. 'I should have drowned you when you were born.'

I'd already guessed Pang Tai had been drowning her girl babies. Now I saw she felt no regret.

'But, Ma, we need Mei Mei to do the cooking!'

I almost laughed.

'Ssh, Danny,' Mei Mei said. 'It's all right.'

I realised that in his clumsy way Danny was trying to save his sister's life while Mei Mei wanted to deflect their mother's anger from him.

'Danny! Don't talk so much!' Pang Tai yelled.

I held my breath as Danny's aim switched to his mother.

'Get rid of the *pai-kah* first. She's the most nuisance.'

'It's no use!' Larry said groggily. 'The police are coming!'

'Police?' Danny laughed. 'In your dreams!'

'I told that taxi driver to go for the police once I saw what was happening. Gave him all the cash I had and told him to go as fast as he could.'

'You're so stupid,' Danny said. 'You gave him his money so why would he want to come back?' He pointed his gun at Larry.

'No! Don't!' I cried, which made Danny turn to me.

I shut my eyes and heard the gunshot. I was still standing, which meant Larry had been shot.

But when I opened my eyes, Larry was staring at Danny who was screaming and clutching at his thigh. He was still holding the gun and he started to raise it, but there was another shot. He crumpled and collapsed.

'Danny!' I jump-crouched towards him, shocked into automatic concern. Then I remembered he'd been about to kill me. I kicked away his gun and put one foot heavily on each of his wrists.

Pang Tai was screaming orders but Danny was in no position to do anything and Mei Mei and Larry were staring at the top of the trail where the shots had come from.

It was only then that I saw Jack Wilson standing there, holding a gun.

Jack Wilson had shot Danny Pang. Now we were all going to die.

To my surprise, Le Froy and Fahey appeared behind him. Wilson must have run up the track, leaving the others to follow.

'I did it again,' Wilson said, horror written on his face. He stared at the gun in his hand. 'I didn't mean to. It was a mistake. I swore I never would again . . .'

'You weren't kidding when you said you shot locals,' Larry said, sitting up. 'Ow, my head. You're a hero. Thank you.'

Wilson didn't look like a hero. He was sitting on the ground like a little boy, arms wrapped round his knees, eyes tight shut. I've noticed most *ang mohs* can't squat, which would have been a better position on ground that wasn't very clean. Now he raised his gun and put it to his mouth. I knew he was going to kill himself.

Killing people changes a person. It had made Pang Tai feel powerful and invincible but had left Wilson feeling guilty and condemned.

'No! Don't!' I cried, scrambling to my feet, but I was too slow.

Le Froy got to him first. 'Shooting to prevent murder is the opposite of reckless use of firearms.' He put a hand on Wilson's shoulder. 'It's the opposite of what happened in Indonesia.'

I don't think Wilson heard him because Mei Mei pushed Le Froy out of the way and wrapped her arms around Wilson, rocking him. He dropped the gun and Fahey picked it up.

'I didn't mean to,' Wilson said, sobbing into Mei Mei's shoulder.

'Everything okay.' Mei Mei was speaking English! My over-stimulated brain took a moment to be shocked. 'Everything okay. Don't cry. Danny not dead. Danny not so easy to kill.'

She was right. Danny was trying to roll over, moaning and swearing. He was nursing his bloodied right arm.

'Ma!' he called.

'Useless!' Pang Tai said. 'You're all useless!' Pang Tai glared round at everyone then returned to Mei Mei. 'You are the one I should have killed when you were born,' she said. 'I knew you were going to bring bad luck to the family.'

That was something I'd heard all my growing-up years. Till now I'd thought being cursed as a disappointment and the bringer of bad luck was unique to me. It wasn't. Maybe all girl children were cursed at birth for not being sons, but that didn't make it any better.

'My son needs a doctor!' Pang Tai said. 'Take him to hospital! You are police, you must arrest that man for shooting my son.'

'Don't listen to her! She killed Ah Kok and Stinky!' I shouted. I needed to tell them the facts before Pang Tai could twist everything. 'She made Danny help her. She killed her husband and Ah Kok's father also.'

'You useless busybody!' Pang Tai yelled. 'How dare you get in my way?'

She launched herself at me, forgetting her injured son, forgetting all the people, and threw the loop of wire around my neck, crossing and pulling on the handles to tighten it against my throat. She'd killed Stinky, Ah Kok and who knew how many pigs, but I wasn't going to let her get me without a fight. I shoved my cloth pouch between the deadly filament and the front of my throat. I could feel the line slicing into the sides of my neck and the wetness of blood soaking into my thin shirt. It would buy me only two or three seconds, but that was enough time for Le Froy and Fahey to get her off me.

Fahey came over. Wilson scrambled to his feet even though Fahey was gesturing to him to stay down.

'I prefer to be arrested on my feet.'

'No!' Mei Mei said. 'You cannot arrest him! He is sick. And he saved us!'

'It's always right to stand up when something needs to be done.' Fahey held out a hand. 'Thank you, sir.'

Wilson looked taken aback, as though he'd expected a jibe but none came. He took Fahey's hand. 'Thank *you*, sir,' he said.

Then, with Mei Mei's help, he sat down again.

'Mei Mei is a protector,' a familiar voice said. 'Nasima said so too. Because even when Nasima was cleaning her blisters, Mei Mei didn't want to let her touch her feet because for Muslims the feet are unclean.'

'Ah Ma? What are you doing here?' I was shocked to see my grandmother on Hakim's arm. 'You got Hakim to follow me?'

'Only in case you needed transport home.'

'I'm going to learn to drive,' I said.

'I'm sorry,' Le Froy said to Ah Ma. 'I know Pang Tai was an old friend of yours.'

'Sorry for what?' Ah Ma said. 'I can't stand that woman. I knew all along she cannot be trusted.'

'But you used to tell your contractors to buy granite from the Pang quarry,' I said.

'Chinese must help Chinese,' Ah Ma said.

I must have heard her say that a hundred times, but I was suddenly furious, 'So even if you don't like her and she can't be trusted, you wanted me to marry her Danny? Danny, who tried to kill me just now?'

'Who said I wanted you to marry that Danny? I told you not to believe anything that one says. Anyway, you are going to marry that *ang moh mata-mata*, yes?' Ah Ma directed her snort over my right shoulder.

'I hope she is,' Le Froy said, from behind me. Right there, in front of my fiercely Chinese grandmother, he put an arm around me. 'You're trembling.'

'Of course,' Ah Ma said. 'That Danny! Wanted to marry her then to kill her. Many men are like that. Many women don't find out until too late.'

Le Froy's arm tightened around me.

'I'm all right,' I said. 'I know why you said Pang Tai had had too many daughters. Those were her daughters in the Death Pool.'

'After your parents died Pang Tai offered to take you as a favour to me,' Ah Ma said. 'You would have drowned in a week and that woman would have blackmailed me for life. I am sorry I let you come here, Lin-Lin,' Ah Ma said. I couldn't remember the last time she'd called me by my baby name. 'If your *ang moh mata-mata* wasn't standing here waiting to report me, I would throw her and her whole family inside their damn quarry and set off dynamite to make sure they stayed there.'

'I wouldn't report you,' Le Froy said. 'I'd offer to help, but I'm guessing you don't need help from an *ang moh mata-mata.*'

He mimicked her pronunciation and the little *moue* she made when she was talking about him. Ah Ma stared at him, mouth open in shock. She couldn't believe he was mocking her to her face. She, Chen Tai, the mother of Big Boss Chen and manager of all the Chen family holdings. Then she shrieked with laughter. 'Yes! You can help me.' She told Le Froy. 'but you'd better make sure you look after my granddaughter or I am coming after you.'

'Absolutely,' Le Froy said.

'I don't need looking after,' I said.

'Then you can look after your grandmother and me.'

Hospital Visit

———◆———

When Le Froy and I went to visit Larry Leask in the hospital ward, we found Jack Wilson there. A couple of days ago, this would have been uncomfortable. But just then I was too happy to be alive to mind seeing anybody anywhere.

There were four beds in the ward, but the other three were empty. Larry was leaning back against at least four pillows, some clearly pilfered from the other beds, in a thin white singlet with a bandaged shoulder, a bandaged and elevated leg, bruises on his forehead, and the shaved portion of his head showed a centipede of stitches running through an ugly bruise.

Wilson got to his feet, and for a moment I thought he was going to bolt for the door.

'Excuse me for not getting up,' Larry said.

'I didn't realise you two knew each other,' Le Froy said. 'No, please don't go. We just dropped in to see how the patient is doing.'

OVIDIA YU

'Chaplain Leask here is truly a man of God,' Wilson said. 'The most truly Christ-like man I have ever met.'

'You told me to find out what was giving him nightmares,' Larry said to me.

Both Le Froy and Wilson looked surprised.

'I might have forgotten to mention that,' I said to Le Froy.

'I'd like to hear more,' Le Froy said.

We commandeered two of the single upright chairs that stood by the unoccupied beds.

'The hospital won't mind,' Wilson said. 'They told me I could take the pillows to make him more comfortable.'

'Anyway, we hadn't really been introduced, but I thought we might have a drink and a chat so I went and introduced myself to Jack,' Larry said. 'Offered to buy the man a drink.'

'Chaplain Leask was the first man to ask me out for a drink since I got to the island,' Wilson said. 'We went to the Shackle Club on Beach Road.'

'The British servicemen's club?' I was surprised. It was an expensive place that catered mostly to recent arrivals, who hadn't yet discovered local dives where the same drinks cost less than a third of the price.

'It's near Jack's office,' Larry said. 'And I thought he'd be more comfortable there.' That was probably because the only locals allowed into the club were the staff. 'Anyway, we wanted to talk and it was quiet.'

'What nightmares were you having?' Le Froy asked Wilson.

'Just – Indonesia,' Wilson shrugged. 'Hell on earth.'

'What happened in Indonesia?' Le Froy asked, as though he'd heard nothing about the shooting of the flood evacuees.

314

'Insurrection. Chaos,' Wilson said. 'Complete breakdown of civilisation and social order. Those people are savages. Britain is trying to civilise and bring culture to the world, but do people appreciate it? No. They want to stay in the mire, bogged down in their ignorance. We were only there to accept the Japanese surrender and stabilise things before handing it back to the Dutch, but the Indonesians made clear they didn't want us there and didn't want the Dutch back. They were throwing things at us, stealing our belongings!' This was clearly a familiar rant.

'Yet you said you felt guilty.' Larry pulled him back into the present.

'You said I did,' Wilson said. 'I don't know how you picked it up.'

'I've spent a lot of time talking to troops,' Larry said. 'It's understandable. Anyway, we were just chatting, friends having a couple of drinks . . .' Larry's voice – his whole manner – had changed. Even propped up in bed, he gave off an air of non-judgemental acceptance that Wilson leaned into.

'Maybe white men have made some mistakes. We're not perfect. But you have to stick with what you've been born into, right?'

'I was born in South Queensferry,' Larry said, with a smile.

Wilson wasn't diverted. 'I'm talking about duty, responsibility, authority.'

'Take up the white man's burden,' Le Froy quoted.

'Exactly!' Wilson missed the sarcasm. 'Let me tell you something – confidentially. Singapore was a kind of test for me. I was sent here to prove myself.' He looked at Le Froy and hesitated.

'We agreed you'd think about coming clean with Le Froy.' Larry nodded towards Le Froy. 'He almost throttled me.' He put his good hand to his throat, which still bore the signs. 'Pretty much threatened to kill me. He's got good instincts. You can trust him.'

That seemed enough for Wilson. 'The thing is,' he said to Le Froy, 'I came here believing you were a cad and a criminal and I fully intended to destroy you. What if I had?'

'Why didn't you?' Le Froy asked.

'I tried. Couldn't find anything on you that would stick,' Wilson said. 'It was supposed to be a cut-and-dried affair, unethical practices. All the evidence in your files, all I had to do was compile it. But . . .' Wilson shook his head.

'The definition of unethical varies with who you're talking to,' Le Froy said.

'Unethical means unethical!' Wilson said.

'Tell Le Froy who sent you after him,' Larry said.

'Instructions came straight from the Home Office. A confidential request on behalf of Governor Evans himself. And a local contact, but the poor man's dead now.'

'Might I have ministered to him?' Larry asked.

'No, not one of ours. A local chap, so probably Hindu or Muslim.'

'George Peters?' Larry guessed, though surely the Peter patronymic ought to have alerted Wilson to the man's religion.

Wilson nodded. 'He said he knew the Pangs were processing opium and paying Le Froy to warn them of spot checks. That kind of information could have put Le Froy away. Only I needed to document the opium processing to pressure them to give him up. But that was a huge fiasco.'

'Why didn't you just give the police Peters's information?' Le Froy asked.

'Peters told me that was how things are done here,' Wilson said. 'He said the Pangs bribed the police to ignore information, which was why I had needed evidence documented with witnesses present. He couldn't be a witness because he'd got the opium evidence from the Pangs.'

'The opium you tried to plant on the Pangs actually came from the Pangs?' I said, just to make sure I understood.

Wilson nodded. 'That's where Peters got it. I wouldn't set up innocent people. But then people started turning up dead. I tried to see Governor Evans. My appointment came directly from him, after all. But he wouldn't see me. All day every day the man's "busy", "in a meeting", "not available". I was sure his assistant – a local girl named Miss Rozario – was blocking my messages and calls, so I went to Government House and said I would sit there, outside his door, until the governor was free to give me ten minutes. That's reasonable, isn't it? I came to Singapore because Evans summoned me personally. The least he could do was give me ten minutes, right? Then this Miss Rozario called the guard to chuck me out and reported me to the police for trespassing.'

Wilson's voice rose, and Larry said, in his calm chaplain voice, 'But the police let you go.'

'They had to. All I did was go to a public office to see a public official. Anyway, I filed a complaint on the Rozario woman keeping the governor isolated and I sent a carbon copy direct to London, along with my report on the Pang quarry. It's no use expecting the local police to do anything.'

'Tell them what you found out about the Pang quarry,' Larry said. When Wilson looked warily at Le Froy and me, Larry added, 'Your report's already en route to the Home Office.'

'The Pangs are storing raw opium balls and processed packs in their disused quarries and using their granite trucks and barges for transport. Their processing was carried out in their old warehouses now taken over by the Bukit Timah fire station.'

'What?' I couldn't help myself.

Wilson nodded. 'I looked into why work on the fire station had stalled and learned Peters had reported unsafe ground conditions and flooding. I confronted him and told him he would do better as a witness for the Crown. The next thing I knew, the fire station was burned down and Peters was dead.'

'And you heard back from the Home Office,' Larry prompted, 'about your assignment from Governor Evans?'

Wilson ground his thumbs into his temples as though trying to dampen the pain there, 'I heard back from Harold Sims, who happens to be married to the younger sister of Mrs Governor Evans. You know Mrs Evans is back in London?'

'Some ladies can't take the climate out here,' Le Froy said.

'Mrs Evans is staying in her brother-in-law's townhouse in London. Harold Sims, a senior auditor with the Home

Office, said she arrived on their doorstep and remains despite increasingly pointed hints that she set up her own permanent establishment. Mrs Evans paid multiple calls to various departments of the Home Office, demanding Le Froy be sacked for his high-handedness, even though he was no longer employed by the Crown Colony administration. Her demands that her husband be given a better posting in a more civilised climate also came to nothing.'

I could imagine Mrs Evans's frustration upon realising she was a very small fish in the English pond. At least in Singapore she had been the governor's wife.

'Convinced that Le Froy feared her and was keeping her out of Singapore, Mrs Evans swore that once he was gone she would return to her husband's side. Anyway, her beleaguered brother-in-law admits he issued the directive to get Le Froy out of Singapore.'

'So, mystery solved. It was Mrs Evans, via her brother-in-law at the Home Office, who was responsible for having Jack assigned to Singapore to get rid of you,' Larry Leask said. 'Once I heard all that, I told him I was going to walk him over to Police HQ where he would tell them exactly what he had told me.'

'And I thought that after hearing my confession a chaplain was supposed to say, "Go, my son, and sin no more,"' Wilson said.

'That's for the Roman Catholics. We Anglicans have to put things right,' Larry said. 'To be honest, I was afraid you might kill yourself once I left you alone. At least the cops would keep you alive overnight, even if they had to lock you up and take away your shoelaces.'

'I admit I thought of it. Many times. But I'm too much of a coward,' Wilson said.

'You're no coward, Wilson,' Le Froy said. 'That's not why you were removed from your post in Indonesia. And it wasn't because of that shooting incident.'

'It wasn't?' Larry said.

'Once Wilson realised they had gunned down unarmed civilians with children, he ran into the line of fire trying to halt the attack, almost getting shot himself. He tried to get his own men to go down to the flooded village to help with the evacuation, but by then the Indonesian military were setting up to defend themselves from further attack and it would have been pointless.'

Wilson didn't deny it. 'How do you know?'

'I have my sources too,' Le Froy said. 'And the police listened to you this time?'

'They didn't want to,' Larry said. 'But once the corporal on duty heard Jack call me "Chaplain" it was no problem. The Church clearly outranked the military police. I told the corporal to let Fahey know and also suggested they get hold of you,' this to Le Froy, 'and let you know what was happening. I don't claim to be psychic but I had a bad feeling about the girls and wanted to check on them.'

'The girls?' Wilson and Le Froy said at the same time, Le Froy glancing at me.

'Life is hard for girls, don't you think?' Larry said, 'Anyway, I went back towards Hill Street. I felt I might have done Jack some good.'

'You did!' Wilson said fervently.

'But I saw something as I passed the alley backing onto his office building. It was dark, but it looked like a man forcing two women into the back of a pickup. He was a big chappie with a gun and I thought the women were tied up. I hid behind a car parked at the foot of the dark alley. Look, I'll admit I'm the coward, not my friend Jack Wilson. A big part of why I joined the Church was to avoid fighting and encounters with guns, and I wasn't about to throw it all away just because the war's over.'

Wilson laughed as though it was a joke.

'I almost jumped out of my skin when I realised the car wasn't empty. This man was sitting in it. My first thought was that he was the look-out for whatever was going on and I was dead. But then he said, "I cannot drive you. I must wait to drive Missy Chen home," and I realised he was a pirate taxi driver.'

'Hakim!' I said. 'He was watching me?'

Larry nodded. 'He said your grandmother pays him to watch you, in case you need a ride home – hey, don't get angry with the bearer of protective news. Anyway, we heard the engine of the pickup splutter. Hakim told me to get in quickly and get down. I climbed in and we both ducked as the pickup went past.'

'And you followed the pickup we were in,' I said.

'Couldn't think of anything else to do,' Larry said. 'We followed with the headlights off. It was terrifying. I found myself really praying for the first time – and not just for myself. When the pickup stopped I got out. I told Hakim to go for Le Froy and tell him what was happening. I reckoned that was the fastest way to get help. Then, like an idiot, I just tried to stall things till help came.'

'You weren't an idiot,' I said. 'You were a hero. Thank you.'

Postscript: The Angsana Pool

———◆———

Danny ended up in Changi Prison. There they discovered that he couldn't read English or Chinese, not even signs, because his brain didn't process words. His eyesight was fine, but just as some people are colour blind or tone deaf, he had word blindness. He'd tried to hide it all his life but it was exposed in prison when he was tested – fortunately for him, because as he was 'disabled', he was spared the death penalty.

The last I heard, Danny was training to work with engines and became quite a good mechanic – but would probably spend the rest of his life sleeping in prison even if he was allowed to work outside.

Pang Tai was sent to the mental hospital at Wood Bridge, named after the old bridge near the hospital. She continued to claim that (a) she had never done anything wrong, and (b) she had been forced by her late husband and wicked children into doing those things that she had never done.

Even in the asylum Pang Tai managed to poison a fellow inmate with disinfectant (the woman survived) saying the woman deserved it for being lazy and stupid and smelling bad. Also because she wanted the woman's ceramic-flower hairpin: 'She's so ugly she doesn't deserve to wear it, but she wouldn't give it to me so I had to get rid of her and take it.'

I don't think even she knew how many people she'd killed without thinking it wrong. Mei Mei continued visiting her brother and mother.

The Pang quarry would come to Mei Mei and her younger sisters. Mei Mei said they would put it up for sale once the documentation had cleared. It wouldn't be a problem since buildings and roads needed granite and gravel, labourers needed work and granite-quarrying was a solid business, even if it didn't pay as much as opium. They would probably keep the house, with its access to the Angsana Pond, as Mei Mei renamed the Death Pool. Names do make a difference, even if living on Mountbatten Road didn't feel much different from living on Grove Road. She set up stone shrines (in granite, of course) under each of the trees so the dead wouldn't be forgotten.

It wasn't just the half-starved, opium-drugged workers who were grateful to Mei Mei for trying to help them when they were released from their dormitory. Wilson thanked her for seeing him as a damaged man in need of help, even without knowing he'd become addicted to the opioids prescribed for his insomnia and terrible nightmares after the shooting.

Fortunately, once it was revealed that Mrs Evans had been responsible for Wilson's assignment to Singapore to get rid of Le Froy, the appointment was cancelled and Wilson was allowed to return to England on leave for medical attention.

We heard more about Mrs Evans from Deirdre Rozario, who called at Chen Mansion on behalf of Mrs Cooper, formerly of Ridout Road (named in honour of Major General Sir Dudley Ridout, who had set up Singapore's first Secret Service), now returned home to Sussex. Apparently Mrs Cooper had made multiple attempts to contact Uncle Chen using our old Grove Road address. The problem wasn't only that Grove Road was now Mountbatten Road, but that there was another Grove Road in George Town, Penang, and since she had addressed her letters to 'Grove Road, Malaya,' that was where all her letters had been forwarded.

'Mrs Cooper wants to buy a full trousseau bedding set for her daughter, who's getting married in June,' Deirdre Rozario said. 'She says she bought her sheets from you and her daughter loved them so much when she and her fiancé came to visit that she wants to give them three master-bedroom sets and two guest-room sets. I can assure you that Mrs Cooper will pay you, but if you're worried, I'll advance you the money myself.'

'Don't worry about the money,' Uncle Chen said. 'I remember Mrs Cooper. Very nice lady. Pure cotton, two hundred and forty thread count with birds on bamboo, yes?'

'Pay first is good,' Ah Ma said.

'Mrs Evans didn't always remember to pay,' I said. 'You were her assistant, weren't you? She used to have her dresses made by Mrs Shankar and she was always forgetting to pay.'

I wasn't trying to make Deirdre Rozario feel bad. I found I liked her and I knew she'd been clearing up the accounts Mrs Evans owed at various local establishments.

'Mrs Shankar is giving me a list,' Deirdre said. 'I'm very sorry about all of that.'

'It can't have been easy working for her,' I said.

Deirdre smiled. 'Mrs Evans demanded I pay my own passage to England to work for her because English servants were rude, expected to be paid every week and ignored her when she woke them in the middle of the night to fetch her a drink.'

'Servants, these days,' I murmured.

'Quite. Anyway, Mrs Evans was sure that her husband and Government House were falling apart without her fulfilling her duties as the governor's wife. There are decisions to be made about the daily running of Government House, choosing flowers, complaining about fish, hosting guests and planning meals for the governor and his guests. But I had already been taking care of these things as Mrs Evans's personal assistant. Now I was seeing to them as Governor Evans's personal assistant, but things were running quite as smoothly – more smoothly, in fact, because we didn't have to deal with her.'

'So she won't be coming back?' I might almost have felt sorry for Mrs Evans if not for what she'd tried to do to Le Froy.

'It's not easy for her now,' Deirdre said, with a small smile. 'Now it's come out that she's been trying to blackmail her and her husband's connections, the governor is only sending her money via official channels – purely to keep the accounts transparent, of course.'

'Of course.'

'The governor's office sends her a monthly allowance of exactly double what whole families of five or six live off and he no longer pays off debts she accrues in London, meaning she's having to find other ways to raise funds to cover her and her son's lavish living expenses.'

'I don't think she'll like that very much.'

'My main responsibility now is keeping Mrs Evans's long-distance telephone calls, telegrams and emissaries from bothering the governor at all hours.'

It sounded to me like Deirdre Rozario was a very efficient personal assistant.

'Does the governor flirt with you?' Ah Ma asked. 'Pretty girl like you, old *ang moh* man like him, you must be careful, you know.'

'Ah Ma!'

'Ma, you cannot say things like that!'

Deirdre smiled, not seeming offended. 'I make sure the governor is comfortable. Flirting makes him comfortable, but he doesn't flirt with me. I've explained I am Roman Catholic and managed to turn him down without hurting his feelings.'

'You are a very smart girl,' Ah Ma said. 'Su Lin, you should learn from her.'

*

Three months later Chaplain Larry Leask married Parshanti to Leasky.

Larry Leask had gone into the Church thinking it was a clever way to get out of joining the army. But, as he put it, 'God in His infinite wisdom used my petty cleverness to put me exactly where I needed to be.'

He was right. Just by being there and delaying Danny's attempt to kill me, Larry had saved my life. It had changed him too. Larry Leask had decided to stay in the Church.

I was the bridesmaid, in a dress Mrs Shankar had made with a sloping hem so that when I wore it, with my withered leg, the hemline was straight. It was a dress perfectly tailored to suit the wearer, just like her husband's prosthetics made it possible for Le Froy to stand as straight as any other man. Industrialisation and mass production would never replace such things.

Harry Palin was their best man. After the ceremony, he handed me over to Le Froy, 'Now you see what a good job I do as best man, think of me when it's your turn, okay?'

'We should think about it,' Le Froy said. 'Work out the details.'

'Why? Things are good as they are.'

I wanted us to have future together so much but I was also afraid – absurdly – that talking about the future could jinx it.

'Things will continue to be good, I hope,' Le Froy said. 'Marriage is just the formal contract of our partnership. Like a business contract that's recognised by the social structure we live in.' He smiled but sounded serious. 'It's a new position for me. You'll have to tell me what's expected. As with any new partnership, we'll have to get used to working together and I really want this to work.'

I wanted it to work, too.

'You already know me,' I said. 'I'm new to this, too, but we know we work together well. I don't want that to change. I'm not a vamp or a party girl but I'm not Greta Garbo either. I don't want to be left alone too much. We could have weekly meetings like we did in the Detective Shack. Discuss what's working and what needs more work.'

'You could be a lawyer, you know,' Le Froy said. 'You have a lawyer's brain.'

'So what do you think?' I wasn't going to digress by asking if that was a compliment or an insult.

'I think it's a great idea.' He smiled. I was so relieved that I laughed, and then he was laughing too, and I knew that, whatever happened, what we had together was right and good and precious.

Neither of us had talked about the physical romantic side of things. But then I was (mostly) Chinese and Le Froy was an Englishman, so that was normal.

Acknowledgements

———◆———

As always, I owe huge thanks to Hazel Orme, Amanda Keats and of course Krystyna Green, who supported and guided me through the writing of this book.

Thank you also to the team behind them: Eleanor Russell, Hannah Wann, Kim Bishop, Chris Sturtivant, Simon McArt, Beth Wright, Francesca Banks and especially Andy Bridge whose cover designs are an inspiration.

Finally, thank you to Priya Doraswamy, my wonderful agent without whom none of this would be possible!